THE FOOLISH VIRGIN

THE
FOOLISH VIRGIN

by

MARGARET PENN

La jeunesse est une ivresse continuelle:
c'est la fièvre de la raison.
LA ROCHEFOUCAULD

JONATHAN CAPE
THIRTY BEDFORD SQUARE
LONDON

FIRST PUBLISHED MARCH 1951
SECOND IMPRESSION 1951

PRINTED IN GREAT BRITAIN IN THE CITY OF OXFORD
AT THE ALDEN PRESS
BOUND BY A. W. BAIN & CO. LTD., LONDON

CONTENTS

THE FOOLISH VIRGIN

To R.W.

CHAPTER I

THE NATION OF LONDON

IN the year 1910, on a dark, rainy afternoon in late
October, a young girl, trembling with excitement,
stared out at the receding grey roofs of Manchester
as the train in which she sat gathered speed on its journey
to London. Her name was Hilda Winstanley, and for
fourteen years she had lived, as the foster-child of simple,
labouring people, in the obscure village of Moss Ferry,
fourteen miles from Manchester. Suddenly and surprisingly she had been summoned to London to make her
home with relations hitherto totally unknown to her, her
father's people. This journey to London was the most
tremendous thing that had ever happened to her; and the
wonder of it, though anticipated at fever-pitch for the
past three weeks, was still so overwhelming that her Aunt
Mildred, sitting in the corner opposite, felt apprehensively that at any minute the girl might burst into tears,
in spite of the fact that they were not alone in the compartment. For this reason, in the strangeness of their first
acquaintance, conversation between them was awkward
and spasmodic, and Hilda could not but feel relieved when
her aunt, after handing her a small bunch of grapes and a
magazine, settled down to read her newspaper.

Hilda ate the grapes, the first she had ever tasted,
slowly and appreciatively, but the magazine lay neglected
by her side until, with the closing-in of the day, she could
no longer look out at the country flying past. London!
She whispered it under her breath, the magic word
growing ever larger until it seemed to fill the now brightly-
lit carriage like a banner. The train clanged on, and
Hilda, awed by the calmness with which her aunt

steadily read through the *Daily News*, as if a journey to London were the most ordinary thing in the world, made a polite effort to interest herself in the magazine, but found to her astonishment that the words and the illustrations conveyed nothing: they were all slurred together, and across each page, in rubricated type several inches high, she read: 'I am Hilda Winstanley, from Moss Ferry, near Manchester, and I'm going to live in London. I don't really believe it even yet, but I've left Moss Ferry for ever and ever, and I'm going to London, to live there, with my new relations, ALL MY LIFE! AMEN!' When, quite as a matter of course, Aunt Mildred passed over the newspaper to her, Hilda, from pure gratitude at thus being regarded as an equal, made a conscientious effort to collect her wits and read it as calmly as her aunt had done; but again found she could not concentrate on it. Holding its pages wide and pretending to read, she luxuriated in the marvel of this journey to the great city and in anticipation of the splendours which there awaited her: Buckingham Palace and the King and Queen; the Olympia and the Crystal Palace; Hyde Park and the Tower of London; Oxford Street and its great shops; the Horse Guards in a place called Whitehall; the Houses of Parliament and Westminster Abbey; St. Paul's Cathedral and the River Thames; the National Gallery and Kew Gardens. The enchanting pictures glowed and flickered across the sober pages of the *Daily News*. Why, she might even see the Prime Minister, Mr. Asquith, and the Alhambra in Leicester Square, not to mention the world-renowned Gaiety Theatre, where the most beautiful girls in England sang and danced their way into the heart of an adoring public until, ultimately, an eager and discerning peerage besought them in marriage. Back in Moss Ferry she had accumulated a magnificent collection of cigarette-cards which depicted these charming young

ladies: Cissie Loftus and Evie Greene; Zena Dare and Edna May: all lovely, and loveliest of them all, with a face as delicate as a harebell, Lily Elsie. Mrs. Winstanley, her strict, chapel-going foster-mother, had gazed reverently upon the picture of Miss Lily Elsie and had found no fault in her, though she had deplored the necessity which drove all these young ladies to earn their living in so godless a place as the theatre, and expressed the most fervent thankfulness and approval whenever one of them was persuaded to grace a stately home of England and thus remove herself for ever from Temptation.

Hilda looked shyly over at her aunt, who was leaning back with her eyes closed. How dignified and handsome she was, with long, beautiful hands, and dark, good, quiet clothes, the sort of clothes they sold in the fine shops in St. Ann's Square, Manchester, in one of which Hilda had spent several happy months with a view to astonishing the world, at some subsequent date, in the role of a properly accredited court dressmaker. For the first time since leaving Manchester her thoughts returned to Moss Ferry, and she wondered if her foster-father was home again after handing her over to Aunt Mildred at the Central Station. If so, the family would be having their special Saturday tea of newly-baked tea-cakes swimming in butter and topped with golden syrup, Saturday being baking-day. They would of course be talking about her and asking each other if she could have got to London yet. Her foster-mother would cry and accuse her of black ingratitude for having left them so eagerly after all they had done for her. Her husband would tell her not to take on so, and repeat many times the undeniable truth that Hilda had got into good hands and that there was no call for uneasiness about her new relations, he having had the honour of meeting one of them. Lily, her foster-sister, would be spiteful with envy; Jim, the youngest

son, would be glad to be shut of her la-di-da ways and provoking tongue, and would frankly say so. The elder son, John, would miss her, though he was so taken up with Edie, his sweetheart, that it would not be for very long. John had always been fonder of her, Hilda reflected complacently, than of Lily, his own sister.

What letters she would soon be writing them! She was already beginning to think out her first, telling them how happy she was in her grand new home, when she felt the train slackening speed. London! Here it was at last! Aunt Mildred opened her eyes and smiled at her.

'Here we are, Hilda. This is London. St. Pancras Station. It won't be long now before we are home. We live in Chiswick, near the river. We take the Underground from here, and we shall be there in no time. Get your basket down, child, and put on your hat. Do you feel excited?'

Hilda, almost crying with joy, could not trust herself to answer save by a nod. St. Pancras Station, London! Chiswick! The river! The Underground Railway! When she lived in Moss Ferry, London had always seemed so absolutely unattainable — right across the world — and now here she was actually in it, surging along with hundreds of other travellers, and keeping so close to her aunt lest she should lose her that she was a menace with her rush-basket to more than one hurrying passenger on the crowded platform. She had never before been in such a scene of bustle and confusion, not even in Manchester, now disloyally dwindling in her mind to the status of just an ordinary town.

Aunt Mildred walked quickly to a wide brilliantly lighted entrance which announced itself in enormous lettering as UNDERGROUND, with Hilda, too bewildered to be aware of anything but noise and light and hurry, almost running to keep safely alongside, so great was her

terror of getting lost in the crowd. Manchester was nothing to this. People there pursued their business in a quiet, leisurely fashion, like responsible human beings. Here everybody seemed mazed and frightened, as if they had come from nowhere and were going nowhere, but all in such a tear that one would think the Old Lad himself was after them and they had to go forward or be dragged back by him into the darkness.

Her aunt, sensing Hilda's fears, took her arm and moved less quickly, assuring her that there was no need to feel nervous. London was always like this, she explained, but one soon got accustomed to it. Within a week Hilda would feel as if she had lived in it for years. Hilda, however, was not so sure. Fearful tales came into her mind of young girls like herself who had disappeared in London and never been seen again by their families. She recalled her foster-mother's urgent warnings never to allow a stranger, man or woman, to speak to her in any circumstances whatsoever. Afraid of appearing stupid in her anxiety not to get lost, she mentioned these warnings to Aunt Mildred.

'Mrs. Winstanley was quite right, Hilda. You must never let *any* stranger talk to you in London, but you're a big girl and should be able to look after yourself. People in London are just the same as people in Manchester, the only difference is that there are more of them.'

By this time, however, Hilda's terror of London was so great that her disloyalty to Manchester had vanished, and she privately concluded that, in spite of its crowds, London had nothing whatever over Manchester. Folks there, even in a crowd, looked like folks, and not a gigantic jumble of liquorice all-sorts. As they went down the wide steps to the fabulous Underground, terror seized upon her like a palsy, and at that moment she would gladly and humbly have abandoned all her dreams of

becoming a citizen of London if by some miracle she could have got into a north-bound train and back to the safety of her home in Moss Ferry. But in no time at all they were waiting on their proper platform, and Aunt Mildred, realizing her niece's agitation, assured her once more that they were nearly home, and here was their train. Hilda stood spell-bound as it emerged from the tunnel, and would have missed it had not her aunt pushed her quickly in. The conductor clanged-to the iron gates, and once again Hilda found herself sitting opposite Aunt Mildred. The fear occasioned by the crowds began to leave her, and she looked about her curiously. How bright the long carriage was and how quickly they came to the different stations, and how funny that no matter how many people got out just as many seemed immediately to get in! When they came to Holborn, Hilda called out the name, and coloured painfully at the smiles this simple act evoked from people sitting near. Aunt Mildred smiled too, but in a friendly way, and came quietly to the rescue.

'You don't pronounce the "l", Hilda. It's the same with Chiswick — you leave out the "w". Don't worry. There are lots of little things like this in London and it doesn't matter in the least if you get them wrong at first. Take no notice if people smile. They wouldn't do any better if they came up against some of your Lancashire names.'

Hilda, reassured, fixed her grey eyes steadily on the nearest of the barbarians, and, though the effort made her feel quite shaky inside, stared back until they in their turn grew embarrassed and retreated behind their evening papers. This strange, brilliant journey through the very bowels of London ended far too quickly, and she kept very close to her aunt as they emerged once more into what seemed to her a monster fair-ground of light and movement and noise.

'Hammersmith Broadway,' explained Aunt Mildred. 'Look, there's our bus. Keep near to me, child,' she urged unnecessarily, 'and do try to walk more quickly. Everybody in London is always in a hurry and you just have to keep up with them or get left behind.'

Hilda obediently quickened her steps. In her whole life she had never witnessed such a scurry as in this last half-hour, and she was immensely relieved when they got off the bus and made their way down a quiet road.

Taking her arm, Aunt Mildred too seemed relieved. 'At last we can really talk,' she began. 'I expect your Grandma has told you that we are your real relatives, your own father's people. He was our eldest brother. There are three of us at home — myself, my sister Helen, and her husband, Phillip Shepheard. When your Grandma wrote and told us how restless you were getting, we thought it would be nice to have you make your home with us. But here we are — Glynne Mansions. Our flat, No. 40, is right at the top, looking over the Thames.'

Hilda, awed by the vast size of the building they had entered, followed her aunt nervously up its wide stone stairs. She had no conception of what a flat was like, though she knew from her reading that people in big cities lived in such queer places instead of in proper houses. The stairs seemed endless, but at last they were at the very top, and, shaking anew with excitement and fear, Hilda stood in the square windowless hall of her new home. Before she had time even to glance round, a door opened and a deep, penetrating voice called out: 'Welcome home, Hilda! I am your Aunt Helen, and this is my husband, your Uncle Phillip.' Hilda, confused, and crimson to the ears, was drawn into a warm, beautiful sitting-room and kissed by her new relations, who then just stood and stared at her as if she was the first young girl they had ever seen. She did not know what to say or where to look. Despite

their affectionate greeting, for the first time in her life she felt utterly alone and helpless, and, unable to check herself, burst into tears.

Aunt Helen was the first to act. Taking her hand, and pretending not to notice the tears, she led her into another room which, she explained, was her bedroom, her very own. Hilda, between her sobs, looked about her and wondered what her aunt meant by bedroom, since there was no sign of anybody ever having used it for the simple purpose of going to bed. Along one wall there was a low couch covered with a brocaded cloth and piled with matching cushions. Hilda took this to be positively the last word in fashionable sofas, but Helen called it a 'divan', and, observing her niece's puzzled stare, explained: 'This is your bed, Hilda. All you have to do is to take off the cover, slip two of the cushions into pillow-slips, and there you are. We want you to feel that this room is absolutely your own, to come to whenever you like. There's not as much room in a flat as in a house, and consequently every inch of space has to be utilized. That's why we've made your room look like a sitting-room. This built-in cupboard is for your clothes. I'll show you the bathroom, and when you've had a wash and tidied up, we'll have supper.' She turned away, calling over her shoulder: 'And please put out the light, Hilda. Always remember to do this whenever you leave your room.'

Hilda, all obedience, looked up fearfully at the light, and wondered how she was going to reach it. This was her first contact with electricity, for the workroom and shop in Manchester had been lit throughout by gas, and in her bewilderment at her new surroundings she had not noticed her aunt switch the light on by the door when they entered the room. Helen, waiting in the hall, called out impatiently: 'Come along, Hilda. Whatever are you doing?'

Hilda jumped on to a chair, steadied the parchment shade between her hands, and blew vigorously. Nothing happened, and she blew again, growing hot and cold with anxiety at being unable to perform the first little thing her aunt had asked of her. Helen, overhearing these extraordinary exertions, came back to the doorway, and at the amazing sight exclaimed under her breath: 'Is it possible? Is it really possible?' Hilda, quite breathless, looked down at her and said apologetically: 'It won't go out, although I've blown ever so hard.'

Helen smiled. 'All right, dear. Get down. See, this is all you do.' She switched the light off and on, and Hilda, covered with shame at her own ignorance, smiled propitiatingly and followed her to the bathroom.

'Here we are,' said her aunt brightly. 'When you want hot water you light the geyser, like this. There, turn the tap on yourself. Now off. And don't go trying to blow the gas out, Hilda, or heaven knows what will happen. It's simple enough, isn't it? When you're ready, come back to the sitting-room. And don't feel worried or frightened about us. You'll soon settle down.'

The instant she was alone, Hilda gingerly approached the geyser, half expecting to be blown to smithereens as she lit the pilot jet. The bathroom itself did not intimidate her, for it was not so very different from the one at the Vicarage in Moss Ferry where, in a voluminous sacking apron, she had earned her first pocket-money. But the geyser was pure magic. What a letter she would be able to write to Moss Ferry about it! Hot water gushing out by merely applying a match! At the Vicarage they had to light the big kitchen range and get a great fire going before the water was even warm. They simply wouldn't believe it when she described this miracle. She could hear her foster-mother's incredulous 'Nay! Ah never did!' when Lily read out the startling news. Having washed

her hands and face, she drew her palms along the smooth white surface of the bath, already impatient for the night to come when she could legitimately get into it. That of course would not be for a whole week yet. This was Saturday, and before the kitchen-fire in Moss Ferry she had only last night had her wash all over for the week. If only she had known, she would have waited another day and had it in this clean, shining room; it had not yet occurred to her that perhaps her new relations, like the Vicar in Moss Ferry, washed all over every day, and not with ritualistic thoroughness once a week as they all did in the cottages.

Her admiring eyes took in every luxurious detail — the thick, white, soft towels, the scented soap, the mat by the bath made apparently of little corks stuck together; the forest of sponges, nail-brushes and tooth-brushes, the wooden pegs on which the towels hung, an initial over each peg, and, glorious to behold, a newly-painted 'H' over one of them for her. Her own room, and her own towel! To say nothing of the flush lavatory which, though familiar by virtue of her service at the Vicarage and her work at Hankinson & Sankey's in Manchester, here took on a new splendour because it was actually in her own home. Though nature did not exact it, she could not resist giving the chain a possessive pull as she went to face the ordeal of getting to know her astonishing new relations.

As she crossed the little hall, Hilda, hearing her own name mentioned, stood and listened at the door. She knew that this was a shocking thing to do and that listeners seldom heard any good of themselves, but for once this maxim proved wrong. Her Uncle Phillip was talking about her, and the tone of his voice arrested her attention.

'Of course she's gawky and awkward,' he was saying, apparently to Aunt Helen, 'but then most girls of fourteen

are, and this is a bit of an ordeal for her. But what a pair
of eyes, and did you notice her hands? They're just like
Mildred's. I'm glad you decided to bring her up here.
It would have been damnable to leave her in that god-
forsaken village.'

Hilda, greedily drinking this in, flushed with pleasure.
Fancy Uncle Phillip noticing her hands! Nobody but
herself ever had, in spite of the care she lavished on them
when it occurred to her to do so. As for her eyes, she had
never, until this moment, even thought about them. She
must take a good look at them. She stayed there for a
little longer, hoping to hear further pleasant revelations
about herself; nothing more was said, however, and trying
to appear as calm and ladylike as possible, she knocked
timidly and went in. They all smiled reassuringly, and
Hilda, gratified by her uncle's remarks, began to feel
more like herself. The sick, lost feeling had gone from
the pit of her stomach, and she sat down gravely in a
corner of the big sofa.

Aunt Mildred, saying that she would see to the supper,
went out, and Aunt Helen began to talk to her, while
Uncle Phillip just sat and looked at her.

'First, Hilda, don't knock when you come into a room,
for this is your home now. We want you to feel this
straight away. Do you think you are going to like it — and
us?' Without waiting for a reply, she continued: 'Mildred
tells me that she has told you a little about us. Your
father died when you were quite a little girl, and asked
us to look after you as well as we could until you were old
enough to stand on your own feet. But you mustn't get
romantic notions into your head about us. Your father
left nothing, and, though we are comfortable enough, we
have nothing much to spare and want you to think about
making a career for yourself — once you've really settled
down, of course. In the meantime, we shall have to get

to know your tastes. When your Grandma wrote to us she said that you loved reading, as we all do too. Indeed, your Uncle Phillip sells books at his shop in the City. There's always plenty to read here, and there's a good public library quite near. What books have you read so far?'

Hilda, remembering the Co-op. library near Moss Ferry, repeated the titles of every book she could think of, excluding, however, *Chatterbox* and her Sunday School prize-books. Aunt Helen, she felt, would regard these as ridiculously childish.

'I've read *The Channings* and *Robinson Crusoe* and *East Lynne* and *Tess of the D'Urbervilles* and *Pilgrim's Progress*. And I'm learning French too,' she added importantly. It was a bitter disappointment to her to find that this last most spectacular accomplishment seemed to make no impression upon her aunt. Uncle Phillip, however, smiled at her and interposed: 'That's splendid, Hilda, and if you would like to learn German as well I'll give you some lessons. I expect I can help with the French too, though I know German much better. Would you like that, child?'

Hilda, thrilled by the prospect of such riches, awkwardly mumbled her thanks. Whatever would they think in Moss Ferry when they heard that she was learning yet another foreign tongue! Her foster-mother would be terribly upset and think she had gone clean out of her mind — got above herself so much, in spite of her new status, that nature could not endure it. Learning French was bad enough, Mrs. Winstanley would say, but learning German on top of it was just plain sinfulness. Better not let them know about the German, Hilda decided prudently. Aunt Helen was speaking again: 'About your reading, Hilda. You can help yourself of course to any books in the flat, though perhaps you had better not choose them quite at

random. Ask one of us first. Do you like Dickens and Scott?'

'I don't know,' replied Hilda. 'I've not read any yet, but I like everything, really.'

Aunt Helen moved over to a shelf of books and picked out two. 'Well, here are *Great Expectations* and *Ivanhoe* to begin with. After supper perhaps Phillip will read aloud to us. He often does, and I don't suppose you'll want to go to bed much before ten, unless you're tired after your long day.'

Hilda eagerly reassured her. What an exciting life she was now going to lead! Coming to this beautiful home, where everyone read all they wanted to as a matter of course, was like a fairy tale.

She kept a tight hold over herself throughout supper, afraid of appearing common and provincial. Her new family, however, did not seem to think that her table manners were any different from their own, so careful was she to do exactly as they did. She noticed, with a spasm of uneasiness, that nobody asked a blessing, and to be on the safe side said one in her mind half way through the meal. She was surprised, too, at the amount of talk that went on all the time. Uncle Phillip said all kinds of extraordinary things, and once he and Aunt Helen got quite heated over somebody called 'Vargner' and a song called 'O Star of Eve'. Her uncle maintained that it was not a good song and Aunt Helen said that she begged leave to differ. She sang a verse of it, and challenged her husband to say *now* that it was not a lovely tune. But he stuck to his own opinion and said no, even though she sang it so beautifully. And then, noticing Hilda's embarrassment at what appeared to her to resemble a quarrel, her aunt laughed unconvincingly and told her husband that he was quite impossible and asked what Hilda would think of them arguing so fiercely about a mere song, as if

it mattered anyway. But Uncle Phillip said it mattered very much indeed.

'Far be it from me,' he said emphatically, 'to belittle Wagner, but he came a cropper over that, and you ought to know it, Helen.'

'All right, Phillip. Let us agree to disagree,' Aunt Helen answered in a tone of benign finality. Her husband flushed, but made no further comment; and Hilda, greatly relieved, wondered who 'Vargner' could be, and was sorry that Uncle Phillip had not really had the last word.

Aunt Mildred, Hilda observed, spoke hardly at all, and they had not even asked for her opinion of the song. It was plain that Aunt Helen was the person who counted most, and Hilda decided that she must be very careful not to get on the wrong side of her. It was plain also that she hated to be contradicted.

When they were back in the sitting-room, Aunt Helen took another book and showed it to Hilda.

'See, Hilda. *The Pickwick Papers.* If you like this you'll like all Dickens. Would you like Phillip to read it to us?'

'Oh, yes, please,' said Hilda excitedly.

Turning over the pages, Phillip said that he would read about the skating party at Manor Farm. Hilda, at Sam Weller's introduction of the Sawbones, pealed with laughter, and the more Phillip read the longer and louder she laughed. She had never heard anything so funny in her life, and her aunts, laughing too, watched her delightedly. Mr. Winkle's frantic clinging to Sam on the ice made her laugh until the lining of her stomach was sore, but when, after Mr. Pickwick had fallen in, Mr. Tupman set off across country madly screaming 'Fire', she was compelled to bury her face in a cushion in a vain attempt to hide the fact that every atom of self-control had deserted her. Her collapse was so abandoned that

Phillip had to stop reading until some measure of composure came back to her. When he had finished the chapter, Aunt Helen, remarking that it was very late, decided that Hilda must go to bed, and he closed the book regretfully. As for Hilda, she could have listened for hours; she was not in the least tired, for a new magic had come into her life — a magic that sustained and exhilarated — the magic of Charles Dickens.

As she was saying good night, Helen, divining that she found it difficult and strange to address them easily as 'Aunt' and 'Uncle', suggested that she should call them by their Christian names, a suggestion which profoundly shocked Hilda. If she had dared to do any such thing in Moss Ferry, her foster-mother would promptly have boxed her ears for forwardness to her elders. Phillip, perceiving her reaction and anxious that she should not feel bothered, told her not to worry but to please herself. All that mattered was that she should feel absolutely at home.

She was unpacking her rush basket when Aunt Mildred came in to help her. As together they lifted out her clothes, Mildred asked if she had brought a dressing-gown, and Hilda was paralysed with shame at being obliged to confess that she had never possessed such an idle and useless garment. Nobody had one at home in Moss Ferry, for nobody had ever seemed to need one there.

'It doesn't matter, child, for a night or so. You can use your coat instead, and we'll soon get a dressing-gown for you. On Monday we're going to take you to Barkers, in Kensington, and fit you out. Helen wants to buy you a nice winter hat and coat, and Phillip said he would like to give you some new boots — brown, high-laced ones. They'll look smarter and neater on your long legs than your buttoned ones. I'll leave you now. Don't forget to switch off your bedside light before going to sleep. And

there's no harm in your reading for half an hour if you want to. Good night, dear, and sleep well. You do feel you're going to like being with us, don't you?'

Hilda, stunned by the dazzling prospect of a visit to Barkers in Kensington; of becoming the proud owner of a dressing-gown; of being able to read in bed by electric light, said shyly: 'I'm going to like everything, Aunt Mildred, and especially you.'

Mildred kissed her, and, as the door closed behind her, Hilda jumped on to the divan, making no move to undress for some minutes. She could still scarcely believe that only that same morning she had been wakened early by her foster-mother in Moss Ferry urging her to hurry so that she might make a good breakfast before starting out on the great journey to London. And now here she was with the incredible luxury of an entire room to herself. She plumped one hand into the divan and marvelled at its resilience after the lumpy, unyielding flock mattress she had always until now shared with her foster-sister. And how lovely the room itself was with its cream walls and glossy cream paint! The floor was covered with a thick, unpatterned blue carpet, and the window curtains were of heavy plain serge to match. Against one wall was a dark oak coffer with a vase of yellow chrysanthemums on it. Against another was a big bookcase packed with neatly arranged volumes. One shelf was entirely taken up with little, dark red books which Hilda, upon investigation, found to be the plays of William Shakespeare. Another shelf contained nothing but poetry. On the mantelpiece were several pieces of delicate blue and white china, and a number of tiny carved ivory figures which seemed to her extremely ugly, and very queer ornaments indeed to have in a bedroom. A stout gate-legged table in the centre, a couple of oak chairs and a small table by the divan completed the furnishings, except for the pictures.

In her bare little room in Moss Ferry the only picture had been a gaily-lettered text — THOU GOD SEEST ME — but though there were several pictures in this new room, they failed signally to remind her of God. They were mostly photographs of statues, very outspoken statues indeed without so much as a stitch on them. 'Shameful!' her foster-mother would have pronounced them. As she began to undress, savouring to the full the glory of doing this alone for the first time in her life, she gradually became conscious of the noise outside — many noises all blending together into a continuous dull roar. She raised the sash window and leaned out, frightened at the enormous height from which she looked down into a deep well, its walls starred with lights. She could actually see people in their kitchens, washing up or cooking things on stoves, not minding whether they were observed or not. It was like living in the street, she thought disapprovingly, and suddenly horrified by the knowledge that if she could see them they too could see her, and in her nightdress at that, she quickly lowered the window and drew the curtains.

For a moment she debated whether she should say her prayers in bed or out of bed, finally deciding that on this, her first night in London, sheer gratitude demanded some slight tribute of discomfort even though it could hardly be called discomfort to kneel on a thick, warm carpet instead of on thin, cold linoleum. She remembered them all at home, even the hateful Lily, but when she came to her new family she hesitated, feeling that it would be a little presumptuous to pray for them before she knew them properly.

In bed at last, revelling in her freedom from Lily, she opened *Great Expectations* and read avidly until the permitted half-hour was up; then reluctantly she switched off the reading lamp, but immediately switched it on again,

and for some seconds played with it as childishly as she had played with the magical geyser. She lay awake for what seemed hours, reliving every moment of the day, recalling every word her new relations had said to her and to each other, and marvelling afresh at her great good fortune in coming to this beautiful home. Finally, with enchanting visions of Barkers in Kensington, the River Thames and Chiswick Mall, merging into musings about 'Vargner', the promised dressing-gown, and the further joys yet to come from Arabella Allen and her fur-topped boots, Mr. Tupman, Pip, and Sir Walter Scott, slightly mitigated by an uneasy feeling that she would have to be very careful indeed not to upset Aunt Helen, she played with the lamp a little longer, and, mentally composing a glowing letter to her old home in Moss Ferry, fell asleep.

CHAPTER II

SUNDAY: NEW STYLE

HILDA was never to forget her first Sunday in London. It was the sharp, taut line which cut her off completely from the world she had hitherto known. It was during breakfast that the first shock came. Aunt Helen, peeling an apple for her husband, looked intently at her niece as the bells of a nearby church began to ring, and inquired whether in Moss Ferry she had gone to church or to chapel on Sundays.

'To chapel,' Hilda replied, unprepared for the coming thunder-bolt.

'And do you like going to chapel?'

'Oh, yes, but I was christened in church. Nearly everybody in Moss Ferry goes to chapel. I went to Sunday School in the morning, and then to afternoon and evening service.'

'I see,' said Helen quietly. Then, after a slight pause, 'We want you to please yourself now whether you go or not.'

Hilda, not fully grasping the significance of this remark, confided that she had all her life wanted to attend church instead of chapel, but that her foster-mother would never hear of anything so unnatural.

'She used to say that church didn't do you half as much good as chapel, but I'd like to come to church with you,' she said gratefully, unable to conceal her joy at this prospective social advancement.

'I don't think you quite understand me, dear,' said Helen, with a curious glance at her husband and sister. 'What I mean is that, unless you want to, you need not go either to church or to chapel. We don't go ourselves,

and we feel that you're old enough to please yourself about this too. Mind — we've nothing whatever against your going. You are just to please yourself about it.'

Hilda flushed with pride at the flattering assumption that, in the matter of religion, she was considered old enough to know her own mind; but it also so astounded her that she took some minutes to realize its full implications. Anxious to please by doing, or rather by not doing, as her relatives did, she was tempted to proclaim the instant annihilation of the whole of her religious beliefs. Habit, however, was too strong; she felt in her bones that if, without grave reasons, she let Sunday pass without attending some place of worship, dire calamity must necessarily befall her not in this world only but also, even more certainly, in the next. She therefore said sedately that, if they didn't really object, she would like to go to church. To evening service.

'Of course we don't object, Hilda,' said Aunt Helen with an edge in her voice. 'Haven't I just explained that you are a free agent in this matter. Why should I say so if I don't mean it? There's Chiswick Parish Church quite near. Phillip will show you how you get to it from here; he's going to take you out this morning and show you the river and the Malls. And this afternoon we've planned to take you to the London Museum. We often go on Sundays. And as it's your first day in London, we'll have tea out, for a treat.'

Hilda, quite dazed, could only stammer a shy thank you. Things were happening so quickly in this amazing new life that she had some difficulty in sorting them out clearly. First, religious freedom, a matter so staggering in its immensity that she was afraid there must be a catch in it somewhere. Nobody in Moss Ferry had ever been able to get through life without going regularly to church or to chapel. True, there had been a few back-

sliders who only went occasionally, but at any rate they
went sometimes. Had they been hardened recusants,
life would have been made so unbearable for them by
their more law-abiding neighbours that they might just
as well have destroyed themselves. Then, as if religious
freedom was not sufficient for one day, and that day a
Sunday, she was actually going to visit a museum, and,
please God, have her tea in a shop, to say nothing of the
promised walk with Uncle Phillip by the River Thames.
But exciting and pleasurable though the day promised to
be, she had many uncomfortable twinges about doing all
these happy things on the Sabbath, and was thankful
that she had compromised by electing to go to church that
evening. That, at any rate, was something she could tell
them about quite honestly when she wrote to Moss Ferry;
even so her foster-mother would deplore her immediate
and snobbish departure from the good chapel-going ways
in which she had been brought up. It was an established
belief in her old home that a church-goer, no matter how
ardent and regular in his worship, ran a terrible risk of
not finding salvation in the end, a risk no true chapel-goer
need ever worry about. In spite of these disturbing reflections, Hilda hoped that her compromise would stand her
in good stead in the world hereafter. She hoped also that
her relations would be impressed by the fact that she had
not readily abandoned her faith.

When she had made herself ready to accompany her
uncle, it at once became obvious that there was something about her appearance which her aunts thought
peculiar, for she caught them exchanging meaning
glances. It was her hat, of course, a white chip straw
trimmed with yellow marguerites. She had known, even
as she started from Moss Ferry, that there was something
about it unsuited to an October day, but her foster-
mother had persisted that it made a better showing than

her last year's winter felt. Aunt Helen, not meaning to be unkind, asked if she had not brought another with her. Hilda, reddening, shook her head.

'Well, for one day it doesn't really matter. We'll get you a new one tomorrow, but it may be rather windy by the river. Off you go and look at old Father Thames, but I do wish you hadn't — but never mind. Enjoy yourselves!'

Hilda, self-conscious and appalled at the stupidity of wearing a summer hat with a winter coat, felt her eyes prick with tears, but, as soon as they were out of the flat, Uncle Phillip took her arm affectionately and assured her that she had nothing whatever to worry about. He said it was a pretty hat and suited her down to the ground. It was surprising how easy and comfortable she felt with him; there was something about Aunt Helen's peremptoriness which made her feel clumsy and stupid.

Walking along arm in arm with Phillip, Hilda gazed about her in ecstasy. Here she really was, at eleven o'clock on the Sabbath Day, taking a walk in London, and only one week ago, at this very minute, she had been in her Sunday School class in the United Methodist Chapel near Moss Ferry. It was stupendous, and, in spite of the white straw hat, she knew herself to be the luckiest girl who had ever lived. From time to time she glanced up admiringly at Phillip, so distinguished-looking with his pale face and dark eyes and gay smile. She would have given much for Moss Ferry to see her like this, escorted by a real gentleman, and he her own relative by marriage; and there was no doubt that Phillip was also enjoying himself, for, every time he caught her looking at him, he squeezed her arm and smiled. As they turned down a narrow, stuffy alley, Hilda caught the dark gleam of water and her heart began to beat faster. The great River Thames! She had read so much about it, but had

little thought that one day — this day — she would actually see it.

'Here it is, Hilda,' said Uncle Phillip proudly as they emerged on to the Mall. 'The Thames. London's own river. Liquid history, as somebody has called it. One day soon you must come up to the City with me and I'll show you London Bridge and the Tower. We're on Chiswick Mall now. Going upstream you come to Kew and Richmond and Windsor. Downstream lies Westminster and the Pool of London, and so on to Greenwich, and beyond there's the sea. That ugly pile is Hammersmith Bridge. We'll walk as far as that. You'll like some of the houses on Hammersmith Mall. They're lovely. When you want a fascinating walk you can cross by ferry from here and go up to Kew, or cross Hammersmith Bridge and go towards Putney. I hope you like walking.'

Hilda assured him eagerly that she liked nothing better, and chattered freely of the great walks which she had taken by herself around her old home, or with her particular friend, May Woodville, the schoolmaster's daughter. She thought of the River Mersey. In spite of its big foreign ships, how little and black it seemed now in comparison with this wide and sparkling Thames.

'Do the foreign ships sail up here too?' she asked, anxious to show that she was interested and wished to learn.

'No. Not as far as this. The Pool of London is the place for seeing them. Up here it is mostly barges and pleasure-steamers. But in the Pool you will see ships from all over the world. London, as I daresay you know, is one of our great ports.'

'Oh, yes,' agreed Hilda quickly. 'I know that; and I know about the Tower of London, and Windsor Castle too. That's where the King and Queen live sometimes, isn't it?'

'That's right, though Windsor is mostly used for State

occasions. And I forgot. You go upstream to Hampton Court. That's a wonderful place, built by Cardinal Wolsey for himself, and then . . .'

'I know. I know,' she interrupted quickly. 'The King got jealous and Cardinal Wolsey had to give it up to him.'

'That's the way it went. I see you know your history. What king was that?'

'Henry the Eighth,' Hilda answered proudly.

Phillip looked at her and smiled. How fresh and bright and eager she was! It was going to be very pleasant work indeed forming her mind, and he only hoped that Helen wouldn't interfere too much. She would of course do her share in the good work, but she was so dominating, and he had already perceived that the girl who, with her, was shy and self-conscious, was, with him, quite natural and childishly unembarrassed. Well, he would always be there to stand up for her, and he knew that he could count on Mildred too. For all her pathetic youthfulness and her feminine desire to please and make a good impression, he foresaw that Hilda was not going to be easy to handle. She had a mind and a personality of her own, and it would be a shame if Helen's natural 'bossiness' dammed her up as effectively as it had dammed up Mildred.

They strolled along in a leisurely way, Hilda's eyes darting everywhere in her anxiety not to miss anything. Even the monstrous ironmongery of Hammersmith Bridge filled her with admiration, and she was frankly puzzled that her uncle should think it ugly; with the sun glancing on its gilded pinnacles it was really beautiful, and the people passing over it, silhouetted against the clear October sky, seemed to confer upon it the delicate precision of an etching.

Phillip drew her attention to the houses they were passing: some of them tall and narrow, with long shining windows and frilled muslin curtains. He said that they

had been built mostly in the eighteenth century and were as lovely as any in London and chock-full of history. Hilda had never heard anyone talk about houses like this. In Moss Ferry there were only two gentlemen's houses — the solid big Vicarage, and the old red-brick house in which the Farnham family lived, that was noted chiefly for its steamy and exotic glasshouse.

On the way home, Phillip asked her many questions about life in Moss Ferry, and many more about her experiences when she was learning the dressmaking in Manchester, all of them leading up to what he really wanted to know. He felt his way cautiously, for it would never do to give the girl the impression he was in any way disloyal to Helen. But he was finding that he liked her enormously, and was quite determined that, when the time came for her to train for a career, it should be one she wanted for herself and not one that Helen wanted for her. His wife had already hinted at the Civil Service as a safe and worthy, if not lucrative, profession. If Hilda thought so too, very well: but if not, it would be cruel to force her into it.

'We shall have to have a talk about your future some time, Hilda. Your Aunt Helen thinks perhaps the Civil Service might interest you. Or teaching. Of course you would have to study hard for some years, for there would be examinations to pass. What do you think yourself?'

Hilda, a dreadful chill creeping through her at the word 'examinations', looked at him miserably, all the joy of the morning instantly vanishing. Examinations would mean arithmetic, the one thing at which she was, if not positively stupid, by no manner of means bright. Given time and encouragement, she felt equal to holding her own with other girls in everything but arithmetic. Somehow, in the Church School at Moss Ferry, she had always managed to scrape through her written sums, and even, sweating

35

blood, through the agonies of mental arithmetic, but Uncle Phillip was speaking of real examinations, where she would have no affectionate and interested teacher to give her personal encouragement. It would be terrible if she failed, and fail she surely would in open competition with strangers, and then what a fool Aunt Helen would think her! The prospect was appalling, even unthinkable, yet, anxious as she was to demonstrate that she was not quite an ignorant savage, she knew that here and now she must take her stand and be absolutely truthful if she were to enlist Uncle Phillip firmly on her side. In a voice unsteady with embarrassment at the painful confession, she said timidly: 'I don't think I should ever pass in arithmetic. I'm best at history and composition and geography. And scripture too,' she added hopefully. 'Couldn't you explain to Aunt Helen for me?'

Phillip, realizing what this appeal had cost her, smiled. 'Don't get upset about it, child. I was never much good at sums myself. Mildred isn't either. Helen's the only really clever one in the family. We'll settle things all right, so don't worry. It's time we were getting back to lunch now, or Mildred will be cross. Let's think of our jaunt this afternoon, and blow the arithmetic.'

Hilda, a great fear lifted from her, breathed naturally again. What a wonderful person Uncle Phillip was! He seemed to understand everything, even his wife. She smiled at him gratefully, confident that she had nothing further to worry about as far as the black tortures of arithmetic were concerned, no matter what Aunt Helen might say or do.

Profoundly happy in the knowledge that Uncle Phillip was her friend, and that Aunt Mildred, though in a different way, liked her too, Hilda did full justice to the first Sunday dinner she had ever eaten out of Moss Ferry. The meal, beautifully cooked by Mildred, was simple,

and no different in quality from what they would now be sitting down to in her old home. It all looked so different, though, that Hilda could scarcely credit even yet that she would never again have to eat at an American-cloth-covered table, flowerless and bare of all but essentials. Moreover, it was so strange to hear Uncle Phillip and his wife talking continuously, as if this was not the great and solemn occasion of Sunday dinner, which one consumed in reverent silence, but a mere weekday affair. As at supper the previous night, she followed the progress of the others, being careful not to finish before they did, for she had read that it was impolite to eat too quickly in company and be left with an empty plate while others were still eating.

'Have a little more, Hilda,' said Uncle Phillip genially, when she at last laid down her knife and fork.

'No thank you, Uncle Phillip. I've had an excellent sufficiency,' she answered gravely. The walk had given her a keen appetite, and she certainly could have eaten a little more, but she felt that good manners demanded this self-denial.

'Nonsense, child! Pass up your plate. I'm sure you could manage another helping.'

She obeyed happily. What a dear, thoughtful man Uncle Phillip was, she reflected in a glow of self-confidence, a glow which faded immediately when Aunt Helen, helping her to vegetables, said reprovingly: 'You must never say you have had "an excellent sufficiency", Hilda. If you really don't want more just say, "No, thank you". That is quite enough.'

Hilda, reddening at this public reproof, was now so nervous that she could not eat at all, and, divining her embarrassment, Phillip looked coldly at his wife. To him the stilted and fantastic phrase had a charmingly archaic sound. Poor child! What on earth did it matter? What did

Helen expect from a girl brought up in a labourer's cottage at the back of beyond, educated in a national school, and not so bad an advertisement, he decided, of either? She was charming to look at in spite of her lankiness: really most attractive with her fine brown hair, clear, delicate skin and widely-set grey eyes. How eagerly she had taken everything in during their walk! She was receptive and intelligent right enough, and quite acutely sensitive. 'An excellent sufficiency' — he smiled to himself. Helen of course was entitled to correct her, but not in front of them all. The child was bound to commit all sorts of gaucheries before the rough-cast of village life crumbled away from her. He decided to speak to his wife at the first opportunity and ask her to be more tactful. She would resent it, but fourteen was a difficult and impressionable age, and it was up to them all to do their utmost to make things easy for Hilda.

Meanwhile Hilda, feeling extremely wretched and deflated, had an unpleasant foreboding that she was going to dislike her Aunt Helen just as fervently as she liked her Uncle Phillip and Aunt Mildred. And what was the matter with 'excellent sufficiency', anyway? she asked herself, resentful of the downright correction. Her instinct warned her, however, that she must give no sign of her resentment, for it was clear that Aunt Helen would always have the last word, and that both Uncle Phillip and Aunt Mildred were resigned to this depressing fact. And though she did not think that Aunt Helen, unlike her foster-mother, would ever box her ears if she dared to answer back, there would be an edge to her voice that would be infinitely worse. Hilda looked at her, and then at Mildred; the satisfaction would have to remain locked within her for ever, but the comparison gave her great comfort. Aunt Helen, she summed up, was clever, and bright, and good-looking, but Aunt Mildred, with hardly

a word to say for herself when her sister was about, was really beautiful. One would listen to Aunt Helen, indeed one could not help listening, but it would be her sister one would enjoy looking at. 'And let Aunt Helen put that in her pipe and smoke it,' thought Hilda to herself, vulgarly.

The meal over, Aunt Helen announced, in tones which anticipated a chorus of approval, that she would make the coffee, after which they would be off to the London Museum. It seemed that Aunt Helen's coffee was something very special indeed. Hilda, accustomed to coffee made immediately out of a bottle, was impressed by the importance which her aunt attached to this simple business, and flattered when invited to watch the process. The great secret, her aunt explained, lay in the pinch of salt to bring out the full flavour, and in never allowing the milk to boil. The result certainly justified these unusual precautions, and Hilda, aware that it was expected of her, expressed sycophantic approval. It was lovely coffee, but had it tasted like wormwood she would have pronounced it beyond compare in her anxiety to keep on the right side of Aunt Helen.

In due course they arrived at the London Museum. Hilda was in a dither of excitement, for this was her first visit to a museum of any kind; but, happy though she was, she could not altogether subdue an invading tide of guilt at enjoying herself so enormously, and apparently so lawfully, on the Sabbath. Even the number of people surging around them, all of them seemingly untroubled by any twinges of conscience, did not entirely reassure her. But although the guilty feeling persisted, she felt also a most unchristian pride in her new importance as a Londoner, made free, in her own right, of the fascinating treasures to be perceived on every hand. Uncle Phillip, taking special charge of her, pointed them out to her one after another,

discussing them as knowledgeably and proudly as if he owned them. He spoke quietly, seldom raising his voice, so that everything he said made a deep impression and she knew she would not forget it. In spite of all she had read about the great London museums, she had not realized, until now, their full magnificence, and when Phillip, delighted by her sparkling eyes and awe-struck expression, said there was no reason why she should not come here whenever she wanted to, if her studies permitted, her stare of joyful surprise made him laugh. It was not until they reached the brilliantly-lighted glass-case containing the wedding-dresses of Queen Victoria and Queen Alexandra that she found her voice. Queen Victoria's bridal-gown, so fairy-like, drew from her one ecstatic 'Oh!', but Queen Alexandra's rose-spattered dress loosened her tongue, and, heedless of people who glanced at her curiously as they heard her Lancashire accent, she related at length how Queen Alexandra and King Edward had once passed through Moss Ferry on their way to stay with Lord Derby at Knowsley. Phillip, pleased that she had broken through her self-consciousness, encouraged her to go on, and, her eyes feasting on the froth of lace and jewels before them, she described that sunny, never-to-be-forgotten morning — Queen Alexandra's parma-violet frock, her heavenly smile, her lovely, lovely face. And to think that now she was actually gazing at Queen Alexandra's wedding-dress, the most fascinating thing among all the wonders she had seen that afternoon. It was with obvious reluctance that she turned away, reminded by Aunt Helen that it was nearly closing time, and that she could, as Uncle Phillip had just told her, come again at any time she liked.

Tea in the A.B.C. shop seemed to the bewildered Hilda nearly as enchanting as the museum they had just left, and she stared admiringly at the marble-topped tables and black-frocked young waitresses who moved about so

quickly and noisily. Aunt Helen, examining the menu, asked what they would like, toasted tea-cakes or crumpets, and, without waiting for their reply, chose crumpets. Uncle Philip gave the order accordingly, with the addition of cakes and a pot of tea for four.

'No,' Helen interrupted him, 'a pot of tea for three, and might we have an extra cup and saucer, please.'

'Certainly, Madam,' said the waitress with polite sarcasm and a sympathetic look at Hilda, who was making the effort of a life-time to keep back her tears of mortification. Phillip, too, had flushed at the paltry and barbarous request, and observing poor Hilda's miserable face, was unwise enough to show his annoyance.

'Damn it, Helen! What's the matter with you? We're not paupers, and Hilda's not a baby. Really, for an intelligent woman you manage to do some surprisingly unintelligent things at times.'

'That may be so,' she answered frigidly, 'but you know perfectly well that neither Mildred nor myself ever drink more than one cup, and if it is unintelligent to pay for the unnecessary, then we must agree to differ. The waitress doesn't mind giving us an extra cup, so why make such a fuss? And I'm quite sure Hilda doesn't mind, do you?'

Hilda, fortified by Phillip's protest, and from that moment transferring to him all the loyalty and affection of which she had ample store, smiled brightly and falsely upon her aunt and gave the expected answer, certain that he would not despise her for it.

The waitress reappeared with a loaded tray, and the incident, as far as her uncle and aunt were concerned, appeared to be closed. But it had made an unfortunate impression upon their niece. 'Fancy Aunt Helen being so near,' she mused sadly. Poor as everybody was in Moss Ferry, not one of them would have done such a thing in public, not if they had had to go without tea for

41

a month of Sundays afterwards. Making a fuss about tuppence, for that, by furtively scanning the menu, she discovered to be the precise difference between a pot of tea for three and a pot for four. Had she dared she would have offered to pay for her own tea, for she had not been suffered to come to London penniless.

No sooner were they home again than it was time for Hilda to be off to church. Aunt Helen again inquired if she was quite sure that she wanted to go, and Hilda, who had not yet shaken off the disquietude which had afflicted her in the museum, answered firmly that she did. She was, moreover, exhilarated with her new status as a permitted church-goer, and, with an affectionate warning from Phillip not to lose her way, set out proudly. Running light-heartedly down the stairs, she narrowly avoided a head-on collision with a tiny Japanese gentleman on his way up, who took off his hat, bowed very low, and smiled as they passed. Hilda beamed at him and descended more slowly, this being more lady-like when a gentleman was looking back at her, though in point of fact this gentleman, as he resumed his ascent, was congratulating himself on his narrow escape from being bowled over by this lanky specimen of English girlhood, whom he devoutly hoped it would not be his misfortune to meet again, either on the stairs or elsewhere. The Japanese gentleman, Hilda presumed, was the one who lived in the flat next door, for she had noticed the outlandish name — T. Tomashi — on his brass plate, and had been told by Aunt Mildred that he was something in the Japanese Embassy; also that he was the perfection of all that a desirable neighbour should be because he was wonderfully quiet and hardly ever visible, an observation which struck Hilda as so odd that she suspected Mildred of concealing something, for what was a neighbour for if not to be neighbourly?

She entered the church timidly, seated herself right at

the back, and looked curiously about her. It was wonderful, she told herself, to be worshipping in this old London church; wonderful to sit beneath brilliant lights instead of the dim, swinging oil-lamps of chapel; wonderful to let her eyes roam along the walls, so thickly encrusted with tablets and plaques and funny, old-fashioned effigies, the like of which she had never before set eyes on. And it was enthralling to watch the quick and fashionable Londoners coming in and to remind herself yet again that, in spite of her offending summer hat, she too was now a Londoner. But long before the service was over she began to feel chilled and lonely, conscious that there was something missing. There was no friendly warmth here as there had been in the chapel at her old home. The sermon, cold, scholarly, delivered in an even, passionless tone, did not stir her, and compared but poorly with the full-blooded denunciations she was accustomed to enjoying in chapel. Even the measureless social ascent implicit in the fact that she was in church and not chapel, failed to comfort her, since there was nobody of her acquaintance to witness it. Had Uncle Phillip or Aunt Mildred accompanied her it would have been quite different. It was consequently with relief that she heard the Blessing and slipped out, dejected and unrewarded, feeling that she might just as well have stopped at home, lost and happy in *Great Expectations*, or pursuing the further adventures of the young lady with the fur round her boots.

CHAPTER III

AUNT HELEN AND AUNT MILDRED

WHILE Hilda was at church, her new relations, conscious in their different ways that she had brought a somewhat disturbing atmosphere into their busy lives, sat round the fire discussing her. In theory it had seemed plain sailing enough when, after much serious discussion, they had decided to bring her to London. The decision taken, Helen had written to the girl's grandmother, asking various searching questions, and had received from that stern but honest woman a letter in which she summed up Hilda's character frankly. She wrote that the girl was tall for her age, gradely-looking enough, sharp as a needle at her book-learning, good-natured and affectionate, but self-willed and head-strong, the latter characteristic passed on, she admitted, from the mother. Furthermore, the letter continued, ever since through village tittle-tattle the girl had discovered that the good folk who had reared her were not her real parents, she had grown increasingly above herself. This lamentable tendency to uppishness had for some time been a source of great disquiet to her foster-family, and there was no doubt that the child would need careful watching. In conclusion, Mrs. Stringer reminded them bluntly that for fourteen years they had shown no particular interest in their niece beyond sending the agreed sum for her keep; that the foster-parents were as fond of her as if she had been their own flesh and blood; that she herself, in spite of Hilda's restless ways and aggravating if laudable desire to be always bettering herself, shared this affection, and that if anything went wrong at London there would always be a home for her in Moss Ferry if she wanted to

come back. 'Not,' the letter ended, 'as us thinks she will, but no harm done in speaking plain.'

When Helen had read them this uncompromising epistle which had taken Mrs. Stringer the better part of a week to compose, they had, though appreciating its directness and honesty, smiled at one another. An intelligent child of fourteen, they argued, could scarcely need the strict supervision Mrs. Stringer seemed to think so necessary. Helen fastened on the phrase 'sharp as a needle at her book-learning', and said that was the great thing to remember, that and the pleasant inference that Hilda was not without physical attractions. Had Mrs. Stringer informed her that Hilda was of homely appearance and not notably bright in her intellects, no amount of sisterly loyalty to the girl's father would have induced Helen to adopt her. Mildred, indeed, would not have been influenced by these deficiencies, for she had a softer and deeper nature than Helen, who had always regarded her, though affectionately, as her mental inferior and junior, when in fact there was but two years between them. And because Mildred, awed by her sister's alleged cleverness and easy social assurance, was invariably tongue-tied and nervous whenever they were together, she had been generally regarded as a beautiful nonentity. Only Phillip, and, years afterwards, Hilda herself, realized that Mildred was anything but a gentle fool. Talk easily she could not, for years of reverential admiration for her sister had had their stifling effect, but her natural good sense was considerable, and her judgment of people exceptionally acute. She seemed to possess invisible antennae that instantly perceived the fundamental truth of a character, and if she gave it as her considered opinion that a person was not to be trusted, Phillip would have staked his life on her judgment.

It was the unpleasing strain of parsimony in her sister

which, more than anything, irritated Mildred. Once, as a birthday present, Helen had taken her to Exeter for a week, stressing that there was no need for her to bring any money at all, as it was to be her 'treat'. Poor Mildred trustingly did as she was told, and as a result spent the unhappiest holiday of her life. She, a grown woman, had to ask for every penny, even for her natural needs, Helen pointing out, with sisterly candour, that if their requirements in this direction could be made to coincide, one penny might serve for both, provided no attendant was in sight. And now it was painfully clear to Mildred, from the miserable business of the extra cup and saucer at tea, that Helen was going to adopt an equally grudging attitude towards their niece. Well, she must try and make things easy for the girl, though her own income was slender in comparison with Helen's. Anyway, Hilda would be mostly left to her to take about, for Helen was always rushing hither and thither, and throwing her energies into different 'movements', the chief of which was Female Suffrage. It was a prospect Mildred found pleasant enough; for though neither Helen nor Phillip had ever yet made her feel unwanted, it was natural that they must sometimes prefer not to be burdened by her.

Helen too had thought all this out before giving her casting vote for bringing Hilda to live with them. Not, of course, that Mildred seemed to mind being left alone, for she was continually urging them to leave her out of their excursions. Helen, indeed, would have been surprised and mortified had she known how passionately her sister, at times, yearned for a little freedom. It was small wonder, then, that Mildred felt no surprise when Phillip, making business the excuse, sometimes came home very late; for, though she might be dumb she was by no means blind, and she was absolutely certain that his business 'friend' was a woman. Once, herself unobserved, she had

seen him at the perfumery counter of the Army and Navy Stores buying scent for a quiet, dowdy-looking girl, and wondered for weeks afterwards what he could have seen in her, who was so different from the energetic Helen. The pair of them had looked as happy as a couple of children on an outing, and Phillip was obviously enjoying the frivolity of the occasion: perfume being one of the things which his strong-minded wife particularly detested, on the ground that it was 'useless'. The assistant, a pretty girl plainly aware of Phillip's appreciative gaze, had tirelessly produced an immense variety of perfumes, taking out the stoppers, inviting them to sniff, and finally pouring a drop from the bottle selected on to the girl's handkerchief. Mildred, saddened by the spectacle of her brother-in-law's perfidy, but devoutly thankful that it was she and not Helen who had discovered it, puzzled ceaselessly over the affair. The girl was so very ordinary — so negative and unalluring both in looks and in manner — that for the life of her she couldn't make out what Phillip saw in her. The problem gnawed at her and worried her until, in a sudden flash, she solved it: in contrast to Helen's restless energy, her cleverness, her strength of mind, which had an almost vampirish quality, this plain, dowdy little thing soothed him, gave him a respite and relief from his wife's exuberant vitality; and, though she could not but deplore his duplicity, she found she could fully comprehend it. His affection and admiration for Helen was, she knew, genuine and deep, but he had to have some outlet for his own personality; he needed someone with whom *he* could be clever, and his refuge was in this insignificant-looking girl. Mildred, relieved to have got to the root of the matter, reflected with her usual common sense that, since it had to be, it was a mercy the girl was so ordinary; and even thought of warning him to be more careful in future. But she did not do so; and now her wandering

thoughts returned to her niece, still under discussion.

Phillip, moved more than he would have cared to admit by the recollection of Hilda's bright eagerness of the morning, had boldly suggested that she should be sent to a good day-school for a couple of years, urging that it was only fair that she should be given her chance, even though it might be difficult in view of her education so far.

'It would be an asset for her to get the atmosphere of a decent school, and I don't grudge the fees, as you know. Don't you think so, Mildred?' he asked.

'Yes, I do, but of course a great deal depends on what sort of work she wants to go in for.'

'That's the whole crux,' said Helen emphatically. 'It's senseless to spend money on an extended education if at the end of it she wants to sell hats or something. I'd like her to go into the Civil Service. It's safe and pensionable, and she seems to be intelligent enough for it, though I hope to goodness she won't remain so monosyllabic for ever. You'd think she was frightened to death of us by the timid way she answers a question. I'm in two minds as to whether it's shyness or dullness, in spite of her alleged sharpness at her books. What I really mean,' she ended rather lamely as she caught Phillip's quizzical glance at Mildred, 'is that she is, after all, turned fourteen, and surely old enough to converse freely and naturally. She embarrasses me with her timid monosyllables.'

Phillip, irritated by his wife's obtuseness, here flew vigorously to Hilda's defence: 'You can take it from me, Helen, that she's anything but dull, though I'm afraid we shall have to think of something different from the Civil Service. Something that won't need a fairly stiff exam. She talked freely enough to me on our walk this morning, and if there's one thing she's absolutely terrified of it's figures. And I don't blame her either. But what's the point of her going in for something safe and pension-

able? She's got the sort of personality, even if *you* don't see it yet, that will get her along all right. And I don't mean to be offensive, old girl, but she seems rather afraid of you. She probably thinks you are going to expect too much, though it's obvious that she admires you. If you honestly believe it's too late to send her back to school, then I personally think it would be best to leave matters alone for a year or so. Let her work at French and German. I can help her there. And let's plan a course of reading for her. The first thing to do surely is to get the rough edges knocked off. What do you say?'

Helen, though ruffled by the suggestion that her niece was afraid of her, expressed agreement with these views.

'All right, Phillip. As you say, she must have a curriculum planned for her. But the first thing we must do is to get her some clothes. That awful hat! And that hideous coat — all wrong for her complexion. And we must break the news when she comes back from church about not writing to her foster-parents. We don't want them coming here to see her. It would be very awkward. She'll soon forget them. In fact she must.'

Phillip looked at his wife in astonishment.

'Surely, Helen, you'll not lay down the law too heavily! Of course she'll want to write. And what about them? It would be pretty low-down to leave them without direct news. Think of how they'll be waiting for her first letter! Of course you must let her write to them occasionally.'

Mildred, recalling the misery in his face when Hilda had taken leave of her foster-father on the station in Manchester, backed Phillip up firmly, and, faced with their united opposition, Helen reluctantly compromised.

'Very well. She can write to say she's arrived safely and likes it here, but I simply won't have them knowing this address. I myself shall write to her Grandmother from time to time and let her know how Hilda is getting on;

Mrs. Stringer can give out any news if asked for it, but the sooner the girl forgets Moss Ferry and everybody in it the better — Ah, she's back!'

'Did you like it, Hilda?' Helen asked brightly as her niece went to take off her outdoor things.

'Not very much, Aunt Helen.'

'Why? Was the sermon very dull?'

'Yes. And it seemed so funny being by myself and not knowing anybody at all in the congregation.'

'Oh well, remember that you need not go again if you don't want to. Come and get warm. I want to have a little talk with you before supper.'

Hilda, wondering apprehensively whether she had done anything wrong, for her aunt looked very serious, nervously obeyed, but was reassured when both Phillip and Mildred smiled encouragingly at her.

'It's like this, Hilda. We know how kind your foster-parents have always been to you, and of course we don't want you to forget this fact, but things are different now you've made your home with us. Moss Ferry is over and done with, and need never come into your life again.' Helen paused uncertainly. With the girl's puzzled eyes riveted upon her, she found it more difficult than she had imagined, and neither Phillip nor Mildred seemed disposed to help her. 'What I want to say is this: your life from now on is going to be entirely different. You'll meet different people — educated people. And don't think I am being a snob, but we don't feel it will be a good thing for you to keep in touch with the people up in the North. In a little while you'll find that you have nothing in common with them yourself. You'll speak differently, and dress differently,' she blundered on with a tactlessness that made Hilda redden and Phillip wince. 'It would be just as embarrassing for you as it would be for them. Of course I shall write to your Grandmother from time to

time, letting her know all about you, and she can pass the news on to your foster-mother. But I don't want you to write, except just once to let them know you are safe and happy, and you must promise, now, to obey me in this, and that you will never let them know this address.'

Hilda, terrified of her aunt, and because of her terror all the more anxious to ingratiate herself, gave her promise with a shameful eagerness. She was only too willing to forget her lowly upbringing, but not to the point of forgetting her foster-parents, common though they might be compared with her real relations. The knowledge that nobody from Moss Ferry would ever see her in her new splendour was, too, a bitter disappointment. Still, it was something that she could write at all, even though she might not hear from them.

Helen, relieved that the unpleasant business had passed off so well, gave her husband a satisfied smile, which he did not return. It was to be a long time before the snobbery she had so criminally encouraged in her niece wore itself out, and Hilda saw her clearly for what she was in comparison with the humble folk whose influence she feared so much.

'So that's all right, Hilda. You're a good girl to behave so sensibly and see that we are only acting for your good. And tomorrow Mildred and I will take you to Kensington and fit you up from top to toe. New hat, new coat, new frock, and new boots.'

'And a dressing-gown, too,' put in Mildred quietly, 'a little present from me.'

'And some warm slippers as well,' added Phillip, putting his arm round Hilda, who felt childishly elated and happy at the dazzling prospect of smart, new clothes in spite of her Aunt Helen's extraordinary assumption that she could forget the previous fourteen years of her life in an equal number of hours.

CHAPTER IV

THE FIRST BATTLE

IMMEDIATELY after Phillip had left for the City next morning, Hilda and her aunts set out for Kensington, and, as it was a sunny morning, Helen decided that they would walk along the Malls to Hammersmith and get a bus there. Very conscious, in her Aunt Helen's society, of the unsuitable white hat, Hilda was alarmed by this proposal. Everybody would stare and giggle at a girl wearing a silly straw hat almost in November. She hadn't minded so much when she was out with Uncle Phillip yesterday, but Aunt Helen was another matter. It was, however, again such a lovely and interesting walk that she soon lost her self-consciousness in looking about her, and in marvelling afresh at the immensity and bustle of the River Thames. As they took a short cut through the graveyard of Chiswick Parish Church, Helen pointed dramatically to what appeared to her niece an exceedingly unremarkable grave.

'Do you see who lies there, Hilda?' she asked impressively.

Hilda, thinking it a little odd that a visit to a graveyard should be regarded as a preliminary to the tremendous business of buying new clothes, solemnly read aloud the name *James McNeill Whistler*. Then, aware that it was expected of her, inquired shyly: 'Was he a relation, Aunt Helen?'

Helen laughed. 'Don't I wish he was! No, child, of course not. He was a painter. A very great painter. There's a copy of one of his pictures in your room — the portrait of his Mother. Haven't you noticed it yet? And he painted the river, this river. We'll take you soon to the Tate Gallery and show you some of his work. Have you

ever been to a picture gallery? The one in Manchester, for instance?'

Hilda, until that moment unaware that Manchester even possessed a picture gallery, said she most certainly had been there, lots and lots of times. Helen gave her a suspicious look and asked for details. What pictures had she seen there, and which did she remember and like best?

Hilda flushed and turned appealingly to Mildred, who did her utmost to distract her sister's attention by urging that they should get on. Helen, however, continued to look searchingly at her trembling niece, and in a voice which sounded sad but dangerous, inquired gently: 'Why did you tell me such a *stupid* lie, Hilda?'

Hilda, now reduced to a state of abject confusion, and with enormous tears falling, not in homage but in fear upon the austere tomb of James McNeill Whistler, made no reply.

Helen, her voice gentler than ever, spoke again: 'Well, Hilda, I'm waiting.'

Hilda, her face red and ridiculous under the criminal white hat, made a desperate effort and gulped out: 'It was because of trying to blow out the electric light. I don't like you to think I don't know anything, Aunt Helen. I'm sorry.'

Helen, mollified by this realistic explanation, took her arm and, as they walked on, expatiated upon the stupidity of telling *unnecessary* untruths, a species of distinction which astonished Hilda considerably in view of her familiarity with the precepts of George Washington. It was distinctly comforting to learn that a lie, provided that it was intelligent, need not involve her in any struggle with her conscience. It was a pity, she reflected, that nobody had ever pointed this out to her before and so saved her a mort of trouble. Her admiration for her aunt's cleverness increased, and with it her mortal fear.

All the way to Hammersmith Bridge, Helen talked and Hilda and Mildred listened, as also did, for a fleeting second, every passer-by. There was no doubt at all, conceded Hilda, that Aunt Helen knew an awful lot, quite as much in fact as Uncle Phillip; but whereas he spoke very quietly, his wife seemed as if she wanted everybody around to hear all that she had to say. She did not actually shout, but her voice had a highly penetrating quality. Hilda, with the exception of the denunciatory sermons of the Methodist preacher in her native village, had never before heard anybody talk so positively. Aunt Helen talked just like a book, and, suddenly halting before an old house of warm red brick, she talked of a particular book, unknown to her niece, a book which went by the name of *Vanity Fair*.

'Look, Hilda! Miss Pinkerton's Academy for Young Ladies, where Becky Sharp, Amelia Sedley and Miss Swartz were educated. And this is the very garden into which Becky flung back the Johnson's Dictionary that Miss Jemima Pinkerton had given her as a parting gift. Becky, as she herself confided to her friend Amelia, was no angel, but what a character! I think you're a little young for Thackeray, but *Vanity Fair's* a treat in store, don't forget.' She turned to her sister: 'Can't you just see her doing it? Phillip and I have often wondered whereabouts that dictionary landed. Poor Becky!'

All three of them gazed reverently into the neat little garden, and Hilda, her imagination fired by what she had just heard, made her aunts jump by suggesting that after dark one evening she might very well come and fling a book into the garden, marking the spot where it fell with a white stone, and returning early next morning to memorize the position. It would be so easy, she pointed out, and so nice to be able to show the precise place to Uncle Phillip.

But Aunt Helen turned upon her severely. 'Of course you mustn't do anything of the kind, Hilda. You'd probably crash the book into a window, to say nothing of the infamy of treating a book, any book, with such violence. I'm surprised at your silliness. Put the idea out of your mind!'

Thus reproved, Hilda said no more, but decided that she would do it all the same for her own private satisfaction. On top of the bus, Helen, happily unconscious of her niece's decision, warned her to be on the look-out for Olympia, which they would soon be passing on their left. 'There it is, Hilda — that enormous building — that's Olympia.'

Hilda stared, entranced. The Olympia! She had read so much about it in the newspapers. Something or other was always going on in it, pageants and tournaments and what not.

'The Olympia,' she repeated wonderingly, turning round so as to keep it in view as long as possible.

'No, not *The* Olympia,' corrected her aunt. 'Just "Olympia". From Olympus — the home of the gods and goddesses of Greek mythology. You must read the books of the Reverend Alfred Church. Nobody has written more enchantingly of the old Greek legends. But we get off here. That's John Barkers over the way,' she informed Hilda importantly, as though making her a present of it. 'Nice shop, isn't it?'

Hilda, whose acquaintance with handsome shops, though of short duration, was by no means negligible, politely acquiesced. She could see that John Barkers had style, first-rate, tip-top style, but then so had the grand shops in St. Ann's Square, Manchester. Helen, irritated at her tepid reaction, shepherded them across the road, and they spent a few minutes looking into the windows, Aunt Helen speculating as to whether Hilda would show

to best advantage in brown or in green, and only Mildred thinking it necessary to inquire what Hilda's own preference might be. She, however, was so excited at the prospect of being dressed in the latest London fashion, that she didn't care what colour her Aunt Helen chose for her, and amiably said so. This docility pleased Helen, and surveying her critically she voted for brown.

'It's your colour, Hilda, unless you prefer green. But I think brown myself. It's a colour one never tires of. We'll look for a leaf-brown, a real autumn shade. "Season of mists and mellow fruitfulness, close bosom friend of the maturing sun." John Keats. But I don't imagine you have read much poetry. That's a further treat in store, and if you don't care for it now you will as you grow older. So shall we look for a warm autumn brown for the hat and coat?' she inquired quite unnecessarily, having already decided that brown it was to be.

Hilda, eager to get into the shop, felt no curiosity at all about John Keats. A warm autumn brown sounded lovely, and she followed her aunts tremulously into the big store, miserably conscious, among the crowds of well-dressed shoppers, that in her last winter's coat and unseasonable hat, she looked both unfashionable and provincial.

A good coat of heavy brown cloth was selected fairly quickly, although Helen seemed to think it rather expensive, especially as Hilda would soon be bound to grow out of it. The assistant, however, pointed out the deep hem which could be let down for another winter, and the cuffs, which could if necessary be used to lengthen the sleeves. Hilda was beside herself with joy. It really was a beautiful coat, a young lady's model, and made her look very tall and very smart. While she was turning this way and that before the long mirror, with Aunt Mildred smiling at her vanity, Helen was settling the bill and

astonishing the shopgirl by telling her too about John Keats. Like Hilda, the assistant also had not heard of him, though she kept repeating: 'Yes, Madam, I quite agree,' and from a quick look exchanged with another young lady assistant who was hovering near, Hilda felt sure that she had little time either for Aunt Helen or John Keats. Aunt Helen, however, was so pleased with the girl's apparent interest in the latter, that she asked her if she did not think a brown felt hat just the thing to go with the new coat.

'Certainly, Madam,' she instantly agreed. 'The young lady will look very smart in a brown felt. Shall we deliver the coat or will the young lady be wearing it?'

The question was superfluous, for her experienced eyes had seen at once, even had there been no white straw hat, that Hilda was straight from the country, and that wild horses would not drag the new coat off her. And being a nice young person, she felt sorry for Hilda, now vainly trying not to admire herself too obviously in her new role as 'the young lady', a phrase which fell sweetly upon her ears. But fancy a customer reciting poetry, thought the assistant. It simply wasn't done. It was the first time she had been so assailed and she hoped it would be the last. But she had to be polite to customers, and this one was probably a bit balmy with her autumn colourings and John Keats, whoever he might happen to be.

Having noted the address to which Hilda's old coat was to be sent, the assistant, again remarking how well the young lady looked in the new one, handed them over to the millinery department, a spot to be for ever memorable to Hilda, since it was there that she fought her first pitched battle with Aunt Helen.

'A hat for my niece, to match her coat,' said Helen graciously to the assistant who hurried forward.

'Yes, Madam. This way, please. Perhaps this model

would suit the young lady,' and she took from its stand a soft, rich-looking velour, at the sight of which Hilda's heart gave a great bound. 'It's a perfect match for the coat, don't you think, Madam?'

'Yes. They go well together. But it looks rather expensive, I'm afraid,' and she peered at the ticket inside the crown. 'Ah! I thought so. Will you show us something else, please. I don't want to give so much.'

'Oh yes, Madam. We have a large selection, but wouldn't the young lady like just to try this one on to see if the style suits her? This is best quality velour, of course, and not really expensive for what it is.'

Hilda, her eyes devouring the lovely hat, reached out for it, and the assistant set it deftly upon her head; then, with an appraising smile, she turned to Helen again.

'Made for the young lady, don't you think, Madam? I can see the other lady thinks so too,' she continued, with a flattering appeal to Mildred. With the unerring perception of all who sell, she was perfectly aware of Helen's decision not to buy, and equally aware that Mildred, in spite of the price, was in favour of the hat. And as for its wearer, it was obvious that she ached for it, and certainly they would never find one that suited her better. Opening a huge drawer, she cunningly produced half a dozen nondescript-looking hats of plain brown felt. In spite of Helen, she had made up her mind to sell the velour if possible, and to that end proceeded to try upon Hilda hat after hat, none of which, after the rich velour, became her at all, though Helen, attracted by the lower prices, proclaimed vehemently that they did. Hilda, however, knew better, and when, in a final effort to sell the velour, the assistant placed upon her head a hard, ugly, sailor felt which Helen, anxious to get the business settled, said was the very thing, she turned desperately to Mildred.

'I don't like it, Aunt Mildred. I know it doesn't suit me — not like this,' and she reverently stroked the beautiful velour. 'This is the only one I like.'

'Don't be so ridiculous, Hilda,' said Helen sharply. 'That sailor felt suits you perfectly. And look at the difference in the price. Don't you agree with me, Mildred?' she asked her sister.

Mildred disagreed so emphatically that Helen, who would have liked nothing better at that moment than to give her niece, big as she was, a good shaking, stood irresolute. Hilda, still caressing the precious velour, praying for some miracle to happen whereby it might become hers, heard a gay voice call out: 'How nice to meet you both!' and perceived a lovely figure, exquisitely dressed in unrelieved black, advancing towards them. She gazed, fascinated. She thought she had never seen anyone so beautiful as this unknown lady who was now affectionately saluting her aunts.

'Helen! Mildred! What are you up to here?' The newcomer turned brilliant blue eyes inquiringly upon Hilda, and Helen explained.

'This is our young niece, Hilda. You remember my telling you we were going to bring her from Lancashire. She only came on Saturday. Hilda, this is a very great friend of ours, Mrs. Ashton.'

'How do you do, Hilda,' said Mrs. Ashton pleasantly. 'What's your Aunt Helen up to? Trying to make you wear something she likes and you don't?' She had taken in the situation already — Hilda's flushed and disappointed face, the pretty velour, the hard and ugly felts, the assistant now discreetly hovering a little way off. And she knew Helen's weakness where spending money was concerned. Taking the velour, she placed it once more on Hilda's head, tilting it back, and standing away to admire the result.

'It's perfect. Exactly right for you, and if it isn't the one Helen has chosen I'll eat my own hat.'

Helen, perceiving herself routed, agreed that of course no other hat could be thought of, and, with an amiability she was far from feeling, told Hilda that she might wear it at once with the new coat.

Hilda, overjoyed, looked all her gratitude at Mrs. Ashton. Even Miss Lily Elsie, she decided, could not be lovelier. Mrs. Ashton in her turn surveyed Hilda. Not a beauty, she concluded, as she herself had been at the same awkward age, but unusual and undeniably attractive. She wondered what her friend, Helen Shepheard, would make of her. A prig, no doubt, unless the girl had spirit and sufficient will-power to stand up to her. There was a certain family resemblance both to Helen and Mildred, but the niece, in spite of her present countrified roughness, seemed finer. Chatting pleasantly with her friends, her thoughts strayed to Phillip Shepheard, and she wondered what his reaction to this tall girl would be, for it was common knowledge among their circle that he was not, for all his devotion, quite so single-minded about his wife as she supposed him to be. However, it was nobody's business to open her eyes, and Phillip had many agreeable qualities.

They left the showroom in a body, Mrs. Ashton and Helen talking gaily, Mildred quiet as usual, and Hilda glancing into every mirror they passed, trying to comport herself as if it was quite an everyday affair to patronize John Barkers and come away looking like a lily of the field. Mildred, observing her, was amused by this innocent vanity, and told her how nice she looked in the all-brown outfit, and that she would look even nicer when she had the high brown boots to go with it instead of her present black ones. Hilda beamed at her. The unhappy episode at the grave of James McNeill Whistler was

utterly forgotten, and she even began to warm towards Aunt Helen for having been so generous over the velour, in spite of the knowledge that it was to Mrs. Ashton she really owed it. That lady, turning round, suggested that they should all have lunch together, but Helen vetoed this. They still had several things to buy for her niece, she explained, but she herself would be glad to accept the invitation if only Mildred would be good enough to finish the shopping and take Hilda somewhere for the afternoon. 'In any case,' she continued, 'I simply have to be at the suffrage meeting in Westminster at three o'clock. You'll come along too, Nora, I hope?'

'Not likely,' said Mrs. Ashton. 'A lovely day like this! I'm out to enjoy myself. But we'll have some lunch and you can tell me how horribly I'm letting down my sex by taking no interest in its sufferings. You'll enjoy doing that even if I don't enjoy hearing it.' She said this cheerfully, but with the faintest tinge of malice. She was genuinely fond of Helen Shepheard, but there was no getting away from the fact that at times she could be tiresome. With a mock compassionate look at Hilda she added: 'And for goodness sake don't preach Votes for Women to your defenceless niece. She's much too attractive to be ground down so early. Stand up for yourself, Hilda! And come and see us any time you like with or without your family. I'm sure you and Tom — he's my husband — will get on like a house on fire. And he doesn't believe in Votes for Women either, only in votes for me, which is quite another story.'

Helen laughed. 'Nora, you're impossible. Of course Hilda's going to believe in our Rights, like every other intelligent woman.'

'All right, Helen. You can count me in among the fools, and no offence taken, but don't count Hilda among the grown-ups yet. Have a heart! And remember I'd

like to see her again soon. So long, Mildred. Goodbye, Hilda, and don't forget my advice,' she ended mischievously to the captivated and admiring girl. 'Stand up to her, or she'll have you in jail for breaking windows before you've cut your wisdom teeth.'

CHAPTER V

THE FLOWRE OF CITIES ALL

THOUGH sorry to lose Mrs. Ashton so quickly, neither Mildred nor Hilda was sorry to see Helen go, for they now felt absolutely free to enjoy themselves, and Mildred thoughtfully allowed Hilda to choose for herself the dressing-gown. After trying on every conceivable colour, she selected a deep, cherry-red quilted Japanese silk, bulky as a small eiderdown, but light as a feather, and to her the very summit of indolent luxury. What would they say now in Moss Ferry, she wondered, if they could see her in this glorious garment. It was a simple matter finding warm slippers to match, and the high-laced brown boots also presented no difficulties. They were of soft kid and came almost to her knees, and Mildred had to be firm about not letting her wear them straight away, in spite of Hilda's assurance that they fitted like a glove and were very comfortable.

'You must wear them indoors, Hilda, for a little while. Yes, I know they probably feel all right now, but they won't after we've been walking about a bit. Besides, after lunch I'm going to take you through Kensington Gardens and Hyde Park, and that's quite a step. It's a shame to waste this lovely sunshine. I expect you've seen pictures of the Gardens and the Park.'

'Yes I have,' said Hilda excitedly. 'And I've read about Kensington Palace too. That's where they told Princess Victoria in her nightdress that she was the Queen of England. And shall we see Buckingham Palace as well?'

'Perhaps. Anyway, you shall see Kensington Palace, and the other if there's time. It's a fine walk there through

the Parks. But let's go in here for lunch, and afterwards we'll make a real jaunt of it.'

Hilda, on top of the world, followed her aunt into an A.B.C. What a heavenly new life this was, and how much nicer not to have Aunt Helen bossing them about and interfering with their innocent pleasures. She would even have interfered, no doubt, with their choice of lunch and have selected for them, of course for their own good, something entirely different from what they had wanted. As it was, they ordered poached eggs on toast, with coffee and chocolate cream-buns to follow. To Hilda it was a lovely meal, especially as Mildred, who could only manage one cream-bun, insisted that Hilda must have another, and yet another after that. The thick cream oozed out deliciously over the thin, sweet pastry, and Hilda experienced no surprise when she realized that the schoolboy who shared their table was lunching entirely off these delicacies. Both aunt and niece were fascinated by his progress. He had started with a dish of seven, which, one after another, had vanished like melting snow. As he finished the last crumb of the seventh an expression of distress overclouded his pleasant, rather ugly face, and under cover of the table he began furtively to count his money. Mildred looked at Hilda, and then at the hovering waitress. Suspicion of his inability to pay for his immoderate appetites was written large upon her face, and she was obviously waiting to denounce him as a shameless and greedy defaulter. Mildred, anxious to avert this disaster, leaned towards him and said in a whisper: 'If you haven't quite enough with you, I'll be glad to make it all right. They are nice, I know.'

The boy, blushing deeply, stammered out his astonished thanks and assured her that he was solvent. He had sufficient money, and with an arrogant gesture he summoned the waitress and shattered her dream of retribution by

ordering yet a couple more buns. His distress had been due not to his inability to pay for what he had already consumed, but to the horrible fear that he could not indulge still further. Suddenly aware that his conduct must seem to others a little unusual, he ate the two extra buns defiantly and very quickly, and proudly demanded his bill. The waitress, still hopeful that his appetite might prove bigger than his purse, gave it to him. He examined it carefully, counted his money again, reluctantly concluded that he really could not afford a tenth bun, paid and went out.

The disappointed waitress, making out Mildred's bill, observed sourly that she had never seen anything to touch it. 'We get all sorts in here, and I know it takes all sorts to make a world, but that young man fair takes the biscuit. Nine cream-buns, one on top of another! No wonder he was spotty.'

Mildred and Hilda laughed outright, and Mildred even urged Hilda to have another, but she was afraid of appearing greedy, and politely refused.

In the cloakroom, Hilda, who could not get the lovely Mrs. Ashton out of her mind, remarked thoughtfully, as she re-tied her hair-ribbon, that she wished she too had been born with blue eyes and yellow hair; her own reflection in the mirror seemed dim and ordinary by comparison, and even Aunt Mildred now appeared less beautiful to her than she had before the advent of Mrs. Ashton. Mildred mildly reproved her for these aspirations, and pointed out that although Mrs. Ashton was certainly lovely, she nevertheless owed a good deal to art. 'She makes up very heavily, my dear, and her hair is not natural either, though she makes no bones about it. She's always experimenting with different cosmetics, and thinks nothing at all of dyeing her hair a different colour every once in a while. She once dyed it a deep auburn, but it made her look so sinister that she wore a

transformation for months until the red grew out. But she's a nice woman, and her self-control is something to wonder at. Nothing puts her out. Once, during the transformation period, she was with us in the City watching the Lord Mayor's Show, and her hat, and the transformation with it, got knocked off into the roadway. She was not in the least embarrassed, and calmly asked a policeman to retrieve them. Everybody around was laughing, and only the policeman looked angry. When you do go to see her I think you'll be surprised. She's a tremendous smoker, but keeps always to cigarettes, except at home. There she smokes a pipe, and sometimes even a cigar.'

Hilda opened her eyes wide at this startling intelligence. She had never seen a woman smoke even a cigarette, and she was loth to believe that Mrs. Ashton of all people could be so peculiar.

'Fancy Mr. Ashton letting her do a thing like that!' she exclaimed incredulously.

Mildred smiled. 'Her husband adores her. He wouldn't care what she did. You mustn't let her influence you too much, Hilda. She's always making fun of your Aunt Helen and me. She says we don't make the best of ourselves. She thinks we're old-fashioned and dowdy because we don't use powder and lipstick, but only papier-poudré leaves. She insists that all women are improved by cosmetics. It's part of her creed. Don't take any notice if she thinks they would improve you. You're much too young for such nonsense. Well, we must be making a move if we're going to get through the Parks.'

Hilda, pondering deeply over the worldly and fascinating ways of Mrs. Ashton, looked forward intensely to the time when she might visit her. But for her kindly intervention over the velour, she would now be wearing that ugly felt; remembering this she decided loyally that Mrs. Ashton could do no wrong, and that if she wanted to

smoke a pipe there could be no harm in it, or in a cigar either, for that matter.

'Here we are,' said Mildred. 'Kensington Gardens. I come here such a lot. Winter and summer one never tires of it.'

It was the first park Hilda had ever seen, and it seemed to her far more beautiful than any countryside. There were crowds of stiffly-starched and uniformed nursemaids wheeling expensive-looking bassinettes up the long Flower Walk, and many small, well-dressed children pushing equally handsome dolls' bassinettes, or bowling wooden hoops. She was enthralled by the opulent look that all of them wore. What a comfortable, effortless world this was, the *real* world she had so often dreamed about when she lived in the hard-working world of Moss Ferry. It was as entrancing as a magic-lantern picture, and the knowledge that she was actually in it, and on a week-day too, made her feel quite humble. Could it be possible that barely two days ago, among the scurrying crowds on St. Pancras Station, she had felt hideously afraid of what might await her in London? How terrible if she had gone back to Lancashire and had never seen Kensington Gardens! In her new humility she even felt compassion towards her hated foster-sister, doomed to live out her days in Moss Ferry. She thought too of her foster-parents. How they would enjoy themselves if they could come here on an Outing! Her foster-mother would sit spellbound, watching the swaying bassinettes and commenting admiringly on their rosy, spotless occupants, while severely censuring their parents for leaving them to the mercy of the uppish young ladies who wheeled them hither and thither. Her foster-father would just sit contentedly, never saying a word, but taking it all in. That very evening, she determined, she would write to them and describe this paradise, for her heart ached at the thought of

what they were missing. Aunt Mildred, after showing her the Flower Walk, turned back and showed her a statue of Queen Victoria, which she said was always known as the Big Penny, because that was how the Queen looked on some of the pennies still in circulation. Hilda gazed at it reverently, for though in her fourteen years she had lived under three Sovereigns, and the old Queen had died when she was scarcely in her fifth year, the name Victoria still evoked the deepest respect in one brought up in a country village so far from London. Her aunt showed her the little Dutch garden, explaining that it was planted entirely with bulbs and was a joy to behold all through the spring and summer and autumn, and worth the tribute of a visit even in the depths of winter. Hilda was agreeably surprised at the easy manner in which her Aunt Mildred now talked, for if Aunt Helen had remained with them she would hardly have spoken. Aunt Helen would have done all the talking and instructing, expecting continual admiration for her knowledge, and her sister and niece would have been reduced to spasmodic monosyllables. As it was they were enjoying themselves enormously, like a pair of children released from school. Mildred was charmed by Hilda's response to the spell of London, and amused by her awe-struck expression at the sight of Kensington Palace. To Hilda, who had been taught to believe absolutely in the divine right of kings, it had something sacred about it, particularly when she learnt that Queen Victoria's youngest daughter, Princess Beatrice, actually had a suite of apartments therein. She recalled a picture she had once seen in *Chatterbox* of a girl but a few years older than herself being awakened in the dead of night in that same palace and informed that she was Queen of England. And to think that that young girl's daughter was living here now! Before they turned away, her eyes searched keenly along the line of windows

in the hope that Princess Beatrice, conscious of the homage being paid to Royalty as Royalty, would look out, but the windows remained blank.

Retracing their steps, they halted next at the Albert Memorial, which the ignorant Hilda thought even more wonderful than the Palace. Mildred, however, said she didn't think much of it, and even pronounced it to be downright ugly, a statement with which her niece diffidently ventured to disagree; but Mildred did not seem to mind, saying tolerantly that she could not yet be expected to know good work from bad.

'You must ask your Uncle Phillip about it, Hilda. He really hates it, and thinks it's a positive outrage in these beautiful gardens. He says it ought to be in Berlin, draped with antimacassars.'

Hilda took a long look at Prince Albert beneath his marble canopy, and for the life of her she could not understand her aunt's unflattering remarks. It was all very puzzling, and she wondered fearfully how she was ever going to learn the difference between what she might admire, and what she might not. Prince Albert seemed to her a most noble-looking man, and the impressive canopy filled her with the profoundest admiration. She was deeply concerned over her lack of taste, for Aunt Mildred could hardly be mistaken, and if Uncle Phillip also despised it that settled the matter.

As they crossed over into Hyde Park, Mildred, looking at her watch, decided that there would not be time for all she had hoped to do.

'It's nearly three o'clock, Hilda. I think we'll just walk down Rotten Row and get a bus home from Hyde Park Corner. I'll take you to see Buckingham Palace another time, and Whitehall, and the Abbey. There's so much for you to see, and it's a pity to rush things, don't you think?'

Hilda agreed, since there would be all the more to look forward to. Something different to admire every time she came out, to be savoured slowly, like extra special sweets. She confided this sentiment to Mildred, who smiled and said: 'That's exactly the way I still feel about London, though I've lived here for years. We're in Rotten Row now. I daresay you've seen photographs of it.'

'Yes, and I've seen a picture of an actress called Lily Langtry driving through Hyde Park — it called her "The Jersey Lily".'

'That's right. I've seen her myself many times, and I've also seen people stand on their chairs to get a better view of her: they used to clap and cheer as her carriage drove by. She was exquisite. Helen and I think Mrs. Ashton is very like her.'

Hilda warmly concurred, but her thoughts were diverted from the memory of Mrs. Ashton's beautiful face by the sight of three riders, a gentleman and two ladies, cantering abreast up the Row. She stood quite still as they passed, laughing and chattering, and remained so until they wheeled and rode back. Her eyes, straining after them, filled with tears, which made her feel silly, for she had no notion why the sight had moved her so deeply; the riders had about them that same magic-lantern enchantment which she had experienced at the first glimpse of the Gardens. They were at the far end of the Row now, tiny, luxurious figures framed in the avenue of trees as if in a picture, and the stout iron rail against which she leant enhanced this illusion. It was all so different from anything she had ever known that she could not help the lumpy feeling in her throat, and, praying that her aunt would not notice, she dabbed at her eyes. Mildred looked at her in some surprise and asked what could possibly be the matter.

'I don't really know,' said Hilda, feeling dreadfully foolish. 'It was those people riding past like that — the horses, and everything. I've not seen people like that before, except in pictures. I know it sounds silly, but they didn't look real. It's all so different,' she ended lamely.

Mildred seemed to think this explanation quite natural, and looking at the sky, said that they must hurry.

'I don't like the way the light has gone so quickly: it looks as if it might rain any minute. We can cut through and get a bus from Knightsbridge.'

Hilda, the spell broken by the ominous word 'rain', hurried along almost in a run, her thoughts now centred wholly on her new hat and coat. It would be terrible if they were spotted, their glorious newness tarnished the very first time she had worn them.

'Not so fast, please, Hilda,' Mildred called after her. 'We shall be all right, and we can both get under my umbrella.'

The first drops fell, and walking as quickly as they could, they were soon waiting in Knightsbridge for the bus; but now it was raining hard, and poor Hilda was in agonies lest her beautiful new clothes should be ruined; and in spite of the umbrella, which Mildred considerately held right over her, her agitation did not cease until they were safely inside the bus. The rain and mist had blotted out everything, and only the lights of other buses were visible. People got in at every stop, all making for the inside, which was packed uncomfortably full; by the time the conductor shouted 'Earl's Court Road', it was obvious that all further passengers would have to sit outside in the pelting rain, but this fact did not deter an aggressive-looking woman, her foot on the step, from asking if she might come inside.

'Sorry, lady,' the conductor answered cheerfully, 'but there's a nice bath-sitting-room upstairs for them as likes

it,' and the woman, threatening to report him for impertinence, resentfully got off.

'No pleasing some people, is there, Miss,' he remarked to Hilda, who was sitting by the entrance. It was her first experience of Cockney humour and she had not the faintest idea how to cope with it; she gave him a grave and sympathetic smile, profoundly thankful that she and Aunt Mildred were safe and dry.

After a cosy tea together, Hilda suggested to her aunt that perhaps she ought now to write to her foster-parents and tell them all her wonderful news. She had spent only two days in London, but had already seen marvels beyond all imagining, glories that far surpassed anything she had ever dreamed of. She wanted to write it all out, omitting nothing but her stupidity at the grave of James McNeill Whistler and her Aunt Helen's astonishing meanness over the tea on Sunday. She would not like them in Moss Ferry to think that anything whatever was begrudged her by her new relations. It would not sound well, for they might get the impression that perhaps these same relations were not so grand after all. Mildred agreed that it was a good time to get her letter written: 'Just tell them about the journey, and that you are well and happy, and of course you can mention your new outfit, but there's no need to say much about us. After all, they don't know us, but they do know from your Grandma that we shall look after you properly.'

Hilda, slightly dashed by this restraining advice from her dear Aunt Mildred, did her best to remember it, but, carried away by her desire to show off her new family to the utmost advantage, wrote as follows:

Dear Mother and Father and All: I write this in the hope that it finds everybody as it leaves me at present. I had a very good journey to St. Pancras Station, London, and

from there on the Underground Railway to this beautiful flat, where I now live with Uncle Phillip, and Aunt Helen and Aunt Mildred. Uncle Phillip is a gentleman and he is married to Aunt Helen who is very handsome and very clever. There are hundreds of books in this flat, and everybody reads a lot. It seems funny living in a flat after a proper house, but it is just like a house except that there is no upstairs. I have a bedroom all to myself which doesn't look like a bedroom because the bed is called a divan. All the furniture is old-fashioned and there is a lot of pretty blue and white china everywhere. There is a bathroom with hot and cold water and a W.C. and I can have a hot bath whenever I like by lighting the geazer. Uncle Phillip has a cold bath every morning of his life. He says he likes it. He keeps a bookshop in the City of London and says he will show me all over the City and the Tower of London. Yesterday I went to church because there is not a chapel near. There is a Japanese gentleman called Mr. Tomashi who lives in the flat next door and he smiled at me on the stairs but I did not speak to him. I have already been to the London Museum and seen Queen Victoria's and Queen Alexandra's wedding-dresses. Aunt Helen and Aunt Mildred took me to Barkers, Kensington, this morning and bought me a brown coat and a real velour hat to match. It is a mushroom shape and doesn't spot in the rain because it is so good. A friend of theirs called Mrs. Ashton, who has yellow hair like Florrie Woodville, said it suited me to perfection. She has invited me to go and see her. I have a new pair of boots — high-laced ones, and they are brown. And I have a cherry-coloured silk dressing-gown, but it is very warm as it is lined with cotton wool. Aunt Mildred says it comes from Japan, Mr. Tomashi's country. I have a pair of red felt slippers to match, and I am now set up for the winter.

Will you please tell Elsie Entwistle and May Woodville about my new clothes and all the books I can now read. Perhaps it would be best for you to show them this letter and then they will know all about London, which is a lot bigger than Manchester. Somebody called Mrs. Sherman comes every morning to do the cleaning but I am going to help Aunt Mildred with the washing-up and the shopping. I must close this now but I will write again soon and let you know how I am getting on. I have not made up my mind yet what I want to work at, but Uncle Phillip says there is plenty of time. With love to all

From Hilda.

P.S. I forgot to tell you that I have an electric lamp on a table by my bed and I can put it out just by turning a switch, and Aunt Mildred does all the cooking on a gas stove, it is much quicker and cleaner than cooking on a fire.
I like living in London very much. With love

From Hilda

Pleased with her letter, Hilda asked Mildred to approve it so that she might post it at once. Her aunt, however, being busy at the stove preparing the evening meal, asked to be excused, and said that in any case Helen must see it before it went. Hilda's face fell, for though she was confident that she had written nothing she ought not to have done, there was no telling how her Aunt Helen would react. Mildred, stirring an egg custard, assured her that Helen's attitude was all for the best, and impressed upon her that she must always try to please Aunt Helen, since it was entirely due to her that she had been brought to London. Obediently laying the letter aside, Hilda offered to watch the custard, and was enjoying this pleasant little task when Helen's key was heard, and she came into the kitchen.

'Well, my dears, had a nice day?' she inquired brightly

as she took out her hatpins. 'Nora Ashton thinks you're the image of Mildred, Hilda. I can't see it myself, but it's no end of a compliment to you. We had a splendid meeting. The Central Hall was packed and I've never seen Mrs. Pankhurst in better form or looking so attractive.' Her eyes fell on Hilda's letter. 'Hello! Have you been writing to Moss Ferry? You don't mind if I just look through it, though I'm sure it will be all right.'

Hilda watched her read the letter with some embarrassment: it made her feel so childish to be unable to send off a letter without first getting another person's approval; but Helen soon handed it back to her with a smile, saying it was quite all right except that 'geyser' was spelt wrongly, and she could run out and post it.

'How did you get on after I had left you?' Helen asked as her niece left the room. 'I was furious with Nora Ashton in Barkers this morning. The velour was much too dear, and Hilda looked just as nice in the felt. I don't want her to get the impression that she can have just what she wants. It's bad for her, and anyway she can't. Where did you go after lunch?'

Mildred, decorating the sweet with almonds and angelica, related the events of the afternoon. 'She enjoyed absolutely everything, even the Albert Memorial, and she was thrilled to death when she learnt that royalty still lives in Kensington Palace. She cried a bit in the Row.'

'Good gracious! Whatever for?'

'I don't quite know. At least I do, but I can't explain it properly. I think it was the unexpectedness of it. She's read about it, and seen photographs of it, and I believe it was actually being in it which moved her so much. Three riders were cantering up as we entered. The horses were lovely, and Hilda stared at them as if she could scarcely believe they were real.'

'Well, thank God it was Rotten Row and not Albert that overcame her,' said Helen humorously. 'I could have boxed her ears this morning for telling me that stupid lie about the Manchester Art Gallery. It was stupid, don't you think?'

Mildred, perfectly aware that her sister was now ashamed of the tyrannical way she had forced Hilda to confess her ignorance, thought it expedient to agree. 'I'm glad you approved her letter. She was so pleased with it, and she'll feel happier now that it's gone. She's very good company, and she likes to help and to do things on her own. She loved washing up the tea things and making that custard, which is more than you would, you know.'

'All right, Mildred, all right. I loathe housework, and I don't care who knows it,' and Helen retreated before her sister could say anything further.

CHAPTER VI

SPRINGTIME

THERE now began for Hilda an unforgettable time.
It had ultimately been decided by her family that it
would be an excellent thing for her to spend her first
year in discovering London, devoting some part of each day
to properly planned study, and, within reason, roaming at
will through the books in the flat and the nearby public
library. In this way, they argued, her provincialism
would quickly fine down and her Lancashire accent
gradually disappear. Hilda was enchanted with this
decision. One whole year to play in! It was bountiful
indeed, and she assured her Aunt Helen earnestly that
she would learn all she could. She *wanted* to learn, to
become exactly like them, she said gratefully. Helen,
pleased with her young enthusiasm, decided that the first
thing she must improve was her handwriting; to this end
she gave her a page of her own writing, together with
a page of Phillip's, as a guide, with the result that Hilda,
anxious to write like both of them, succeeded in doing
neither, but evolved a style peculiar to herself alone. It
was by no means distinguished, but Aunt Helen, after a
few weeks, pronounced it to be reasonably 'educated',
and praised her for her industry. She spent an hour every
day in practising this new calligraphy, copying out for
both profit and pleasure, long extracts from Dickens and
Scott; and also each day, at her uncle's suggestion, a
part or the whole of a poem, which she learnt by heart
and repeated to him. In this fashion she came to know
many of the loveliest poems in the English language, and
she found that in some mysterious way this memorizing
of verse deepened the pleasures of reading generally, and

made her see with new vision whenever she and Mildred went exploring.

Sometimes her relations gave what they called an 'evening' to their numerous friends, many of whom 'did' something, such as singing or reciting poems. Aunt Helen, who recited frequently and with vehemence, asked her niece at the first of these evenings which she attended to repeat any little piece she could call to mind, and Hilda, tremendously flattered, obliged with John Masefield's:

> I have seen dawn and sunset on moors and windy hills
> Coming in solemn beauty like slow old tunes of Spain:
> I have seen the lady April bringing the daffodils,
> Bringing the springing grass and the soft warm April
> rain . . .

It was a nerve-racking experience, standing there before a roomful of friendly but grown-up people, and her voice shook; but everyone was very nice to her, especially a strange-looking man whom they called Dermot, who made her colour even more violently by crying out, when she had finished, 'Bravo!' He conversed in such a low, staccato voice that it was difficult, from where she sat, to catch what he said, but whenever he did speak those near him shouted with laughter, and Hilda soon discovered that he was the most interesting and most amusing person in the room, just as Mrs. Ashton, who sat next to him, was the most beautiful. Hilda thought Dermot McGilray was the darkest person she had ever seen, for he had strong, thick, black hair, and very fine, brilliant dark eyes topped by immense black brows. His face was long and almost ugly, but so full of character and distinction that the ugliness became an asset and the more one looked at him the more one wanted to look. He had fine manners too, and Hilda felt quite envious of Mrs. Ashton's good fortune in sitting beside him. It would be four years

yet, she reflected sadly, before she could really call herself a grown woman, and have a gentleman paying her as much attention as Mr. McGilray was now devoting to Mrs. Ashton. That lady, smoking one cigarette after another, looked even more wonderful to Hilda than when she had first seen her in John Barkers millinery department. She wore a black velvet djibbah, and her face, framed in bands of corn-coloured hair, made Hilda think of a water-lily swaying in a pool. She would cheerfully have added decades to her existence if by so doing she could have looked like Mrs. Ashton, beautiful, self-assured, courted and admired by all men, and with an adoring husband into the bargain. Aunt Helen, also wearing a djibbah, of silvery-grey velvet, looked handsome enough, but there was no woman in the room who could hold a candle to Mrs. Ashton. And not only was she beautiful, but Aunt Helen said that she was also a first-rate amateur actress, and often played with her husband in Shakespearean productions at Toynbee Hall. In response to many requests they consented to do a scene now, but, as it was the balcony scene from *Romeo and Juliet*, insisted that they should play it in the hall just outside the door of the sitting-room.

'Without proper make-up it is better at my age to be heard and not seen,' Mrs. Ashton remarked softly to the enchanted Hilda, 'but that won't apply to you for years and years, lucky girl! Go and sit by Dermot while we're doing our little act. He's been saying some very pretty things about you to me.'

Hilda, overwhelmed with self-consciousness at this unexpected compliment, remained glued to her chair, afraid to look in the direction of Mr. McGilray, who must have heard the remark. She was delighted to think that she had attracted his attention, and wondered excitedly what kind of pretty things he had said of her. It

made her feel important to have a gentleman interested in her, and she experienced a sudden spasm of gratitude towards Aunt Helen for having bought her a new frock for this and other special occasions. It was of emerald-green ninon, with a rucheing of white ninon round the neck, and tiny puffed sleeves, and she wore with it a Liberty-designed pendant of amethyst and silver, lent to her by Mildred. The dress was quite long, right down to her black velvet slippers. It was the prettiest frock she had ever had, and the very first to have a real 'evening' look about it. Her hair, parted in the centre, was drawn softly back and tied with an immense black velvet bow in the nape of the neck. At first Hilda had protested at the unusual width of this hair ribbon, for which she could find no precedent, but Helen had explained that it was a 'Mozart' bow, and as such perfectly normal; also, she added, very becoming to a young girl. Aunt Helen had then given her a little dissertation upon Mozart, and had shown her a book containing a picture of him, so that Hilda might see for herself the origin of her bow. To her astonishment, her aunt became quite worked up about Mozart, especially when she related the shameful fact that he had been buried as a pauper in a common grave, and that by the time his friends heard of this appalling circumstance it was too late to recover his body.

'Think of it, Hilda. The composer of the Jupiter Symphony thrown into a common grave!'

Hilda, now also full of the tenderest compassion for Mozart, looked inquiringly at her aunt, whose eyes were brimming with tears, and did not understand her at all for in some curious fashion she seemed to be enjoying her emotion, indeed revelling in it.

'Poor Mozart,' ventured Hilda softly. 'I've never heard any of his music. Is it very beautiful, Aunt Helen?'

'You shall judge for yourself, my dear. I'll take you

one night to a Promenade Concert, and then you'll
appreciate better the full horror of what I have just told
you.'

When the applause for the Balcony Scene had died
down, Helen asked Dermot McGilray if, as a great personal
favour, he would sing an Irish song, well knowing, as did
everyone except Hilda, what it would be. As the mournful
wail of *The Wearing o' the Green* floated round the room
Hilda sat up tensely. It was a tune she had heard
hundreds of times, away back in Lancashire during the
potato-lifting season, when most of the farmers hired
Irish labourers to help with this important harvest, but
she had never before heard it sung like this. Mr. McGilray
had a terrible voice, harsh and unyielding as a corncrake's,
but he put into the song such a searing passion for Ireland
that instead of a single unlovely voice it sounded as if a
whole sobbing orchestra was playing, mercilessly determined to harrow and pursue them all to the very rim of
the world. Hilda heard her uncle whisper to Mrs. Ashton:
'There it is again, all the unnecessary sadness of Ireland!'
and made a mental note to ask him what he meant by this
puzzling remark. It was a relief when the song ended
and, in response to many requests, Dermot, with a gallant
wave of his hand towards Hilda, made amends by dashing
into the rousing:

Here's to the maiden of bashful fifteen;
Here's to the widow of fifty;
Here's to the flaunting extravagant quean. . . .

Hilda sat enthralled. It was such splendid fun, her first
real, grown-up party. The talk glowed and crackled like
a well-laid fire, for everybody but herself and Aunt
Mildred seemed to have something amusing or interesting
to say. To hide her own ignorance and shyness she zeal-
ously helped to hand round the sandwiches, while Uncle

Phillip filled the glasses generously with a claret cup which he alone, he boasted privately, could make to perfection. She had watched him make it and had marvelled at the complexity of the operation. 'It's got to taste like liquid rose petals,' he had told her, and that was how she thought it did taste. When she had finished her glass she felt quite equal to standing up and reciting every poem and ballad she had so far memorized, including Lord Macaulay's *Horatius*, and was disappointed that nobody asked her to perform this feat. Listening eagerly, she caught names now and then that were not unfamiliar, such names as Granville Barker and Lillah McCarthy, whom one of the men described as a glorious creature; Gaby Deslys and Isabel Jay, Lily Hanbury and Evelyn Millard. Uncle Phillip professed a reverent adoration for Miss Julia Neilson, and sadly deplored her execrable taste in descending to Nell Gwynne melodrama after the splendour of starring as Rosalind with George Alexander. Aunt Helen was saying something about Lily Langtry. 'I saw her once, I think it must have been about the time you were born, Hilda, going into Covent Garden Opera House. She was then in her maturity, but she was perfect — "a vision splendid", but *not* in the first rank as an actress, poor dear.' Everyone seemed to have a favourite actor or actress, and there was much good-humoured disagreement about their respective claims. Somebody mentioned Miss Ellen Terry, at the sound of whose name a small, quiet man jumped up and solemnly gave the toast:

To our Ellen.

Instantly they were all on their feet, and even the ignorant Hilda thrilled as she raised her glass to the absent queen. It did not even strike her as odd that she, who had been brought up to regard the theatre as the haunt of the devil, should be drinking the first toast of her life to an actress.

Aunt Helen murmured dreamily: 'Dear Ellen Terry. "Beauty and anguish walking hand in hand, the downward slope to death." Tennyson, Hilda. *The Dream of Fair Women*. You must learn it.'

'Don't forget to see that she learns to laugh as well, Helen, before she takes the "downward slope" herself,' said Mrs. Ashton half-mockingly, confirmed in her belief that the unfortunate girl, if someone didn't save her from her earnest, sententious and quotation-mad relative, would grow into an appalling prig. She turned a brilliant blue gaze upon Hilda, and invited her to share the chesterfield between herself and Dermot. It was a gesture calculated to provoke Helen, who was extremely attached to Dermot McGilray and not at all pleased to have her niece regarded as of equal interest to herself. It was long past eleven, and Hilda, conscious of her aunt's disapproval, murmured that perhaps she ought to go to bed.

'No, child. Enjoy yourself a little longer. You wouldn't be able to sleep, anyway.'

And so Hilda, tongue-tied but happy between Mrs. Ashton and Mr. McGilray, was made much of, and tingled to the roots of her hair when Mr. Edgar Jepson, in a high-pitched voice, suddenly exclaimed: 'Why, what lashes the child has!' Unaccustomed to such compliments, she searched among the laughing faces and singled out her Uncle Phillip, who smiled and told her to take no notice of Mr. Jepson's nonsense because he simply could not help it. Not to be outdone, Mr. McGilray too became very flattering; and Mrs. Ashton, pretending to be put out at all this admiration for a mere schoolgirl, reminded him that Hilda was not sweet seventeen yet, even if, under Helen's misguided earnestness, she might soon begin to talk as if she were twice that age.

Helen, feeling that it was now high time her niece retired before her head was completely turned, lured her

out of the room on the pretext of helping with the refreshments, and said she must go to bed.

'But I must go back and say good night to everybody,' Hilda protested. 'If I don't they'll think I'm rude, especially Mrs. Ashton and Mr. McGilray.'

'Don't be so silly,' Helen said sharply. 'It would be different if there were only two or three people, but a whole roomful! Why! they won't even notice you've gone. Run along now. I'll say good night for you. Everybody will understand, my dear. And you mustn't get puffed up because people say nice things to you. They don't always mean them, I'm afraid. It's just a pleasant thing to do. Still, you do look nice in your new frock, and I'm glad you've enjoyed it all so much. Off you go. And you can read as long as you like. Good night, dear, and thank you for helping Mildred with everything. I won't forget to say a special good night for you to Mrs. Ashton and Mr. McGilray,' she ended reassuringly, aware that the girl was genuinely distressed at the possibility of being thought lacking in good manners.

Hilda went dejectedly, thinking hard thoughts about her cruel Aunt Helen. Whoever heard of anybody leaving a party till the very last minute! In her own room she dawdled about, stopping repeatedly to examine herself in the mirror. Why had that nice Mr. Jepson said what he had about her eyelashes? They seemed to her no different from anyone else's. She brushed and plaited her hair and then, in the cherry-coloured dressing-gown and with an empty tumbler in her hand, opened the door a crack, ready to dart across the lighted hall into the kitchen if the sitting-room door should open. Though all the canons of her upbringing informed her that it was not a proper thing to do, she hoped passionately that one or other of the gentlemen would come out. She stayed by the door for a long time, listening enviously to the buzz of

talk and laughter. Then the other door opened and in
a flash she was out, walking sedately towards the kitchen
to get a glass of water. She knew instinctively that it was
a man behind her, but modesty, genuine enough this
time, prevented her from looking round in spite of her
curiosity. The steps, however, did not turn into the bathroom, and no sooner had she switched on the kitchen light
than she heard her uncle's voice: 'Goodness me, why aren't
you in bed, child? What a little Gretchen you look with
your pigtails. Quite different from the young lady who
recited John Masefield. The claret cup has made you
thirsty, I expect. Here — have some soda-water, it's
more quenching.'

He filled her tumbler, and while she drank stood smiling
at her. Hilda smiled back, pleased with the success of her
little stratagem, though sorry it was only her uncle when
she would have preferred it to be Mr. McGilray or Mr.
Jepson. She felt vaguely frightened too at the strange way
in which he was looking at her. As she turned to go, he
put his hands round her and muttered something about
the absurd bulk of the dressing-gown and what a narrow
little waist it was hiding. His voice changed abruptly,
and he bade her sharply to go to bed, adding that Helen
would be very angry if she knew she was still up. Hilda
ran back to her room, and lay awake, not reading but
wondering why her uncle stared at her so intently at times,
and what he could possibly have meant by that funny
remark about her waist. Haunted by Mr. McGilray's
unearthly singing of the familiar Irish melody, she finally
slept and was not disturbed by the intermittent leave-
taking of the guests, for the very good reason that she was
no longer in the flat. She was flying, high up over the
river, higher still over Hammersmith Bridge, dipping and
soaring, waving triumphantly to the trams and buses
crawling beneath her like golden caterpillars, so easily

did she outdistance them by this marvellous power which had been given to her. London lay below her like a diamond-spattered carpet, with the river threading through it and shining with the velvety blackness of coal. This was the first of her flying dreams, and the memory of it was so beautiful that every night she prayed for the miracle to repeat itself. How she left her room and returned to it was never revealed to her, for the dreams always began with an upward flight and dissolved when she was high above the river. She kept them jealously to herself, afraid even of letting Aunt Mildred into the secret. It almost seemed to her that if she spoke of them to anyone she might be deemed guilty of some subtle treachery, the punishment for which would be the loss, for all time, of her mysterious and splendid gift.

CHAPTER VII

PROCESSES OF EDUCATION

THAT first year in London was crammed so full of splendours and discoveries that Hilda's thoughts turned less and less frequently to her old life in Moss Ferry. It was now all so far away and long ago that it seemed as though it had been the life of some other girl only faintly related to her, so quickly did she adapt herself to her new environment. She was, too, financially independent, for one day, with the air of bestowing upon her all the wealth of the Indies, Aunt Helen thus addressed her: 'I've been thinking, Hilda, that you ought to have some money regularly of your own, for such things as fares and sweets, so I am going to give you half a crown every month for pocket-money. I think you should manage to buy your hair-ribbons out of this as well. It will teach you how to spend money wisely, I hope.'

She waited, in a glow of self-approbation, for her niece's response, which Hilda, though considerably taken aback by the smallness of the allowance, did her best to make enthusiastic. Half a crown a month was not much, but at any rate it would be her own, and luckily most of the sights of London were free; luckily, also, both Uncle Phillip and Aunt Mildred were generous, while in a large multiple sweet-shop in the Chiswick High Road, coconut candy and coconut ice could be purchased at four ounces for a penny.

She helped Mildred with the shopping, and kept her own room clean and comparatively tidy, though one morning, when she had thoughtlessly stayed out too long, leaving her bed unmade, she was mortified to find on her

return that an envelope was pinned to her door, and in Helen's writing she read the dreadful words: ENTRANCE TO CHORES. Hilda tore it down resentfully. She had, after all, only left her bed to air, and Mildred had dinned into her the necessity for beds to be thoroughly aired before being made. Helen never referred to the incident, but from that day Hilda became horribly afraid of her aunt's sarcasm, and did all she could to avoid such reprimands.

As for the processes of education, she spent many happy hours in the nearby public library, reading widely. At Helen's suggestion, she read all the works of the Reverend Alfred Church and was enchanted by his gods and goddesses. Other books in which she revelled were by Harrison Ainsworth, Talbot Baines Reed, Robert Louis Stevenson and Alexandre Dumas; while at home she lost herself in the pages of Charles Dickens, Sir Walter Scott and Thackeray. She tried to read *Zuleika Dobson*, which her Uncle Phillip said he had greatly enjoyed, but she found it impossible to understand; and she was equally bewildered by *The Picture of Dorian Gray*, which appeared to her to have no meaning whatever. She continued to read and memorize poetry, and her uncle, seeing how genuinely interested she was, suggested that she had better investigate William Shakespeare. This, however, was not an immediate success although, eager to please Phillip and increase her self-importance, she diligently read through the plays selected for her. It was not, however, until she had actually seen a Shakespeare play that she read him because she wanted to and not because she felt it the proper thing to do.

Encouraged by Aunt Helen, who said it would be excellent training in independence and general knowledge, she went about a good deal by herself, exploring the Chiswick and Hammersmith Malls, often walking as far as Barnes Common and back for the pleasure of seeing the

stolid little houses in Castelnau, with their white-painted woodwork and lace curtains and wide stone steps. Thanks to Phillip, who had taught her how to use her eyes out of doors, a walk in London, no matter where, was never dull. There was always something lovely to be discovered, a dentilled cornice or an elegant fanlight; a smooth red arch with neat white mortar joints, or a fascinating door-knocker. It became like an enjoyable game to look out for these attractions, and within a few weeks she could have described from memory the façades of nearly every house along the Chiswick and Hammersmith Malls. She had, of course, already fulfilled her great ambition and seen Buckingham Palace. She had gazed hopefully into the forecourt, praying that the King and Queen would drive out, but the thrill of seeing them had been deferred until the visit of the much-talked-of German Emperor, Kaiser Wilhelm. When it became known that during his visit to the King and Queen there was to be a semi-state drive, Aunt Helen decided that, for Hilda's sake, they must make a day of it, and so they had waited for hours, in glorious sunshine, to see the Royal Procession go by. It was Hilda's first experience of a densely-packed, good-humoured, and patriotic London crowd, and it was alto-gether satisfying. The sun danced on the helmets of the Life Guards; and the German Emperor, a majestic white cloak sweeping from his shoulders, was an impressive figure on his richly-caparisoned horse, though it was obvious that the loudest cheers were for his host, King George V, and the other English royalties. Queen Mary, a gracious figure in her open carriage, had her young daughter by her side, and to Hilda she seemed like a princess out of a fairy tale with her clear, rosy complexion, shining golden hair, and white lacy frock. But she looked so grave, so much more grown up than Hilda herself, though they were almost of an age, that Hilda remarked

on this to Aunt Helen, who said it was enough to make any girl look serious to have to follow behind that peacock of an Emperor. All this pomp and colour, she explained to her niece, was part of the wonder that was London; and having seen the King and Queen, 'like Shelley plain', an allusion lost upon Hilda, she promised that when the winter Courts came on she would take her one night to watch the débutantes drive up to and into the Palace. 'It's worth seeing once, at any rate. I used to think it was hard on the girls to be stared at by sightseers, but on the whole I think they enjoy it as part of the excitement of being presented: they know they look as attractive as human ingenuity can make them with their lovely frocks and fans and headdresses. A girl would have to be quite hopelessly plain not to look nice in such trappings. Ah youth, youth, how pitiful it is! Whenever I see these young things going to make their curtsy, I feel so sad for them, and always think of those heartbreaking lines:

> Gather ye rosebuds while ye may,
> Old Time is still a-flying:
> And this same flower that smiles today
> Tomorrow will be dying.

Robert Herrick. Make the most of your youth, Hilda! It's the most precious thing you will ever possess, for:

> Golden lads and girls all must,
> As chimney-sweepers, come to dust.

Shakespeare — our own Will Shakespeare.'

Hilda, regarding her aunt with astonishment, passionately disagreed with these revolting sentiments. The years could not fly too quickly for her. As for making the most of her youth, she felt it was going to be a difficult business on half a crown a month, in spite of all that

William Shakespeare and Robert Herrick might say. If Aunt Helen really wanted her to enjoy it so much, surely it was up to her to provide for it a little more adequately. However, as her aunt so frequently pointed out, nearly all the most interesting sights in London were free, gratis and for nothing, and Hilda made the most of this.

Aunt Mildred loved exploring too, and if the day was fine Hilda could always tempt her to an outing. They would take sandwiches for lunch, and have tea out. One of their favourite jaunts was to go by bus to Barnes Common, walk over the Common and up Priory Lane into Richmond Park, and there spend the whole day, ending up with tea in Richmond. On several occasions, when Phillip and Helen were away, they rose very early, had a cup of tea only, and breakfasted in Richmond Park. It was tremendous fun making tea and boiling eggs on a spirit stove, and no breakfast ever tasted more delicious to Hilda. She used to lie out in the sun, reading or daydreaming, and occasionally trying hard to fall asleep in the hope that she would have one of her flying dreams, but she never experienced this joy in the daytime. She would shut her eyes and imagine herself flying over the Park, but it was a poor substitute for the effortless floating of her true dream. Some days, if they felt particularly energetic, they walked straight on through the Park to Richmond and ate their lunch on the Terrace, going on from there to spend the rest of the day in Kew Gardens.

The first time Hilda had been to Kew was on a fine spring Sunday with her aunt and uncle. The daffodils were in full bloom, and immediately they entered the Gardens, Aunt Helen, spreading a proprietorial hand over the first bed she saw, began to recite:

Daffodils! that come before the swallow dares,
And take the winds of March with beauty.

Several passers-by looked at her curiously, but she was not at all embarrassed, and encouraged by their obvious interest she quoted yet a further passage about violets and Juno's eyes and somebody else's breath. Hilda wished that Aunt Helen would quote a little less loudly. It was lovely poetry: she could feel that deep within herself, but it seemed to her the kind of poetry to be enjoyed secretly, like the vision of the three riders in Rotten Row, and her entrancing flying dreams. She could not have shared these joys with anyone, and the more secretly she hugged them the deeper was her pleasure. Aunt Helen, however, only appeared to enjoy poetry when she was proclaiming it publicly, and Hilda had often noticed her Uncle Phillip flush when he observed people staring at his reciting wife and then exchanging significant looks with each other. Her compassion for him was, on such occasions, considerable, and she would have given much to possess the awful courage to tell her aunt to *shup up*, an imperious command she had once heard a tiny girl, scarlet with rage, hiss at her teasing elder brother. It was sad to think that nobody, not even Aunt Helen's own husband, had the temerity of that four-year-old child.

One memorable Sunday, Hilda was taken on her first visit to Hampton Court. Phillip, who loved the place and knew every corner of it, started in his quiet way to explain it to her, but as usual Aunt Helen quickly took the lead and discoursed fluently on everything they came to. Halting before the portrait of Lady Castlemaine, she gave her niece, and the surrounding sightseers, an instructive résumé of that lady's history, and, to Hilda's extreme horror, informed her that, if dressed in the fashion of the period, she, Hilda, might herself be taken for a Lely portrait. Phillip, regarding the embarrassed girl with that queer light in his eyes which made her feel so uncomfortable, whole-heartedly agreed. So far as her aunts

were concerned it was an ordinary, affectionate, and mildly appraising glance, but Hilda conceived the mad idea that it was a look behind a look, as if quite a different pair of eyes was shining through his own. For once she was thankful when Helen, slowly and gravely and loudly, launched herself into the inevitable quotation — the dying speech of the fallen Cardinal. She chanted it directly at Hilda, and was enjoying herself immensely when another female voice was raised in shrill protest: 'Crikey! Who does she think *she* is! Come on, Fred, let's get out of this!'

Hilda, experiencing a pleasant twinge of satisfaction that Aunt Helen had at length got what she was asking for, turned round in time to see a young man and woman, arm in arm, go giggling through the door.

Helen, showing only by a slightly heightened colour that she had heard the interruption, finished the speech, and made a few loftily sarcastic comments upon the bad manners of the average tripper: 'Really!' she exclaimed, 'I can't conceive what they come here for!'

'To enjoy ourselves, Missus, not to hear yore blooming recitation,' said an inoffensive-looking man with unexpected truculence. 'When we wants to hear Shakespearean Dramma we goes and hears him — proper. And since that was my sister as 'as just gone out, I'll thank you not to go calling people out of the name they was christened!'

Helen, startled out of her complacency, took refuge in an icy representation of dignity, and in a cutting voice, which so terrified Hilda that she actually trembled, expressed her regret for having been audible. 'I may say that I was merely quoting the speech for the benefit of my niece,' she explained coldly, and, taking Hilda's arm, she swept away.

'That's all right, Missus,' came the benevolent reply. 'I'm sure you can't help it, but it's a bit rough on the

poor kid,' and with this parting shaft, and a friendly wink at Hilda, off he went in pursuit of his relatives. Aunt and niece also found it necessary to go in search of theirs, for both Phillip and Mildred had sidled away in the most cowardly fashion and were discovered in rapt contemplation of an indifferent picture at the far end of the gallery. Helen, aware that she had had the worst of the encounter, suggested tea. She felt she needed a space in which to regroup her forces, and so it was unfortunate, though quite in the perverse nature of human affairs, that both the inoffensive man and his relatives should seat themselves, a few moments later, at a table directly behind the Shepheard family. Helen and Mildred had their backs to the trio, but Hilda and Phillip faced them, and, horrible to relate, were treated to a vulgar series of winks whenever Helen's voice rose above the clatter of china and the buzz of talk. They were friendly winks, winks void of all malice, and both uncle and niece presently felt an alarming desire to return them. So severe grew the temptation at last that one of the undoubted pleasures of life, tea out of doors at Hampton Court on a fine, sunny day, became positive torture. It was a relief to the guilty pair when Helen decided it was time to be up and doing, and hustled Mildred and Hilda into the Ladies' Cloakroom, where, since there was an attendant in charge, Helen's single penny was unable to do the work of three. Tidying her hair, Hilda wondered if Phillip, free for a few minutes, would so far forget himself as to return at least one wink. She rather hoped he would, but she naturally made no inquiries.

Before going to sleep that night, Hilda lazily called up the pleasures of the day, so that they streamed before her in the darkness like a many-coloured panorama. From her earliest years she had found this a most gratifying habit. In far-away Moss Ferry, the really golden days

had been rare — the Sunday School Treat — the Whitsun Walk — the annual Outing to Southport or Rhyl or Llandudno; but here in London, where everything was a thrill and an adventure, she went to sleep in the glorious certainty that the day had not ended at all, that the coloured ribbon would unwind itself endlessly, and that at any minute she might find herself soaring at will over the great city. And so it was on this occasion, but, for the first time since her bewitching dreams had commenced, she flew over the river in terror. Something or someone, also with this same magic power, was pursuing her, determined to catch up with her. It was something evil, and, in her endeavours to evade it, she dipped and circled frantically, dropping like a plummet straight towards the gleaming water, skimming over it for a second or so, and rising again desperately, the pursuer exactly following her every movement. She had never known such deadly fear. Mile upon mile she flew, always over the river, which broadened and narrowed as she swooped and rose again. She looked despairingly down for landmarks, but she had never before flown so far up the Thames as this, and the unfamiliar landscape stretched dark and silent to right and left. In a final, supreme effort to get free, she plunged madly down towards the land, uttering piercing screams for the help that was not there. She woke up crying and trembling, unable to realize for a minute or two that she was safe in her own bed. As she became fully awake there was a loud knocking on her door, and then the light was switched on and her Aunt Helen came towards her, while in the doorway stood Mildred and Phillip.

'Hilda! What on earth's the matter? Your screams were enough to wake the dead. I've never heard anything like it. Are you all right?' Helen asked indignantly.

Hilda, still trembling, looked beyond her to Phillip. He was smiling at her affectionately, but, silly though she

now felt at having caused all this commotion, she glimpsed again that strange, flickering look which he had given her in the picture gallery that afternoon, and she knew, beyond all doubt, that it was from him she had fled so madly in her dream.

'I'm sorry, Aunt Helen. I was dreaming,' she answered, feeling extremely foolish.

'It sounds more like a nightmare to me, though I can't think why after such a lovely day. Can you tell us what it was?'

Hilda shook her head, and mumbled again that she was sorry to have wakened them up. Whether her dreams were good or bad, she did not want them to stop, as stop they would, she was sure, if she were ever to divulge them.

'Well, whatever it was, I hope it won't happen again, or we shall have Mr. Tomashi and the other tenants thinking we're ill-treating you,' her aunt laughed. 'Good night, and pleasanter dreams if you must have them.'

CHAPTER VIII

HILDA ALONE

IN August that year, Phillip and his wife went to Devonshire for three weeks, whilst Mildred went to visit friends in Cheshire. Phillip worked hard to persuade Helen to take Hilda with them, but she was adamant in refusal; neither would she entertain the idea of her accompanying Mildred. Devonshire, she pointed out, was expensive, while Cheshire was much too near Hilda's old home across the Mersey. She argued that it was not as if the girl needed a change, for she was the very picture of glowing health and perfectly happy and contented. As for being left alone in the flat, she emphasized that any natural girl would thoroughly enjoy the responsibility of keeping house. Both her husband and sister, helpless where Helen's parsimony was concerned, avoided looking at one another as she explained the position to her niece, asking graciously if she would look after things while they were away, and set their minds at rest by washing the delicate blue and white china herself; this was a task not to be entrusted to the rough-and-ready Mrs. Sherman, who was, as she herself frankly admitted, 'a regular smasher'.

'I shall leave you thirty shillings, dear, for food — ten shillings a week — more than enough. You'll be able to go about and enjoy yourself out of that. And if you think you'll be nervous sleeping here by yourself, I'll ask Mrs. Sherman to let her eldest girl sleep here too. And be sure to cook yourself a good meal every day, a chop or steak, with potatoes and a green vegetable, and eat plenty of fresh fruit. And don't be out at night, or sit up too late. And why not go occasionally to a suffrage meeting. You

should take more interest in your rights. It's important for your future. Now I'm sure you'll be all right, won't you?'

Hilda, overjoyed at the novelty of keeping house by herself, amiably agreed and assured Aunt Helen that she was not at all afraid of sleeping alone. It never occurred to her that there was anything unusual in everybody going off for a holiday while she was left behind, and she was of course ignorant of Phillip's and Mildred's views on the matter. All she visualized was a glorious three weeks of doing absolutely as she pleased; and who wanted to go to the country anyway when there was all London to roam in? Pleased with her reaction, Helen praised her for being such a sensible girl, said that she would send her a tin of Devonshire cream each week, and promised that next year she too should have a change.

Clutching the three half-sovereigns which Helen gave her just before they set off, Hilda said goodbye brightly and happily, and was immensely surprised when her Uncle Phillip, on the pretext of having forgotten a particular book to read in the train, breathlessly reappeared and presented her with another golden coin.

'Just a little secret between you and me, child. Not a word to your Aunt Helen, you understand. Goodbye, and take care of yourself. Goodbye.'

The door shut behind him and Hilda gazed ecstatically at the four yellow talismans in her palm. Two whole pounds! Never, in her whole life, had she handled so much money. What a heavenly time she was going to have, and, she reflected gratefully, what a splendid, generous person her Uncle Phillip was even though he did frighten her sometimes.

Waiting for Mrs. Sherman to arrive, she roved importantly about the flat, made the beds and washed up the breakfast things. She was impatient to get out and spend

some of her lovely gold, and decided that a pound of coconut candy, the necessary chop for her dinner, a box of dates and a Fuller's chocolate cake would be the most suitable articles for which to break into her first half-sovereign. And even then she would still have limitless wealth for cups of coffee and cream buns in the A.B.C. teashop at Hammersmith Broadway, or, should she prefer to go further afield, in Kensington High Street, not to mention ice-creams and other delicacies. Even allowing for three weeks' food, she would be rich enough to have at least one abundant tea in the Maid of Honour shop in Richmond. As for Aunt Helen's advice to learn more about her rights, she dismissed this as unnecessary, for ever since she had heard Mrs. Ashton make fun of Helen's absorbing passion, she had been divided in her loyalty. She knew that her Aunt Helen was brilliant and serious-minded, for she was always proclaiming this fact, but though Mrs. Ashton laughingly denied even a suspicion of cleverness, she appeared to Hilda to have everything in the world any reasonable woman could desire, and to grow up like her became her dearest ambition.

After the first few days, the novelty of doing as she pleased began to pall a little, and Hilda, after her solitary breakfast, found herself waiting eagerly for the bustling Mrs. Sherman, who made no secret of her belief that 'they' had no business to leave the young lady all alone while they went off holiday-making.

'It don't seem right to me, Miss,' she said sympathetically, 'and with that foreign gent living next door too. I can't think what you do with yourself all day long. It's a pity you don't know nobody of your own age to keep you company, though Mrs. Shepheard did ask if I'd let my Betty sleep 'ere if you wanted 'er. She's my eldest, and if she 'adn't bin at school when young Rodney was born, that steak and kidney pudding wouldn't never 'ave bin

ruined.' Mrs. Sherman paused significantly, a look of mournful reminiscence stealing over her cheerful face.

Hilda, brimming over with self-pity at this motherly interest, ostentatiously dabbed at her eyes, and smiled bravely. Then, consumed with curiosity about the birth of young Rodney, she encouraged Mrs. Sherman to continue.

'Well, Miss, Mr. Sherman went off to work, looking forward to the steak and kidney pudding I was making for 'is dinner, and it was nicely on the boil when a pain come on and I 'ad to ask my neighbour to send for Mrs. Meadows, the midwife. And do you know, Miss, Mrs. Meadows 'adn't bin in the 'ouse five minutes before young Rod just slipped out. She said it was the quickest confinement she'd ever seen; but the pudding was ruined. It went off the boil and was as 'eavy as lead. Mr. Sherman said it lay on his stomach all afternoon and there was no shifting it.'

'What a shame!' exclaimed Hilda warmly. 'But I didn't know a baby could be born so quickly. I always thought it took all night.'

'Bless you, Miss, so it does in the ordinary way. Sometimes the pains goes on night *and* day, though that's not often. But this won't get the work done, so if you'll pardon me I'll be getting on,' and she began to sweep vigorously.

Hilda left the room reluctantly. Mrs. Sherman was the first person who had ever told her about the actual birth of a baby, and she would have liked her reminiscences to have continued a great deal longer. However, there was plenty of time for further confidences before her relatives came back, and with this pleasing reflection she went out to do her shopping.

The days sped happily enough, and, though always by herself among the crowds in Kew and Kensington Gardens, or in the teashops she frequented for the consumption of cream buns, she did not feel lonely. It was all such a tremendous adventure, and she enjoyed every

minute of it when she was out of doors. Lovely postcards arrived from Aunt Helen and Uncle Phillip in Devonshire, and from Aunt Mildred in Cheshire, and Phillip also wrote her a charming letter describing places called Bolt Head and Hope Cove and Salcombe, and said how much he was looking forward to showing them to her next year. It was only at night, in the empty flat, that she gradually began to feel sorry for herself, and to have uneasy tremors lest she should have a *bad* flying dream, like the one which had awakened the whole household. This calamity, however, did not occur, for during the entire three weeks that her family was away she did not dream at all.

By the beginning of the third week she was alarmed at the rapidity with which her little fortune had melted. Certainly she had enjoyed herself while it lasted, but the quiet evenings dragged in spite of her passion for reading. One night, to beguile the tedium, she decided to try on all her aunt's clothes, and she was admiring the effect of Helen's silvery-grey djibbah when the bell rang. Her spirits rocketed. A visitor! Perhaps Mr. McGilray or Mr. Jepson. There was no time to take off the djibbah, and pulling it tightly about her she opened the door in high expectation. It was Mrs. Ashton's husband, and with him was a small, brown dog of dubious lineage but obvious goodwill. Feeling silly in her capacious, borrowed finery, she stared at Mr. Ashton confusedly, and stammered out that everybody had gone away on holiday.

'Well, my dear, do you mind if I come in for a minute? And this is Doctor Livingstone. He's very well-behaved and friendly, and a great explorer. That's how he got his ridiculous name. We call him "Doc" for short. Shake hands with the lady, old chap!'

Doctor Livingstone gravely extended a paw, which Hilda as gravely shook, and both followed her into the sitting-room.

'So you're left in charge, Hilda. What a pity we didn't know your family was away. You could have come to us, couldn't she, Doc?'

Doc gave a confirmatory grunt and sidled up to Hilda, nuzzling into the velvet djibbah so vigorously that, alarmed for its safety, she had to push him away, whereupon, unresenting, he lay down quietly and slept.

'And how long have they gone for?' Mr. Ashton inquired.

'They've been away for two weeks, but they'll be back next Saturday. They've gone to a place called Hope Cove in Devonshire. Look, Aunt Helen has sent me all those postcards on the mantelpiece, and Uncle Phillip wrote me a long letter. Aunt Mildred's gone to Warburton in Cheshire.'

Mr. Ashton surveyed Hilda kindly. There was something very touching about her as she sat there in the floppy djibbah, taking it for granted that it was quite the thing for her relatives to have left her behind. He was profoundly shocked at their callousness, and wished he or his wife had dropped in earlier.

'What about coming back and having supper with us, Hilda? Nora will be delighted. She loves people to drop in. So does Doc, and you can stop with us if you like till your people return.'

Hilda flushed with pleasure. What a nice man Mr. Ashton was, so gentle and thoughtful, and talking to her as if he had known her all her life. The prospect of going back with him to supper was so delightful that she conveniently forgot her promise to Helen not to be out at night. She could not, however, stay with them, she said seriously, because Aunt Helen relied upon her to look after things while she was away.

'I see. Anyway, come with me now, and Doc and I will see you safely home again. It isn't very far. We can

walk it in a quarter of an hour. Doc has rather positive views about travelling by bus, so positive that we never take him in one if we can help it,' at which statement Doc looked up complacently and gave a frightful grin.

'Thank you very much, Mr. Ashton. I won't be a minute. This isn't my djibbah,' she explained.

'I can see that,' he laughed, as she trailed out. She soon returned in her lawful clothes, and presently the three of them were walking briskly along to Bedford Park, where the Ashtons lived.

Mrs. Ashton made a great fuss of her, and, in spite of warning signs from her husband, commented unfavourably on Helen's selfishness in grudging her niece a few weeks' holiday.

'Just like her,' she said tartly, 'to boggle over an extra pound or two. I'll bet she was the one responsible. Phillip Shepheard has his faults, but meanness over money isn't one of them. You must come and see us whenever you like, Hilda. You can take Doc out to the Parks or along the river. He'll love it, and he'll be company for you too.'

Hilda, thus made much of, spent an enchanting evening. Mrs. Ashton was so different from her Aunt Helen; so easy-going and gay, and so wonderful to look at that Hilda could scarcely take her eyes off her. Mr. Ashton, on the other hand, was quiet, but it was plain that he adored his wife, and he carried in all the supper things for her and cleared them away when the meal was over. Doc, replete with various titbits, retired to his own armchair by the window. It was an immense basket chair, nearly falling to pieces where he had chewed it when he was bored, and he lay in it snoring loudly and dreaming, so his master said, that he was winning all the Derbys that had ever been run, so fast did his legs twitch on the shocking old cushion.

Remembering what Aunt Mildred had told her about Mrs. Ashton smoking a pipe, Hilda watched expectantly, and was not disappointed, for after filling his own pipe Mr. Ashton handed his tobacco pouch to his wife. As she helped herself, she turned smilingly to Hilda: 'I hope this doesn't shock you, child. I daresay your aunts have mentioned it. Helen thinks it's rather daring and unnecessary in spite of her belief in equality between men and women. She thinks I do it to create an impression, which is stupid of her. I smoke a pipe because I like it, and if there's a better reason than that I should be glad to hear it. Now talk to us about yourself, Hilda. How do you get on with Phillip, and does your Aunt Mildred ever get a word in when Helen's in the field? I imagine not, but Mildred is a dark horse and not nearly such a nonentity as Helen likes to make out. What a cat you'll think I am talking like this about your relations! I'm not, really. I'm very fond of both your aunts, but don't you get like poor old Mildred. What I'm endeavouring to tell you is that you'll have to hold your own with Helen. She just can't help domineering over everybody: it's her nature. But you're a person too, and if you don't stand up to her you'll be lost. I saw that plainly enough at Barkers over that frightful hat she wanted to buy you. She talks a lot of drivel about the slavishness of following the fashion. She says she would hate to look the same as every other woman, and that's why she goes in for all this "artistic" nonsense. The arguments we've had about it! Anybody can achieve distinctiveness, and what it is worth, by looking dowdy. The real triumph for a woman is to look completely different from all other women when dressed exactly like them.'

The enraptured Hilda heartily agreed. For years, since she was about twelve, she had passionately desired a simple, good coat and skirt, a real tailor-made, but in

Moss Ferry this had been considered altogether too modish and expensive. She had hoped to attain to this distinction in fashionable London, but such hopes had been cruelly dashed when she had ventured to ask her Aunt Helen if one day she might possess such an outfit. Her aunt had been genuinely shocked. 'Do you *want* to look like every other girl?' she had asked scathingly. As this was exactly what Hilda did want, she had frankly said so, whereupon Helen had spoken to her most severely, pointing out that a coat and skirt, in the eyes of all artistically minded people, was a garment utterly devoid of grace, particularly upon a young and slender girl. And from this she launched into a little lecture on the desirability of drapery, of long, flowing lines, of lovely embroidery. A coat and skirt, she emphasized, cut one's figure in half; it was an affront to the female form, and completely opposed to the gracious lines favoured by the classic women of antiquity. Hilda, whose interest in the classic women of antiquity was entirely confined to the pages of the Reverend Alfred Church, agreed with apparent meekness; she was, nevertheless, determined that the very first thing she would acquire when she had money of her own was a perfectly tailored coat and skirt. She spent many happy half-hours dreaming of it, and equally unhappy ones envying other girls of her own age who, thus attired, walked the world freely and proudly. This was one instance where she knew beyond a peradventure that she was right and Aunt Helen hopelessly wrong. Nothing, she was convinced, would become her more,   , as for looking cut in half, she was quite tall enough to stand it. Childishly, she now confided her secret dream to Mrs. Ashton, who encouraged her to hope, adding that it was even possible that some day Helen might change her mind.

When ten o'clock struck and Mr. Ashton suggested that he and Doc should take her home, she rose reluctantly.

'Thank you very much, Mrs. Ashton. It's been lovely,' she said.

'Well — come along any time, child. Bring your book and make yourself at home. There's no need for you to sit cooped up in that flat while they're all away. Look at Doc wagging approval. He's a rational creature and understands perfectly what I'm saying to you.'

Hilda, waggling his ears, promised to come the very next day and take him for a long run by the river.

'That's splendid,' said Mrs. Ashton. 'Come early, about half-past two, and after your walk stay till bed-time. That's a promise, mind!'

Hilda's self-esteem soared high. What delightful, friendly people the Ashtons were to make her feel so welcome, and how utterly different Mrs. Ashton was from Aunt Helen, who always talked at her, and not, like dear Mrs. Ashton, to her.

CHAPTER IX

MR. RUMSEY'S ESTABLISHMENT

As Hilda's days of grace drew inevitably to their close, the important question of her career became the chief topic of discussion. There was little visible trace now of the awkward and frightened girl who had burst into tears on first meeting her new relatives; and, thanks to her industry and natural mimetic ability, her Lancashire accent had practically disappeared, though the pronunciation of a simple word like 'soot' would occasionally embarrass her. She had not lost her clear, bright colour, and because of her height looked older by a couple of years than she was. Reading was still a passion with her; but now, under the influence of Mrs. Ashton, an influence greatly deplored by the austere Helen, her most absorbing interest was in her own physical charms, to enhance which she secretly indulged in the daring application of papier-poudré leaves. She kept the little perfumed sachet in her handbag, and used it only if she was going out alone, vigorously rubbing it off before re-entering the flat. She made the care of her hands a daily ritual, and brushed her hair until it gleamed like copper. It was difficult hair, long and fine, but under Mrs. Ashton's skilful guidance she learnt how to set it with combs and even to achieve the suspicion of a wave.

The day came at last when Helen, looking unusually grave, asked if she had yet made up her mind what she would like to be, and Hilda, for no reason at all beyond that of creating an immediate dramatic effect, replied seriously: 'Yes! I want to be an actress like Lillah McCarthy.'

Helen flushed with annoyance, while Uncle Phillip and Aunt Mildred merely laughed.

'And what makes you think you have the makings of an actress?' Helen asked sarcastically. 'I suppose Nora Ashton's been putting the idea into your silly head. You see far too much of her. She's a delightful woman, but there *are* other things in life, Hilda, beyond admiration and flattery, and the sooner you realize this the better. Take up amateur acting by all means if you want to. I've nothing whatever against that — but as a career, indeed No! We must think of something very different.'

'But you've always said how much you admire Lillah McCarthy,' Hilda pursued tactlessly.

'Of course I admire her! Who doesn't? But Lillah McCarthy is a finished, intelligent and beautiful actress, and you're just Hilda Winstanley, aged fifteen and a bit, and — correct me if I'm wrong — with no pronounced histrionic ability. So please put the stage right out of your head. I never heard anything so fantastic. Don't you agree, Phillip?'

'I'm afraid I do,' he smiled, 'though I believe it's a phase most young girls go through. Cheer up, Hilda! You've got years and years yet if you really want to become an actress, and as Helen says you can always enjoy it as a hobby. What we've got to decide now is something practical.'

Helen again mentioned the Civil Service, which caused Hilda to quake and to look desperately at her uncle for his promised help. He did not fail her, and made it quite clear to his wife that it would be a sheer waste of time and money to force the girl into this profession; but Helen, who hated to be thwarted, argued that, if only Hilda would give her whole mind to the business, a good teacher could get her through her exams — that it was only a

matter of application, and really quite ridiculous to assume that a naturally intelligent girl, given proper tuition, would utterly collapse in the face of a few sums. Hilda, however, knew better, and dreaded the prospect of proving herself, once and for all, a dunce.

Patiently and reasonably, Phillip set himself to convince his wife that their niece was not cut out for the dubious blessings of inadequate wages and lifelong security in the Civil Service, with the result that, finally, she turned to Hilda once more, and asked pathetically: 'Well, what *do* you want to be? I suppose you have given *some* thought to the matter.'

Hilda, mortified by her aunt's unsympathetic attitude, suggested diffidently that perhaps she could learn to be a confidential private secretary, a career which was continually being advertised by a local business college as interesting, lucrative, and altogether desirable; a career, moreover, so the advertisements said, which opened up for its followers infinite and dazzling horizons, and was, in fact, the one and only possible career for any ambitious boy or girl. It was true, of course, that the curriculum, which Hilda had studied on the notice-board outside the college, included book-keeping, but this subject was shorn of its horror by the prefix 'simple', and even Hilda felt herself equal to tackling 'simple' book-keeping. Now that she had to enter into bondage, it was borne in upon her, with relentless clarity, that she wanted the past most glorious year to go on and on, just as it had been, until such time as she was grown up and married to an adoring husband, since this, Mrs. Ashton had declared to her more than once, was the only career worthy of any girl's really serious attention. Her Aunt Helen would have been aghast had she known how cleverly Mrs. Ashton had gone to work to counteract her own influence over Hilda. It was a thousand pities, the Ashtons agreed, that

she had no companions of her own age: it was unhealthy for her never to be in any but adult society.

To Hilda's surprise and relief, Helen took her suggestion of a secretarial career quite seriously, but pointed out that she would still have to work extremely hard.

'Nine girls out of ten nowadays seem to go in for this type of work,' she observed, 'but with application, and luck, you might eventually end up as secretary to a statesman, or an editor, or even a famous author. H. G. Wells, for instance! Wouldn't that be splendid, Hilda? Really worth striving for. There are plenty of openings, and when we women get our rights there will be a very wide field to choose from. You ought to join the Fabian Nursery. You'd meet lots of intelligent and ambitious young people there. All right, it's settled then that you want to become a private secretary. We'll go along tomorrow to that business college and make inquiries.'

Hilda eagerly assented, and a pleasant glow warmed her at the possibility of entering history as personal secretary to Mr. H. G. Wells, whose thrilling book, *The War of the Worlds*, she had just enjoyed. Also, at a meeting of the Fabian Society to which Aunt Helen had taken her, she had heard him speak, and, in spite of his funny, squeaky voice, had been very impressed by the affection in which the audience held him. His attractive blue eyes, Hilda conceded, more than made up for his otherwise not remarkable appearance. Mrs. Wells had been on the platform too, small and brown and quiet; and of course Mr. George Bernard Shaw, ripping everybody to pieces with a virulence that delighted even his victims. Yes, Hilda decided, she would aim at Mr. H. G. Wells. Mr. Shaw, of course, was perhaps even more desirable from the point of view of prestige, but it was Mr. Wells who radiated the warmth. Her heart yearned towards him as it would never yearn towards Mr. George Bernard

Shaw, although Aunt Helen had impressed upon her that she must admire and reverence so great a man, or remain for ever in the darkness of Philistia — wherever that might be.

Mr. Rumsey, the pope and principal of the Business College, received them graciously, and expounded at some length his belief that a year's tuition under him would turn the young lady into the treasure that hundreds of harassed business gentlemen were waiting for. The curriculum, he explained, consisted of a thorough grounding in shorthand, typewriting, simple book-keeping, elementary French or German, and an apparently new version of the English language which he called 'Commercial English'. Aunt Helen started when he mentioned this last subject, and puzzled him not a little by asking what was amiss with the tongue that Shakespeare and Milton had spoken. For a paralysing second Hilda feared that her aunt was going to treat him to a selection of entirely uncommercial prose and verse, but she controlled herself and merely repeated, in a sort of stupor, his horrible phrase — 'Commercial English!'

Mr. Rumsey, rallying bravely, produced a manual devoted to examples of business correspondence, and, handing it to her, showed her what he meant by 'Commercial English'. Aunt Helen, fascinated as she turned over the pages, slowly read aloud and with fine, dramatic effect, the following sample of a correct business letter:

Messrs. The Reinforced (Dorking) Boot Tree Co., Ltd.,
  68, Cosway Street,
    Dorking,
      Surrey.
Dear Sirs: Re your esteemed favour of the 30th ult., for which we beg to tender our best thanks, we have pleasure in informing you that we shall be most happy to quote you

some very attractive prices for the range of goods you are interested in.

Before doing so, however, we should be glad to learn from you, at your convenience, as to whether you wish our prices to be ex works or delivered, either at your premises or the nearest railway station. It is our usual custom to quote f.o.r. or f.o.b., but can also give site delivery in van where this is called for.

May we respectfully add that in the event of any query arising we shall be happy to arrange for our representative, Mr. Potts, to wait upon you without delay.

Thanking you in anticipation of a speedy reply, and assuring you of our desire to at all times quote you the keenest possible market price for what is really a most attractive and saleable line of goods,

We beg to remain, dear Sirs, Yours very faithfully,

CLANK, CRANK & CHIPPENDALE

pp. J. Hanks, Sales Manager.

'So that is "Commercial English",' she remarked thoughtfully, as she handed back the manual. 'Well, I think it is a travesty of our glorious tongue — our birthright — and for the life of me I don't see the point of it. Why cannot even a business man write a letter in *English* instead of employing a language that never was on land or sea? My husband is a business man, but I'm sure he finds it unnecessary to use such outlandish terms.'

Mr. Rumsey looked uneasy, and Hilda, uneasy also, saw that he was anxious for Aunt Helen to complete her business and go. He made no attempt to answer her question. He had been teaching the new tongue to a succession of aspiring merchant princes and lady secretaries for well over a decade, and this was the first time anyone had regarded it as something out of the ordinary. What an overpowering lady this was, he reflected gloomily.

Probably a suffragette! He could think of no other satisfactory explanation for her peculiar and really unladylike
attitude.

Studying the curriculum, Aunt Helen decided that
'Commercial English' was a superfluous accomplishment,
and, eyeing Mr. Rumsey firmly, asked whether he could
not exclude it from her niece's training and reduce his
fees accordingly, or alternatively make it up by allowing
her more time in another subject, book-keeping for
instance. Figures, she emphasized, were not Hilda's
strongest point, and it would be far more profitable for
the time thus saved to be spent on book-keeping. Mr.
Rumsey, however, would make no concessions. If the
young lady was to become a fully qualified and successful
secretary, it was essential, he said, that the mysteries of
commercial English should be made manifest to her.
Without such knowledge she would find herself but ill-
equipped for a triumphant business career and would
soon be outdistanced by her more amenable contemporaries. Aunt Helen, though not alarmed by the
depressing picture he drew, thought it politic to give
way, especially as she would have to pay for the subject
in any case. Mr. Rumsey's dull and heavy features were
beginning to irritate her, and she was just as desirous of
getting away from him as he was for her to go. The
matter, therefore, was settled, the first month's fees paid,
and Hilda duly enrolled.

Before they left, Mr. Rumsey conducted them through
the various classrooms, and the prospective student's
spirits dropped to zero as she surveyed the long tables,
the drab bare walls, and the earnest faces of the boys and
girls pounding away at typewriters, or learning the new
and improved version of the English language. It would
be like going back to school, she thought glumly, though
not nearly so pleasant. She was surprised also to discover

that some of the students were much older than herself, and that one of them was even of a different colour. She noticed him particularly because he looked rather intently at her, causing her to feel self-conscious and thankful for once for Aunt Helen's dominating but protective presence.

Shaking hands with them, Mr. Rumsey assured her aunt that Miss Winstanley would be given every encouragement and personal attention, and that it would not be his fault, or the fault of his staff, if she did not leave his charge a perfectly-trained lady secretary certain of resounding success in the continually expanding arena of English Business.

When they were back in the street, Helen turned to her niece and reproved her sharply for her dejected demeanour and apparent lack of all interest in Mr. Rumsey's establishment: 'Really, Hilda, there are times when I should like to shake you! What's the matter now? Aren't you glad you are going to begin taking life seriously? You couldn't look more miserable if you were at your own funeral. Didn't you like Mr. Rumsey? He's a fool, of course, but never mind. What *is* the matter?'

Hilda flushed but managed to appear composed; she would not have dared attempt any explanation of her low spirits. Mr. Rumsey and his College had filled her with dire misgivings: it had looked so exactly like a vast prison. She did not want to be a business young lady at all unless she could be positively assured that in the fullness of time she would be permitted to minister to the needs of the exciting and lovable Mr. H. G. Wells, or of someone equally unbusinesslike and human. She had seen no colour and felt no warmth in Mr. Rumsey's Establishment. The very thought of it now loomed like a gigantic shadow waiting to engulf her.

'I'm sorry, Aunt Helen. There's nothing the matter

really. It's just that everything made me feel nervous, as if I'd never be able to learn anything properly.'

'Nonsense, Hilda! You'll be all right. Work hard at the College and study all you can at home as well. Phillip or I will always help you, if we can, should you find anything too difficult. Now, there's nothing whatever to worry about, and you have to begin earning your living some time — surely you see that?'

Hilda meekly accepted this indisputable fact, which was not new to her anyway, and her spirits lightened when she remembered that she would be free every day at four o'clock, and that there was no college on Saturdays. By the time she reached home she had already passed with distinction, indeed with outstanding brilliance, from the sombre shadows of Mr. Rumsey's Establishment into those more smiling pastures where — surely — distinguished employers awaited her. Authors even, blue-eyed, warm-hearted, greatly resembling Mr. H. G. Wells.

She had not been many weeks at the Business College before she made the depressing discovery that the process of becoming the perfect secretary entailed a great deal of preliminary monotony, and it was nothing but her fear of incurring Aunt Helen's wrath which kept her, at first, doggedly to her textbooks. The one bright spot in the whole curriculum was the simple French lesson given twice a week by Miss Printon, an ugly little woman with fierce black eyes, frizzy black hair, black kid buttoned boots with very high heels, a fiendish temper and a Cockney accent. Hilda, who had for some years prided herself on her knowledge of the French tongue, entirely self-acquired until Uncle Phillip had given her lessons, was bitterly humiliated when Miss Printon informed her that she didn't know the first thing about it, and adjured her, in her own interests, to forget what she had hitherto been

pleased to call 'French', and to pay attention, instead, to what she, Miss Printon, had to offer, which was the only true and genuine article. Also, she boasted, it was well known throughout the whole College that she had a real flair for teaching, and certainly she had a way of making even the most stupid of them learn something. Hilda, in spite of the uncharitable mirth which the black buttoned boots aroused in her, liked this teacher, and made reasonable progress. Miss Printon returned the liking, and even invited her to tea one Sunday at her little flat in Hammersmith, impressing her guest enormously when, dropping a teaspoon, she exclaimed tragically: 'Ah! Quel dommage! Quel dommage!' It sounded superb, and great was Mildred's astonishment when her niece, having carelessly let some milk boil over, ejaculated with deep feeling: 'Ah! Quel dommage! Quel dommage! Quel dommage!' Pleased with herself, Hilda felt considerably dashed when Aunt Mildred warned her kindly against becoming affected.

Miss Printon, who was evidently lonely, asked Hilda again to tea, whereupon Helen, gratified at this interest, which she regarded as a good augury for Hilda's future progress, allowed her to invite Miss Printon back, mildly curious to discover what kind of person she was. Hilda presented her invitation proudly, for Miss Printon was the first friend she had made in London independently of the family.

When Sunday afternoon came she was all eagerness in getting tea ready, and thrilled with pleasure when Aunt Helen said she might use the green and white tea things, which were so old and fragile that they seldom emerged from their corner cupboard even for Helen's own friends. But this, her aunt said graciously, was a very special occasion, denoting a happy relationship between teacher and pupil. And as a further mark of favour she said that

Hilda should act as hostess. Dear Aunt Mildred had gone to much trouble in making special little cakes, and, as she always did for a tea-party, had bought a Fuller's iced chocolate cake as well. Uncle Phillip, interested as ever in any new feminine personality, was at his most agreeable, and when the bell rang at four o'clock precisely, Hilda, all excitement, ran happily to welcome her guest. But at sight of Miss Printon her heart went into her boots, for there was something quite awful about her new friend's appearance. She was all frizz and billow and incredibly high heels, and literally tinkled with earrings and bangles, while round her neck, long as a small skipping rope, was wound an imitation jade necklace which made Hilda think of plump, newly-shelled peas. Her eyes glittered like onyxes in her plain, heavily-powdered little face, and Hilda felt decidedly nervous as she led her into the sitting-room.

Her family showed no surprise at the startling apparition, but when their greetings were returned in mincing, Cockney accents, and she saw Uncle Phillip look meaningly at his wife, Hilda sent him a despairing appeal for help, to which he responded nobly by giving himself up wholeheartedly to the captivation of Miss Printon. Hilda, busy and important with her duties as hostess, said little, and blushed without joy when Miss Printon informed her family that she was a good and eager pupil, and that if she made as much progress with her other business studies as she was making with her French, she would turn out a lasting credit to Mr. Rumsey's famous college. It was clear that she regarded Mr. Rumsey as a very great man indeed, and her enthusiasm for his qualities at first ousted all other topics from the tea-table. Helen, during a breathing space when Miss Printon was sipping her tea, asked if she had been in the recent great Suffragist Procession, and whether she did not think it was superb of Mrs.

Drummond to lead on horseback her army of forty thousand women.

Miss Printon, her cup suspended, and her little finger sticking out as though waiting for a small parcel to be suspended from it, regarded Helen with surprise. 'Surely, Mrs. Shepheard, you're not going to tell me that you are a suffragette!' she exclaimed in tones of genuine horror. 'I certainly am not. I would not demean myself by being so unladylike. I think they're dreadful, shouting and singing and making such a show of themselves. Insulting our womanhood, that's what I think. What do we want with the vote, anyway? What good will it do us? — Of course,' she added lamely, realizing from Helen's frigid face that she had blundered beyond all hope of pardon, 'I don't mean to be personal. We're all entitled to our opinion, are we not? That's what I always say. What I mean is that you do not *look* like a suffragette, Mrs. Shepheard. I had no idea . . . Hilda never mentioned it.'

Helen surveyed her pityingly, undecided whether to engage in battle or not. Common sense, however, warned her that this was no case for an attempted conversion. Miss Printon was not worthy of her steel. She was just a plain fool, with her gimcrack jewellery and her gimcrack opinions. The Cause was better without such creatures; and Hilda too, she reflected, would be better for seeing no more of her than the French lessons entailed. Pressing her to more cake, she smiled and said pleasantly: 'Of course we are all entitled to our opinions, Miss Printon. But we're all suffragists here, even Hilda. You should come to one of our Meetings some time. We've raised over one hundred thousand pounds this summer for our funds — subscribed by men as well as women. Oh yes, Miss Printon, we have quite a lot of male supporters — great men in politics, literature, the Church, the Peerage, and even in sport. We shall

win, of course. We English always win our wars. It's a habit we've acquired. Don't you agree, Phillip?'

'Indeed yes,' he answered, fussing agreeably over the now wilting Miss Printon. 'You'll have to come in on our side, Miss Printon. You'll be looked on as old-fashioned if you don't, and I'm sure you're anything but that.'

He gave her a charming smile. When he laid himself out to please he was quite irresistible, and Miss Printon, her self-esteem bubbling to the surface again, said archly: 'Of course I'm not old-fashioned, Mr. Shepheard. I'm all for progress, really. Fancy *you* being a suffragette! Isn't it a funny world?'

'It is indeed,' he replied gravely, 'very funny. Try one of these. My sister-in-law made them, and they're worth all the shop cakes that ever were, you can take it from me.'

Phillip, sorry for Hilda, fussed over Miss Printon to her heart's content, and even Helen, taking her cue from him, managed to endure her with fortitude. It was not for long, and need never happen again. For the future, Hilda and Miss Printon must remain in their respective spheres. Mercifully, she could detect no horrible twang whenever their guest uttered a ridiculous exclamation in French, which was often. It transpired that she had taught English privately in Paris for many years, and had naturally acquired her French over there. It was, however, frightful to reflect upon the hundreds of innocent Parisians who must have learnt their English from her. It recalled the shock they had experienced when the Ashtons once brought along a pleasant young Dane they had met at Toynbee Hall, whom they had nicknamed 'Hamlet'. His parents had placed him in what they had fondly imagined to be a cultured English family, and he had learnt to speak the language fluently and with as excru-

ciating an accent as ever proceeded from poor Miss Printon. Mr. and Mrs. Ashton, who had taken a great fancy to him, worked hard to undo the mischief, but it was too late and Hamlet returned to Copenhagen full of loving admiration for the English, and intensely proud of his Cockney accent, which, in due course, he conveyed to his younger brothers and sisters.

The time dragged on and Miss Printon gave no sign of leaving, despite the ominous collecting by Mildred of the tea-things. As a quarter past six struck from the church clock, Helen, calm but desperate, informed her that they would have to be getting ready to go out.

'This evening will be something of an occasion for Hilda,' she confided. 'We are taking her to the O.P. Club to hear Mr. G. K. Chesterton. He's the most fascinating speaker in London, and it's a great feather in the O.P. Club's cap to have got him along to-night.'

Hilda, till that moment unaware of this treat in store, looked beseechingly at her guest, who appeared to be glued to her chair, incapable of moving anything but her trinkets.

'Oh! You lucky girl, Hilda!' she exclaimed enviously. 'What wouldn't I give to hear Mr. Chesterton too. Is it the sort of meeting anybody can attend, Mrs. Shepheard? I would so like to hear him.'

'I'm sorry, Miss Printon,' said Helen firmly, 'but it's for members only. We ought not really to take Hilda, but I want her to have the experience. So I'm afraid we must not keep you any longer. It's been so nice meeting you, and we're all so pleased that you think Hilda is getting on so well.'

She sent Phillip one of her private looks, and he immediately said to Miss Printon: 'You'll let me take you to your bus. Are we all ready?'

Miss Printon, unable to conceal her disappointment, sullenly unglued herself, and after what seemed an eternity minced and jingled away under the protection of poor Phillip. As the door shut behind them, Helen turned to her niece and said kindly: 'It's not your fault, child, but for heaven's sake don't go to see her again. There's something dwarfish, malignant, about her, or it may only be my imagination and she's no more than silly. Those beads! Thank God for G. K. Chesterton. I hadn't meant to take you to the O.P. Club — the Old Playgoers' — tonight, but I feel we ought to make it up to you for your visitor. It's an ill wind, etc.'

And certainly, when Hilda found herself waiting eagerly for Mr. Chesterton's appearance in the bright reception room of the Hotel Cecil where the O.P. Club held its gay and friendly meetings, Miss Printon was more than made up to her. She stayed contentedly in her seat while her relations were greeting various friends, and beamed when Mrs. Ashton, looking absolutely wonderful, waved to her. She was far and away the most beautiful person in the room, thought Hilda proudly, as she waved back, hoping that people would notice that Mrs. Ashton was her friend.

The talk died away in a burst of applause as the President of the Club piloted Mr. Chesterton, who, for all his bulk, tripped as lightly as ever did General Gordon, on to the small platform. Hilda gazed at him reverently. So this was the famous Mr. G. K. Chesterton, about whom her family and their friends were always talking — quoting his poems — laughing at his jokes — telling stories of how he was continually losing his manuscripts and finding them again in the most unlikely places, or rather his friends finding them for him. What a fortunate girl she was! No wonder Miss Printon would have liked to come too. He was the bulkiest man she had ever seen, and it

did not escape her notice that the chair placed for him was quite different from all the other chairs in the room. It was immensely solid, a veritable giant of a chair. She craned forward earnestly so as not to miss a single word of all he had to tell them about the Drama, and so brilliantly did he speak, provoking such continuous laughter and applause, that it was some little time before his youngest listener realized that he was not talking about the Drama at all, but about a certain Don Quixote, and his companion Sancho Panza, names that were vaguely familiar since she had once come across them when glancing speculatively through one of her uncle's books. It had every sign about it of being a dry book, and she had soon replaced it. But here was Mr. Chesterton talking about Don Quixote and Sancho Panza as if they were the most dearly loved of all his friends! Phillip, observing how raptly she hung upon every word, squeezed her arm and exchanged a smile with Mildred. It did him good to watch her enjoyment of this new experience, and her regret when the magical flow ended was written all over her.

'And what do you think of G. K. Chesterton, Hilda?' he asked when the applause had died down. 'Great fun, isn't he? And not one blessed word about the theatre!'

'It was beautiful,' said Hilda earnestly. 'I didn't know that anybody could talk like that. And all about one book too. I shall start reading it tonight if you'll let me.'

'But of course, though I think you should wait a bit. You'll enjoy it more when you're older. At least, that's how it was with me.'

'She must certainly wait,' Aunt Helen interrupted briskly. 'She won't appreciate it for years yet. What an evening! There's nobody like him, is there? I wonder what your friend Miss Printon would have made of him, Hilda? Look, there are the Ashtons waiting for us.

Suppose we all go and have supper at Appenrodts, to celebrate Hilda's first experience of G. K. C.,' she suggested in an unusual rush of extravagance, due, Hilda presumed, to the genial influence of the entrancing Mr. Chesterton.

CHAPTER X

MR. RAM LAL

HILDA's year at Mr. Rumsey's Establishment passed without particular distinction for her. She worked reasonably hard, but her thoughts strayed so frequently to the happy things she would so much rather have been doing, that Mr. Rumsey, in his report at the end of her first term, wrote that though she was intelligent above the average, and could do well if she gave her mind to it, she was both careless and lacking in concentration: grave defects, he pointed out, which she must determine to overcome.

Aunt Helen was so surprised when she read this criticism of her niece, who was continually assuring her that she was getting on 'nicely', that she went to see Mr. Rumsey, to obtain more precise information. She returned in a furious temper and immediately reduced Hilda to tears by accusing her of indolence and black ingratitude.

'You want to be a success, don't you?' she asked bitingly. 'As Mr. Rumsey says, it isn't as though you were a fool, incapable of learning, and since you're not devoid of natural intelligence, why in heaven's name don't you use it? Really, Hilda, you must pull yourself together and learn to keep your mind on what you are doing! Here am I spending all my time, and more money than I can afford, for the Cause, so that you, and all your generation, will benefit, while you are just frittering away your opportunities. Why, lots of girls would give anything to be in your shoes. You don't want me to send you back to Moss Ferry, do you? Now stop crying, and make up your mind to do better.'

Hilda, overflowing with self-pity, escaped to her

room, uneasily conscious that her aunt was justified in her onslaught. It was true: she knew that she was capable of learning, but how to explain that she simply couldn't help her thoughts wandering? It was so satisfying to conjure up Mrs. Ashton's lovely face, and to think of new walks to take Doctor Livingstone; to recall Mr. Chesterton's magic; to quote to herself snatches of stirring ballads, and above all to dwell upon the splendour of her flying dreams. She stood gazing into her mirror, watching with enormous interest the spectacle of herself crying, and wishing that Uncle Phillip or Aunt Mildred would come in and be sorry for her and take her part against Aunt Helen. While she was thus enjoying herself, Helen's ominous remark about sending her back to Moss Ferry shot through her mind, turning her quite sick with fear. It had never occurred to her that such a thing was even remotely possible. One day, when she was grown up and independent, she would return to Moss Ferry for a visit, just to show them all how marvellously a few years in London had transformed the Hilda Winstanley they had known. She had even decided upon the expensive present she would take for each member of her foster-family. But now a very different picture formed itself before her streaming eyes: she saw herself returning miserable and humiliated, with nothing to show for her lovely years in London but different clothes and a different accent. They would welcome her affectionately enough, of that she was sure, but with no special pride as befitting a girl out of the ordinary who was bound to make her way in the world. She might as well drown herself as go back in such circumstances. For a few thrilling moments she dwelt appreciatively upon the remorse which would overwhelm and, very probably, destroy Aunt Helen when they pulled her body, clad only in its nightdress, out of the Thames. It would be far, far

better to do away with herself, she decided mournfully, than to leave London and all its enchantments; never to see Uncle Phillip or Aunt Mildred or Mrs. Ashton again; not even, she admitted honestly, to see Aunt Helen again, to whom it was entirely due that she had been rescued from Moss Ferry. The sobering thought that if she drowned herself she would never have the satisfaction of witnessing Aunt Helen's remorse, called a halt to these self-dramatizations, and she dismissed the possibility of an untimely end as impractical. But she had been thoroughly frightened, too frightened for further play-acting before the mirror, and was genuinely anxious to begin making up at once for all the hours she had wasted day-dreaming in Mr. Rumsey's dreary precincts.

She took out her shorthand manual and set to work with a will. Shorthand held no charms for her, and until now she had always hoped that some day, in a revealing flash, its mysteries would be instantaneously made clear; but after her aunt's outburst it began to dawn upon her that perhaps nothing would be made clear without some slight application on her part. She was engrossed in the manual when she heard her uncle's key, and presently he came in to see what she was doing. She perceived from his expression that he had been told about the interview with Mr. Rumsey, and, feeling nervous and guilty, she started to cry again. With his arm round her shoulders he asked her just what the trouble was. She explained that she couldn't memorize the shorthand outlines, no matter how often she copied them out, and that she couldn't account for this troubling fact when she found it so easy to remember other things — verse for instance, and whole passages of prose.

Phillip smiled. 'There's a good enough reason for that, I think. You like learning poetry, and you don't like learning shorthand. All the same, Hilda, you must be

sensible and master this business. Think of Charles Dickens! He taught himself shorthand, and earned his living through it in the Press Gallery of the House of Commons, though thank God he didn't stop there. I have an idea. Suppose you try learning it out of doors when you're taking a walk. When you see a notice, or even the name of a house or shop, try to transpose it mentally into shorthand. In that way it will fix itself, and gradually you'll gain confidence. It will all come right eventually. Just keep hammering away at it, and one day you'll find it so simple that you'll wonder why you ever thought otherwise. And don't spoil your eyes with crying. I never saw such big tears.' He took her face between his hands and stared down at her. 'You are not in the least like Helen,' he said gravely, 'not in the least,' and with that he released her and went out.

Deeply puzzled, Hilda again looked into the mirror. She had always assumed that she bore a strong family likeness to both her aunts, though she fondly hoped that she was more like Mildred than Helen. How strange of Uncle Phillip! Why, she had once heard him tell Mrs. Ashton that he thought she was very like Aunt Helen, and Mrs. Ashton had answered laughingly that she hoped the resemblance was no more than physical. But although he looked at her so oddly at times, she loved him very much and was passionately grateful to him now for his sympathy with her troubles. To show how truly she appreciated his advice, she would profit by it without loss of time, and, improving upon his suggestion, within five minutes she was slowly pacing the nearest graveyard, scrutinizing the memorials and transposing into shorthand the uncompromising pronouncement GONE HOME — which, surmounted by a large stone doorkey, was the briefest inscription she could find as a beginning. It became quite a fascinating game to go to the graveyard after tea, and

in a few weeks she had acquired a vast and varied store of tombstone verse, and aroused the deepest compassion of the sexton, who came to regard her as a poor young thing sadly afflicted by a great bereavement.

At other times she would take a brisk walk up Castelnau with the lively Doc, turning into shorthand the grandiloquent names of the little Georgian houses, and letting him off his lead if they got as far as Barnes Common. On these occasions she would spend the rest of the evening with the Ashtons, learning from her hostess how to make herself desirable and indispensable to man. Though the heavens fell, warned Mrs. Ashton, she must never affront the world with an unpowdered face. Hilda, eager to demonstrate that she was not such a simpleton as Mrs. Ashton evidently thought, produced her little sachet of papier-poudré leaves, but her friend said they were old-fashioned, and presented her with a box of powder proper, and a puff. Hilda experimented there and then, and had the satisfaction of being warmly congratulated upon her improved appearance. And, before long, moved to even closer imitation of Mrs. Ashton's outward charms, she took a further important step that made it necessary for her to look ahead cautiously in the street lest she should run into some member of her family, for this was a step obvious to everyone. It was a lipstick of raging scarlet, which she handled at first as gingerly as if it were made of explosives. Even Mrs. Ashton was mildly critical of this innovation, and advised her to use it sparingly, for Hilda in her enthusiasm had made herself more scarlet than the woman of Babylon. She was highly flattered by the admiring looks of various passing gentlemen until one of them, more adventurous than the rest, raised his hat, remarked that it was a lovely day, and showed an obvious desire for her acquaintance. But Hilda, her early Methodist upbringing sounding in her ears like a tocsin,

gave him such an annihilating stare that he reddened, muttered, in a most ungentlemanly fashion, what sounded to her like 'damned cheek', and hurried with sinister jauntiness upon his way.

Excepting Miss Printon, with whom, in spite of repeated invitations to tea, her relationship was now on a strictly business footing, Hilda made but one acquaintance at Mr. Rumsey's Establishment. Nobody seemed particularly friendly, or behaved at all sociably, and she was far too self-conscious to take the initiative. The exception was the gentleman from India who had looked at her so intently when Mr. Rumsey had first shown Aunt Helen and herself round the premises. Mr. Ram Lal was rather dark, with a deeply pitted face, and courteous manners. He sat next to Hilda in the class for 'Commercial English', and, in spite of his different colour, she was not displeased by his various little attentions such as retrieving, in a flash, anything she dropped, lending her his blotting-paper when he saw that she had none, and occasionally asking, with a pleasing air of deferring to one of superior race and knowledge, questions as to the correct pronunciation of unusual words in the new language they were both studying. Hilda regarded him, on the whole, with a mixture of fear and curiosity. She speculated deeply on his probable age, which seemed to her about thirty, and wondered for what mysterious reason he had left his own beautiful country to spend his days in this dingy class-room. She pondered too on his reason for studying English at all, since he spoke it at any rate with considerable fluency. As time went by, she could not fail to notice that Mr. Ram Lal always contrived to be leaving the College at precisely the same moment as herself, and, snobbishly afraid of being seen in his company, would wish him a polite good afternoon and hurry away. One day, however, as they were coming out into the street,

Hilda unthinkingly exclaimed aloud that she had forgotten one of her textbooks, and instantly Mr. Ram Lal darted back for it. Blushing deeply, she thanked him, and as usual was beginning to walk rapidly homewards, when Mr. Ram Lal, bowing gracefully, addressed her: 'Please, Miss, may I not walk a little way with you? We go one way together I think, if you please, Miss.'

Hilda stood in awkward silence. It was one thing for Mr. Ram Lal to be attentive in the class-room, under the protecting eye of the teacher, but quite another for her to be seen walking with him, a man of colour, along the Chiswick High Road, disapprovingly observed by her fellow men and women. It would not be so bad, she reflected, if only his complexion had been a shade lighter.

'Oh yes, Miss,' he continued persuasively, 'let us walk together. Why should it not be? Let us begin, please Miss.'

Hilda, crimson to her eartips, moved on quickly, thankful that she had not far to go, and praying that she would not run into anybody who knew her. It would be dreadful if she met her aunts or Mrs. Ashton, and even more dreadful if dear Mrs. Sherman, who lived in one of the nearby turnings, should see her. For Mrs. Sherman had once discoursed to her at length on the unpleasing fact that, in her opinion, there were far too many coloured gentlemen in the neighbourhood, and had remarked tersely that it was a pity they didn't all stop in the land where their mothers had borne them. She had commented unfavourably on the nerve of Mr. Tomashi, their Japanese neighbour, in occupying a flat next door to a respectable English family like the Shepheards, though, so far as she knew, there was not a single thing that was undesirable about him. She had hinted at all kinds of 'goings-on' in his flat, and was firmly convinced that foreigners generally, no matter what their race or complexion, were by nature

inferior to the English, and ought to be treated like fowls, that is shooed away if they impeded one's progress. 'Don't you never have nothing to do with them, Miss. They're always up to some monkey trick or other,' she had warned Hilda.

It was evident, however, that Mr. Tomashi from Japan, and Mr. Ram Lal from India, both, judging by the deference they paid to her, regarded Hilda as a grown-up person. It was true, of course, that Mr. Tomashi never said anything when they passed on the stairs, but he always bowed to her and stood motionless against the wall while she went by. She would have appreciated a little friendly conversation with him on these occasions: it did seem so peculiar to have a next door neighbour who kept so rigidly to himself that they knew nothing about him except his name. Even her family, who had lived next to him for over ten years, knew no more of him than she did. But, though Hilda was curious about him, he did not inspire fear: he was much too tiny. With Mr. Ram Lal, however, it was altogether different, for though slender he was both tall and fierce-looking, and the pits left in his face by small-pox gave him a sinister appearance.

Walking lightly beside her, Mr. Ram Lal piloted her across the main road with such assiduous care that Hilda could not help feeling flattered in spite of her uneasiness. Even though he wasn't an Englishman, it was pleasant to find herself treated as a grown-up woman. She said goodbye to him a little distance from her turning, and blushed again when he took her hand and bowed low over it.

'Goodbye, Miss. It has been much pleasure to me,' he said in his high, thin voice. 'We walk again tomorrow I hope. I give you kind thanks for your goodness. Goodbye Miss.'

He bowed again as she moved away, and, although she resisted the temptation to look back, she felt quite certain that he was standing where she had left him and gazing after her. She had an impulse to tell Aunt Mildred about the little incident, but thought better of it, for Mildred would only look grave and counsel her that a young girl could not be too careful about the company she kept. Anxious for her niece's welfare, she would probably tell Aunt Helen, who would look even graver and begin to quote Mr. Rudyard Kipling:

> Oh East is East and West is West,
> And never the twain shall meet,

and between them they would contrive to make her appear both vain and childish. She therefore kept Mr. Ram Lal's existence a secret, and it became a matter of course for him to walk part of the way home with her, his conversation being highly entertaining after the dreariness of Mr. Rumsey's Business College. He told her many delightful things about India, painting such colourful pictures of life there that she fancied she could actually smell the sun-dried air. She asked him to tell her about the Taj Mahal, and was surprised to learn that he had never seen it. It seemed to her very curious that Aunt Helen, who had not seen it either, should know so much more about it than Mr. Ram Lal. In the sitting-room at home there was a framed photograph of it. 'One of the wonders of the world' her aunt had called it. 'Built for a dead Queen, Hilda. For Mumtaz Mahal, "The Chosen of the Palace". Oh, Hilda, it must be glorious. What a shrine for a husband to build in memory of his wife!' Her eyes had filled with tears, and Hilda, also deeply stirred by the faithfulness of Shah Jehan, had shed a few tears in sympathy.

Mr. Ram Lal had, however, been to Mandalay, which

was something, and, eager to show off her knowledge, Hilda asked him if he knew Mr. Rudyard Kipling's famous poem. Mr. Ram Lal smiled: 'You English people all speak Mr. Kipling. I do not know this poem. You will speak it for me, Miss? I would like to know it from you. Please, Miss.'

Feeling very foolish, she repeated *Mandalay*, not looking at her companion until she had finished. He was still smiling at her, but in a way which made her feel unaccountably stupid. He said nothing for a second or two, and then, as a tramcar rumbled past them, nodded towards it and observed quietly: 'There are tramway cars in Mandalay too — and much dust — oh, very much dust. Thank you, Miss, for speaking Mr. Kipling. It is kind to me.'

When Mr. Ram Lal announced one afternoon that his studies were drawing to an end, and that in less than a month he would be returning to India, Hilda's relief was so great that she was unwise enough to show it, and for the first time his expression, she imagined, was not as deferential as usual. Her association with him had never been comfortable, in spite of the many pleasant things he had said to her about the charms of young English ladies, and, although she had twice allowed him to take her out to tea, it was the refreshment rather than the society which she had enjoyed. Whenever he took her arm to guide her through traffic, she felt a faint revulsion, while she accepted his admiration complacently and as her lawful right.

He was now regarding her so intently that she suddenly suspected him of despising her, and at this shocking thought her self-esteem collapsed, and blushing violently she hurried away. He caught up with her immediately, all deference again, and asked humbly how he could have given offence. He would never do such a bad thing, he protested, to the young English lady who had always been

so kind to him. Indeed he would not offend any English
lady, for he bore in his mind great respect for them.
Mollified by these protestations, Hilda graciously forgave
him his unnatural nationality, and before she realized
what she was doing promised to go to tea the following
Saturday at the house where he was lodging. He had a
good, kind landlady, he said earnestly, who would be
proud to wait upon her, and he had many photographs
of his country which it would please him to show her. He
lived quite near, and he and his landlady would expect
her at four o'clock. He would see that the tea was of the
best, with many sweetmeats.

Not without trepidation, Hilda kept her promise, and
a few minutes after four o'clock rang the bell of No 2,
Beedon Road. The good, kind landlady who opened the
door regarded her sourly, disapproval in every line of her,
and without a word led the way along a narrow, linoleum-
covered passage to a door at the far end.

'That's his sitting-room,' she indicated in tones which
made Hilda want to run straight out of the house; she
had half-turned to do this when the door opened and Mr.
Ram Lal, as if divining her impulse, was welcoming her
warmly, settling her into a massive and dusty armchair,
and ceremoniously inquiring after her health. Hilda
nervously looked about her. It was a hideous room, high
and square, containing so many knick-knacks so closely
jammed together that it was impossible to distinguish one
from another. Apart from Mr. Ram Lal, the only two
things which she took in distinctly were a solid round
table covered with a maroon-coloured chenille cloth,
fringed with bobbles, and the tall, dingy window, through
the lace curtains of which she glimpsed a drab backyard.
Against this background, Mr. Ram Lal, flitting about
and moving books and papers from the table, appeared
darker than ever; and shut in alone with him, the land-

lady's disapproval seeping like fog even through the closed door, Hilda, more miserable than she had ever been in her life, was already vowing that never again would she do anything so stupid as this.

Smiling agreeably, Mr. Ram Lal seemed not to notice anything amiss, and having cleared the table he went into the passage and called for tea, which was quickly brought in by the terrible landlady. She set it out resentfully, gave Hilda a frigid stare, and shut the door after her with such a bang that the cups jumped on their saucers.

Mr. Ram Lal smiled apologetically. 'The poor landlady! She is ugly and old and perhaps after all does not like to wait over a young, beautiful lady. We will excuse her, Miss, if you please. I am honoured that you should visit with me. You must like your tea, please. See — all these sweetmeats are for you.'

He continued to fuss over her, and Hilda made a valiant effort to appear at ease and interested. It could not last for ever, she comforted herself, and anyway Mr. Ram Lal was so courteous that she found it difficult to explain the sick little feeling which disturbed her. Several times, during tea, the landlady clattered about in the yard, throwing an apparently casual glance at the window, and looking even more disagreeable than when she had admitted Hilda. When they had finished their tea, Mr. Ram Lal brought out his photographs, which were all of temples and monuments; they were lovely, but wasted upon his guest, whose eyes strayed continually and in the most unmannerly fashion to the black clock on the mantelpiece. Hilda had never known time to drag so. It was only a quarter to five. She would stay until five for the sake of politeness, but not a minute after, she decided firmly. As the hour struck she rose and said that she must go, or her aunts would be wondering where she had got to. 'I did not tell them about you. They think I am

just out for a walk,' she informed him naively. Mr. Ram Lal smiled, and protested that it was not kind of her to leave so quickly and that he had still not shown her all his treasures. Surely she would stay a little longer? Hilda, her heart thumping so that she could scarcely breathe, turned resolutely towards the door, but before she could open it Mr. Ram Lal had sprung at her, gripping her waist and endeavouring to push his dark face against her own. But she was a strong girl, and though for a second almost paralysed with horror, she beat at him fiercely, revolted at the nearness of his pock-marked skin and flickering eyes. Shocked and terrified though she was, she did not lose her head and scream. She felt that to call for the help of that awful landlady was impossible. Through vanity, curiosity and sheer silliness she had got herself into the grip of this tiger, and now she must get herself out of it the best way she could. Mr. Ram Lal, though obviously mad, must be made to understand that if he did not let her go at once she would scream, and would go on screaming until the whole street came to her rescue. Pushing desperately at his face, which felt like wire-netting against the palms of her hands, she at last managed to impress this intention upon him, and the grasp on her waist slackened. Exerting all her strength she succeeded in pushing him sharply against the table, and in a second was out of the room and the house, but, agitated though she was, she resisted the urge to run. She was safe enough now, and she had no mind to please the good, kind landlady, who was, she felt sure, watching from behind the curtains, by betraying the least sign of panic. She now hated Mr. Ram Lal and was bitterly ashamed of herself for having invited his unwelcome attentions. She had known all along that she had no business to visit him alone, or indeed any man who was not a friend of her family. She thought affection-

ately of her Uncle Phillip. He too often looked at her with that same bright flicker in his eyes, but she did not feel sick when he touched her. The nearer she got to Glynne Mansions, the lighter her spirits became, and in the bright comfort of her home Mr. Ram Lal and his squalid, airless lodging seemed like a bad dream that had happened a long time ago.

But Mr. Ram Lal was not to be defeated so easily, for, in the privacy of her own room, the sickening fear of him returned and pursued her, in her sleep, with a singleness of purpose that sent her flying over London in the brightest daylight. She flew high over the city, higher even than the cross of St. Paul's. She could see it glittering in the sunlight, and far below an angry crowd pointing up at her and shouting fiercely. It was agony to look down at them. She could not imagine what crime she had committed to rouse such frenzy, but she knew with deadly certainty that they were trying to reach her, and that if they succeeded they would tear her to pieces. She could feel them pulling with a malignant, concentrated force against which she was helpless. Her body, until now transparent and buoyant, began to get heavier and heavier, as if she were swimming against the tide in a rolling sea. Suddenly, joyfully, the lovely power flowed back into her, and in a daring second she swooped down over the crowd, poised herself with one foot on the statue of Queen Anne, laughed into the sea of faces, and, as the infuriated throng surged forward to seize her, soared mockingly into the cloudless blue.

CHAPTER XI

THE CAUSE

ALTHOUGH Mr. Ram Lal did not attend the College again, it was a considerable time before Hilda really succeeded in pushing her terrifying experience from her, and for many weeks she went about burdened with a load of guilt and shame. More than once she was tempted to confess her stupidity to Aunt Mildred; but the confession, cunningly rehearsed so that she might appear, by contrast with Mr. Ram Lal, innocent as falling snow, always stuck in her throat, her natural honesty ramming home the irritating truth that she had only herself to blame. In her efforts to attain peace of mind, her heart even warmed towards Aunt Helen, and to please her she asked if there were any way in which she could help the great cause of women's rights. Aunt Helen, delighted at this voluntary show of intelligence, said that the very best help she could give was to work hard at her business studies and thus equip herself for a worthwhile future independent of all effort but her own. She thought, however, that it would be instructive for her to walk in an occasional march of protest; there was, she informed her, to be a most important procession that very week to No. 10 Downing Street, and, as it was on Saturday afternoon, promised that she should take part in it with herself and her friend, Miss Mabel Campbell. It was a happy prospect, for Miss Campbell, although older than Aunt Helen, was gentle and quiet and pretty, not at all like a lady whose entire life was being soured and ruined by the obduracy of Mr. Asquith and his Ministers. These processions, said Aunt Helen, were of the utmost value and profit to the Cause, and every

woman who marched in them was a thorn in Mr. Asquith's side. It was extraordinary, she observed, that a man of his intellectual stature could be so short-sighted, to say nothing of his fascinating and brilliant wife. How, she asked Hilda sadly, could a man with such a wife fail to see that in denying women their rights he was insulting that wife in the deadliest fashion?

'But we shall fight on, Hilda. Let Mr. Asquith and his Cabinet make no mistake about that. And we shall win, you'll see. I hope it's fine on Saturday for your first public appearance as a young campaigner, and I think you'll enjoy yourself, especially as we are hoping that both Mrs. Pankhurst and Christabel will lead the procession.'

And Hilda did enjoy herself. Both Aunt Helen and Miss Campbell wore their prettiest dresses and hats, and assumed such a fanatical air of martyrdom that it might have been the stake to which they were marching rather than No. 10 Downing Street.

When the long, orderly procession reached the Whitehall opening to Downing Street they found, effectively barring their way, a cordon of good-humoured policemen who addressed them benignly and advised them to disperse at once — 'as if we were schoolgirls' said Aunt Helen savagely. Mrs. Pankhurst and her daughter, after a whispered consultation, decided to stand their ground and stop there until the police, as they inevitably would, accused them of causing an obstruction and legitimately moved them on. The procession had now re-arranged itself into a solid square, and, still between her aunt and Miss Campbell, Hilda, to her joy, found herself in front, her chin nearly touching the chest of a young policeman who was exchanging cheerful badinage with several of the demonstrators. And while she was hoping passionately that something really exciting would happen, a com-

plaining murmur arose from the company and she saw a beautiful and charmingly dressed woman being shepherded respectfully by two policemen right into the sacred street itself. The lady was slightly flushed, but not at all embarrassed, and, safe behind the dark blue cordon, she gave the watching women a pleasant and sympathetic smile before disappearing through a door which opened for her as if by magic.

A fierce little woman standing next to Helen, goaded beyond endurance by what she had just witnessed, shouted indignantly: 'Did you all see that? Gone right through! If she can go in why not one of us?' she demanded of the policeman. 'It's a public thoroughfare, isn't it?'

The policeman, whose eyes had expressed frank admiration for the lady who had just passed through, regarded his questioner with dislike. His gaze travelled thoughtfully over the restless crowd of women, and without addressing anyone in particular he said meaningly: '*She's* a lady, she is!'

Aunt Helen, who could not help smiling in spite of this rude implication, also could not help showing off her knowledge, and informed all about her that the lady was Mrs. Winston Churchill, wife of the First Lord of the Admiralty.

'Isn't she a beautiful woman, Hilda? One of the loveliest in London. I wish she would come out on our side — indeed, I wish it of all intelligent women,' she ended, with a belligerent look at the policeman. He, stolidly refusing to be drawn into argument, suddenly noticed Hilda's eager young face, and enraged both Helen and the very fierce woman by advising her to go home and have her tea.

'This is no place for you, Miss,' he said benevolently. 'You don't want to get mixed up with this lot. What did you want to bring her here for?' he asked Helen sternly.

'You grown-up ladies are worrying enough, without letting kids like this in for trouble.'

Hilda was even more shocked than her aunt at this outburst. She, who prided herself on looking quite grown up, to be called a 'kid', and before all these people too. It was too much, and with all the dignity she could command she answered icily: 'I'm *not* a child! I'm nearly sixteen. And I *believe* in Votes for Women. And if I want to walk in processions I'll *walk* in them!'

The policeman grinned, and Helen, too angry even to have the last word, beamed approval at this up-and-coming independence on Hilda's part and left the field to the fierce little woman, who could think of nothing more shrivelling to say than an exasperated: 'Oh! You men! You so-called men!'

At this moment a disappointed buzzing broke out, and Mrs. Pankhurst could be heard commanding everybody to disperse quietly. Helen, surveying with affectionate admiration the frail figure in the becoming black dress, turned to the policeman once more: '*She's* a gentlewoman, too, young man, and I hope you and your colleagues won't ever forget that fact.'

'Don't you worry, Madam. We won't so long as she behaves like one, and that isn't every day,' he replied seriously. 'And take my advice and keep this young lady out of it till she knows her own mind. Downing Street's no place for school-girls.'

'Nor the police force for school-boys,' retorted Helen, thoroughly nettled. 'Come along, Hilda, before I'm tempted to give this young officer a piece of my mind.'

'At which he'd thank you for nothing,' said a hatchet-faced man on the edge of the crowd who had been enjoying the little exchange. 'Soured virgins, every one of you — at least, all bar the girl. And she soon will be if she doesn't take the bobby's advice.' He swept a hostile

glance around, bowed with exaggerated politeness to Hilda, and went on his self-righteous way.

'That's the sort of thing we're up against,' said Helen bitterly. 'I've nothing against the policeman, a nice enough young fellow keen on his job. But, Hilda, just think! That mindless fool who has just moved away has the right, if it so pleases him, to a voice in the affairs of his country — *our* country — while splendid women like Mrs. Fawcett and Mrs. Pankhurst and thousands of others are not considered "responsible" enough to be heard. It's outrageous. Men like that, if you can call them men, deserve anything we can do to them. The procession this afternoon was quiet, but we aren't always like that, my dear. All the same, I don't want anything unpleasant to happen to you, so you must never do or say anything yourself to annoy the police. Just watch and listen and you will be all right. And if Nora Ashton makes fun of us, don't laugh with her. You must never let anybody influence you against the fight for the Vote. I felt proud of you when you stood up to that young policeman. Even dear Mabel Campbell couldn't get the last word that time Mr. Augustine Birrell was so flattering to her. She was with me at a matinée at the Court Theatre, and he, then a Minister, was in a box. Of course it was too good a chance to miss of doing something for the Cause, and as he came out to his car Mabel darted up to him and said quietly: ' "Please, Mr. Birrell, may I speak to you?"

'Mr. Birrell, a little apprehensive, said courteously: "Certainly. What is it?"

' "What are you going to do about the vote?"

' "It will come. It will come. We are doing all we can. You must be patient and wait a little longer."

' "But, Mr. Birrell, we've been waiting forty years already," Mabel protested.

'Mr. Birrell looked at Mabel, gentle, blue-eyed, middle-

aged Mabel, gave her a smile that would have melted Aberdeen granite, and exclaimed incredulously: "Forty years! My *dear* lady, *you* haven't been doing anything for forty years!" and before she could utter another word he had bowed, got into his car, and driven quickly away. It was beautifully done, and we've all had a soft corner for him ever since.'

Hilda laughed appreciatively, thinking that, if only Aunt Helen would be quiet now and then, she might in time grow to be quite fond of her. She felt quite fond of her now. The horrid qualms she experienced whenever she remembered Mr. Ram Lal were eased by the warmth of her aunt's approval, and if by pleasing her she could finally obliterate him, then it was a small thing to devote herself to the cause of her sex.

But both Mr. Ram Lal and the suffrage movement were forgotten that very night, when she was taken to see Mr. Henry Ainley in *Old Heidelberg*. Sitting motionless after the lights had gone up during the first interval, Hilda was roused by her uncle as if from a trance. He smiled at her, but she did not respond. She saw nothing and thought of nothing but Mr. Henry Ainley. Her entire world now revolved around Mr. Henry Ainley. She loved him deeply, passionately, tenderly, and for ever. She was no longer young Hilda Winstanley sitting in a theatre with her bright and talkative relations. She was Kathie. Lowly, enchanting Kathie, dancing in a perfumed garden in faraway Heidelberg, shyly receiving the boisterous homage of the students and the adoration of their leader, the gay young prince who was none other than Mr. Henry Ainley. Against his radiant charm and golden voice, the darkness that was Mr. Ram Lal seemed like something out of the bottomless pit. She shuddered as she recalled that thick, honey-combed skin and high, scratching voice, and she smelt again, but for the last time, the dusty squalor of

his room. Gone, too, was her recent high resolve to avenge the wrongs of her sex. This lovely sensation was quite different from anything she had ever known. It had nothing to do with her vanity. She felt no urge to meet Mr. Ainley. No desire to reveal herself as a passionate devotee. All she wanted was to be left alone, if need be for the rest of her days, to luxuriate secretly in this new and wonderful emotion. It was like floating in a sun-warmed sea, lazily watching ragged little clouds drifting across a deep blue sky. And it was somehow all bound up with the three riders in Rotten Row; with long, idle days in Richmond Park; with the scent of heliotrope in Kensington Gardens; with all the enchantments London had showered upon her; and above all with her flying dreams. But suddenly a chill little wind sprang up; the sea grew grey and choppy, stinging like nettles, and the whole rainbow picture was misted over as she heard her Aunt Helen exclaim laughingly: 'Just look at Hilda! I believe she's fallen in love! And no wonder, seeing Ainley for the first time in such a romantic part. I once heard somebody say that he could read a railway time-table and make it sound like *Paradise Lost*. Oh! What it is to be your age, child! Gather ye rosebuds while ye may! Lucky girl!'

They were all laughing at her, and Hilda, though speechless with resentment at their intrusion, managed somehow to smile back. The uprush of affection which she had felt for her Aunt Helen only a few hours before evaporated. It was horrible of her to laugh and make fun of something so sacred, and it would serve her right, Hilda reflected spitefully, if she went to her grave with the wrongs of her sex for ever unavenged. Anyway, what could they possibly matter in such an enchanted world? She forgot them, and her relations also, as she waited longingly for the curtain to rise again.

CHAPTER XII

EARNING ONCE MORE

THE blessed day came at last when Mr. Rumsey, gravely shaking hands with Miss Winstanley, wished her well in the great world of business which she was now, in his opinion rather than hers, reasonably well qualified to enter. As kindly and as tactfully as he could, he again drew attention to her besetting sin of carelessness, and besought her to eradicate it at all costs. Hilda thanked him, said goodbye to Miss Printon and the other teachers, and walked out of the College on air. It was a glorious day and her thoughts turned to Mrs. Ashton and the delightful Doc. What better way of celebrating her release than by taking him for a run on Barnes Common! She was soon at the Ashtons' house, and Doc, instantly divining her purpose, capered madly about her, rushed off to fetch his lead, and in a transport of gratitude offered her the remains of his dinner, a capably-gnawed marrow bone. As they raced along Castelnau in the singing sunshine, Mr. Rumsey's reference to her carelessness kept intruding uncomfortably, and, when they reached the Common, Hilda sat down and for once solemnly tried to think instead of to feel. Any time now, she realized miserably, she would be called upon to think for several hours each day of each week of each year. She knew that Mr. Rumsey was justified in calling her careless: in her heart she knew that she was even worse, that there were times when she was actually idiotic. She was always waiting for something lovely and exciting to happen that had no relation whatever to Mr. Rumsey's mighty world of business. She wanted the years to fly on wings, faster than her dreams, until she should attain

to the triumphant status of a married woman. She chanted some verses she had just memorized, and when she came to the assurance that even the weariest river flows somewhere safe to sea, her spirits brightened as she applied this happy sentiment to herself. It was clear, however, that no amount of dreaming and wishing would get her safe to sea, *via* an adoring husband, for a year or two. She must accept the inevitable and work honestly and industriously during the dragging interval. Satisfied with this solution, she pushed the encroaching future from her, and, mechanically throwing sticks for the imbecile Doc to retrieve, dwelt tenderly upon the charms of Mr. Henry Ainley in *Old Heidelberg*.

When she returned home, Aunt Helen, looking very serious, was waiting to have a little talk with her about her future, and startled her considerably by announcing that a post had already been secured for her, through the goodwill of Miss Mabel Campbell, with two maiden ladies who ran a typewriting office in the Earl's Court Road. Hilda's dismay at this parochial beginning to her business career was so apparent that her aunt pointed out sharply that she had a long way to go yet before she could hope to achieve a distinguished secretarial position, and that she must be content with this humbler start. The Misses Simpkins, Aunt Helen continued, were good and kind, and, because of their cousinly relationship to Miss Campbell, would doubtless do their best to bring Hilda on. Anyway, she was to take her along the next day for inspection, and if the two ladies looked upon her with favour, then she was to enter their employ on the following Monday. Hilda, who had envisaged herself travelling to the great city of London every day as proudly as she had once travelled from Moss Ferry to Manchester, followed her aunt gloomily next morning up a dark and narrow staircase, at the head of which was a glass-

panelled door bearing in large black letters the announcement:

MISS JOANNA & MISS LUCY SIMPKINS

TYPEWRITING ESTABLISHMENT

AUTHORS' MSS A SPECIALITY

'There you are, Hilda,' Aunt Helen exclaimed brightly. 'Authors! Just the place for a girl like you. Now don't be nervous, and do your best.'

In answer to their knock a gentle voice invited them to enter, and Hilda, feeling about twelve feet high, found herself being looked up at by two of the quaintest and smallest women she had ever seen. She and Aunt Helen towered so much above them that they appeared like a pair of robins; and so bird-like were they in their movements, and with such gentle, twittering voices, that it was not difficult to think of them as robins. There was no difference of feature or colouring between them, and it transpired that they were twins, so indistinguishable from one another that each wore at her throat a brooch of twisted gold wire, one of which said 'Joanna', and the other 'Lucy'.

The one wearing 'Joanna' conducted the interview, and after Aunt Helen had explained Hilda's year at Mr. Rumsey's Business College, and had emphasized her niece's ambition to excel in all work connected with authors, 'Joanna' quietly observed that perhaps the young lady would be willing to take a test; she pointed out that authors were very exacting creatures, and that their manuscripts had to be returned absolutely perfect. 'Indeed,' she added, 'we pride ourselves on sending out *all* our work absolutely perfect.'

Quaking with anxiety, Hilda was placed before an immense typewriter, of unfamiliar aspect, and given a page of manuscript to copy; Miss Joanna considerately

withdrawing herself and Aunt Helen to the far end of the room, where Miss Lucy had now resumed her typing. Hilda endeavoured to do her best by proceeding with extreme slowness: the manuscript was written in a large, bold hand, and was not difficult. It appeared to be some part of a story for children, and she acquitted herself with no more than two mistakes. Miss Joanna read it through carefully, but made no comment. She would like next, she said, to test Miss Winstanley's shorthand, and dictated to her a dull section of the leading article in that day's *Morning Post*, which she then asked Hilda to transcribe on the typewriter. Again Hilda acquitted herself reasonably well, and Miss Joanna, remarking that she of course made allowance for natural nervousness in a beginner, told her that she might consider herself engaged, as from Monday, at a commencing salary of seven shillings and sixpence weekly, and that the hours were from nine o'clock until six o'clock, with one hour for lunch. In the afternoon, she added, a cup of tea was provided, which it would be part of Hilda's duties to make.

Aunt Helen was very pleased, and Hilda, though not enthusiastic, was relieved that she had come through without ignominy. And so she began her business career in London, and did not enjoy it nearly so much as she had enjoyed her few months in the big dressmaking workroom in St. Ann's Square, Manchester, where she had first set about the important affair of earning her own living. Miss Joanna and Miss Lucy were very quiet, and very dull. They typed away earnestly hour after hour, and Hilda found that her own work consisted of re-typing any pages on which they had themselves made a mistake, for it was a point of honour with them never to rub out. Sometimes they sent her on errands, which she welcomed as an exciting distraction in the monotonous routine of the day. By taking a bus, she was able to get home to

lunch, Miss Joanna thoughtfully allowing her an extra quarter of an hour because of the journey, and her rides at midday, and the time spent in making tea, were the brightest spots of the day.

At the end of a fortnight, her fundamental carelessness began to re-assert itself. Neither Miss Joanna nor Miss Lucy wasted any time in conversation. They were always busy, and Hilda found the time weigh so heavily that in sheer desperation, she paid long and quite uncalled for visits to the lavatory, there to indulge in a page or two of *Nicholas Nickleby*; she had secreted this volume at the bottom of a cardboard box crammed with dusty typed documents tied up with green silk, the property, presumably, of Mr. Cartwright, the Commissioner for Oaths who occupied a single office above the Misses Simpkins. Sometimes, when the fascination of Charles Dickens outweighed her respect for Miss Joanna and Miss Lucy, Hilda was absent for so long that, on her return, the two ladies would exchange significant looks, and then Miss Joanna, fingering her brooch, would look over at her and say mildly: 'You've been away a long time, Miss Winstanley. Is it really necessary, my dear?' and Hilda would blush guiltily and count the hours until she could reasonably re-visit *Nicholas Nickleby*. She gave herself up for lost, utterly abandoned to this dreary office where nothing ever seemed to break the monotony. If only an Author would walk boldly in! But nothing so stimulating ever happened, and, as the weeks passed, more and more she indulged her passion for day-dreaming, with the result that her work suffered and one Saturday morning, as Miss Joanna counted out her salary, she said, looking up at her sadly: 'I'm afraid you're not happy with us, Miss Winstanley. We feel, that is Miss Lucy and I feel, that perhaps you ought to work where there is young society. So, my dear, we shall not want you to come again

after next week. I have sent a little note to your aunt asking her to come and see us. Young society — yes — I'm sure that is the trouble.'

Hilda nearly cried with relief, in spite of her fear of what Aunt Helen would have to say. Nothing, she told herself passionately, nothing anywhere could be more deadly dull than the work the Misses Simpkins had given her to do. It was dreadful never speaking a word to anybody, and she was beginning to feel quite old, nearly as old as Miss Joanna and Miss Lucy.

To Hilda's surprise her Aunt Helen, after the interview with the Misses Simpkins, did not say very much to her, although she reproached her for not having tried harder, and Hilda was speculating on what her fate was to be next when she heard something which sent her into transports of joy.

'How would you like to start again in Phillip's office?' her aunt inquired, with apparent casualness.

Hilda could scarcely credit that she had heard aright. She had never thought of anything so wonderful. Why, it would not be work at all to be in Uncle Phillip's bookshop. It could never be dull there, for was he not always full of interesting stories about the different visitors to the shop? As if divining her thoughts, her aunt regarded her sternly: 'Remember, Hilda, that it will only be a beginning. Neither your uncle nor I, after what Miss Simpkins told me, think you are capable of securing a responsible post yet, though I must say that after a whole year at that College you ought to know more than you do. I believe Mr. Rumsey to be a fraud. And because you will be in Phillip's office, that will be no excuse for carelessness and inattention — indeed, quite the reverse. It would be unforgivable of you to cause him annoyance. It will give you a better insight into the routine of an office than you would have gained with Miss Simpkins and

her sister, and I imagine that a bookseller's counting-house is much the same as any other business office.'

Phillip confirmed this, save in one particular. He pointed out to the delighted girl that all booksellers, without exception, paid the most miserable salaries. He had often confided to his wife that, given a free hand, he would have altered this state of affairs at Messrs. Talbot, Reed & Shepheard, but as he was in a minority of one he could do nothing.

Hilda's soaring spirits were not damped by these financial considerations. She did not care in the least what salary Messrs. Talbot, Reed & Shepheard might think fit to offer her. It was reward enough to be away from the Misses Simpkins and in the stimulating society of Uncle Phillip. And surely she too would meet, or at any rate see, some of those queer people who were always visiting him — The New Bohemians as they called themselves and their Club. One or other of them was always coming in to borrow books, for, as he said laughingly, they hardly ever thought it necessary to buy one. Foremost among them was a writer called Arthur Machen, of great learning, whose manners, Aunt Helen said, were the finest she had ever known. On several occasions, long before Hilda came to London, he and some friends, describing themselves as Rosicrucians, had held their meetings in the flat, and he had charmed Aunt Helen by courteously inviting her to become a 'Daughter of the Night', in return for her hospitality. And there was Mr. Edgar Jepson, and Mr. Louis McQuilland, and Mr. Cecil Chesterton. And there had been, too, a strange and moody young man called Richard Middleton, who wrote poetry and had died, by his own hand, in a foreign country, away from all his friends. Her family still talked of him, and on the anniversary of his death her uncle made a point of honouring his memory by reading aloud one

of his poems. 'If only we had known he was in such straits,' Phillip would say sadly. 'Why couldn't he have written to one of us? Any one of us?' And Hilda, who only knew of the dead poet through hearsay, was sad too for her uncle's unhappiness over his lost friend.

It was Phillip who had suggested the new move for his niece after hearing Helen's discouraging report on her instability, and he had defended Hilda stoutly. He admitted that she was careless, but, loyally backed up by Mildred, he disagreed with Helen's growing belief that they had made a mistake in bringing her to London.

'She never *says* anything,' Helen complained continually. 'She's old enough now to take part in any general conversation, but I never know what she is thinking, or for that matter whether she ever does think. I sometimes wonder whether she uses her mind at all, except in a repetitive sort of way — memorizing things, that is.'

Phillip smiled. He knew very well that Hilda was an entirely different young person from his wife's conception of her, for she talked both to him and to Mildred easily enough, but Helen, who liked intelligence to be obvious, had much the same paralysing effect upon her niece as a stoat has upon a rabbit. The relationship between them was perpetually strained. The truth was that Hilda genuinely admired what she called 'Aunt Helen's cleverness', but, feeling herself to be quite inadequate before it, preferred even to be thought stupid rather than say something which might, to her aunt, appear stupid. Also it puzzled her considerably when Helen talked of having a 'real' conversation with anybody. Other people, Hilda noted, talked as naturally as they did anything else, such as eating or drinking. Mrs. Ashton was always making fun of Aunt Helen's passion to instruct. 'She's always wanting to teach me something, Hilda. I know she thinks I'm a frivolous idiot, and I

shouldn't mind if she ever said anything really original. But poor old Helen gets it all out of a book, and even the most stupid of us can do that for ourselves, if we want to.'

The dark, untidy, counting-house of Messrs. Talbot, Reed & Shepheard, which contrasted so oddly with the bright, book-filled shop below, seemed to Hilda a miracle of life and gaiety after the sedate typewriting office in the Earl's Court Road, and she settled down contentedly to work away the years which separated her from her heart's desire. And because she was now thoroughly happy, she astonished everybody, herself not least, by becoming quite a useful member of the staff. In a community hitherto exclusively masculine, she possessed the attraction of novelty, and she found everyone kind and helpful. When the Christmas season commenced she was delighted by being allowed to help, during the busiest hour of the day, in the children's section of the shop. She exerted every ounce of energy to wheedle orders out of parents for such admirable works as *The Would-be-Goods* or *The Treasure Seekers* by E. Nesbit, of which, until then, they did not appear to have heard. When some busy father put away his completed list with a thankful sigh, Hilda cunningly drew his attention to the Nesbit volumes: it would be a grave injustice, she stressed, if he allowed his children to grow up ignorant of such treasures. They had been the chief interest and delight of her own childhood, she romanced, with a note of sadness in her voice for something now so remote. The customer would glance at her curiously, unable to make up his mind whether she was sixteen or twenty; then, anxious to get his shopping over, and not unwilling to please her, he would casually enlarge his order, and leave the shop with the gratified feeling that not only had he made a literary discovery for the benefit of his young family, but that he was not nearly such an old stick-in-the-mud as his wife fancied.

Hilda enjoyed herself so much during these coveted spells that she asked her uncle whether she could not leave the counting-house altogether and work in the shop, but he would not hear of it. He said that she would soon tire of selling, that it could be very dull during quiet periods, and that it was even more inadequately paid than the office work. Though she worked hard every second of the day, and even stayed, as did most of the staff, until nearly midnight, helping to carry up stock from the basement, it was by far the happiest Christmas she had ever spent, and when, as her just reward, she was given a half-sovereign in addition to her salary, there was only one flaw in the bright circle of her days. It was this: for some time she had experienced an ever-growing ache to see her foster-parents again, and Moss Ferry, the village of her childhood. It seemed now to be so far away, so small and self-contained. She thought of it continually before going to sleep. Lying in the dark, it was as if she saw it through a telescope, the people and the cottages and the fields and lanes tiny but very clear. The longing to go back became so obsessing that, in a breath-taking moment, Hilda made up her mind that, at the first available opportunity, she would venture on the journey. It was a serious business, involving much crafty thought. Her chance would come when her family went away again to Devonshire in June. There had been some talk of taking Hilda with them for the first week, for she was shown no special favours at the office, and this first year would have only one week's holiday. Aunt Helen, however, said it would be a pity for Hilda's first visit to the west country to be confined to a single week. Far better, she suggested, for her to wait until she had earned a fortnight's holiday. She might instead, this year, go for a change to Stoke D'Abernon, to a cottage where Helen had stayed several times. The woman, Mrs.

Sellick, was a good soul, and it was lovely country. She would write and arrange it. It was cheap, too, only one guinea a week, and the fare a mere nothing. To her aunt's surprise, Hilda readily agreed, for, much as she wanted to see Devonshire, she wanted far more to see Moss Ferry again. With her family out of the way she could go down to Surrey for the week-end, make some excuse to Mrs. Sellick for leaving hurriedly, and then take the first possible train to the North. She would need to save money in addition to her ten-shilling Christmas box, but she could dedicate herself with vigour to this wearing process. She would economize on her lunches, keeping away from A.B.C.s and Express Dairies and subsisting instead on the kindly fruits of the earth. For tuppence she could, for instance, buy a whole pound of nourishing dates. Or she could lunch off bananas, or a sandwich, or apples and a bar of chocolate. Once Phillip had questioned her, before his wife, on the kind of lunches she ate, and had maintained, to Helen's annoyance, that they were totally insufficient for a growing girl. After this he made a point of taking her now and again to Slaters or to an old-fashioned chop-house, and treating her to a really substantial meal. And although he did not ask her to say nothing at home about these feasts, it was somehow understood between them that they were to be kept secret.

This saving-up was at first as satisfying as are all forms of self-sacrifice, but, though the novelty of it soon palled, Hilda stuck single-mindedly to her course, and by the time her holiday was due had accumulated quite a nest egg. And now, as the momentous week drew nearer, she could think of nothing else: it would be dreadful if anything should go wrong at the last minute. But nothing did. Her family, with many injunctions on the part of Aunt Helen to enjoy herself in Stoke D'Abernon by

taking long walks and experiencing the beauties of nature, departed. Hilda had laid her plans with elaborate cunning, having taken into her confidence a young lady called Miss Preager, who worked in the office next door, and with whom she sometimes lunched and explored the city. Hilda was to leave for Stoke D'Abernon on Friday evening, and on Monday morning, before starting work, Miss Preager was to send to Miss Winstanley at Laburnum Cottage, Stoke D'Abernon, the following telegram:

RETURN IMMEDIATELY AUNT HELEN DIED SUDDENLY YESTERDAY LOVE AUNT MILDRED

Hilda, greatly pleased with this composition, typed it out carefully. It was, of course, necessary to give Miss Preager a valid reason for enlisting her help, and over their lunch on the Friday she related, therefore, the romantic story of an admirer, deeply in love with her, who wished to present her to his family in Manchester. His name, said Hilda, warming to her work, was Robert Lovell. She had met him in a Chelsea studio and had known him for some weeks, but she had to keep him secret from her family, who were very strict, and would certainly ruin both her present and future happiness if they were to learn of his existence.

Miss Preager, gazing at Hilda with mounting admiration, pressed for further details, which Hilda's imagination, now at full tide, willingly provided. Robert Lovell, she informed her friend, was an architect, and was older by some years than herself. He was, in fact, in the prime of life, having just celebrated his thirtieth birthday. He did not, however, look anything like his age and was very young in all his ways.

Miss Preager, deeply impressed, asked what he looked like, and was given a faithful description of Mr. Henry Ainley in person. 'And he has a beautiful speaking

voice,' Hilda threw in for good measure. 'I do believe he could read a railway time-table and make it sound like *Paradise Lost*. So now you can see, can't you, why I don't want to stop in Stoke D'Abernon when I can be with Robert in his own home.'

Miss Preager, full of sympathy, did see, and promised that the telegram would be faithfully dispatched; and, being a nice girl, not given to envy, sincerely wished her friend a very happy time and said that she would be 'all fidgets' until she came back and told her all about the visit.

Hilda was a little dashed by this future contingency, which she had overlooked, but reflected that she would have plenty of time, before seeing her friend again, to construct a convincing picture of Mr. Lovell's home life.

It was charming country at Stoke D'Abernon, and Mrs. Sellick, a cheerful, middle-aged widow, received her kindly. It was quite an adventure, too, for Hilda was the only visitor and was given Mrs. Sellick's undivided attention, which made her feel adult and of consequence. She had a clean and stuffy little parlour all to herself, and a funny little bedroom looking out over a common. In between meals she took long walks, singing the latest popular songs or chanting ballads, and not feeling in the least lonely. Following an inviting path through a glorious pine wood she suddenly came upon a viper and her young family of six or seven, lazing in a broad shaft of sunlight across the path. This pretty little dishful of venom was no more than a couple of yards away when Hilda spotted them and stopped dead, fascinated by the flickering tongues which shot in and out like summer lightning, for the tiny black things reared as bravely and angrily as the mother. Her blood ran cold as she watched them slither into the dense undergrowth, and she turned and hurried out of the wood.

On Sunday evening she accompanied her landlady to church. Given no encouragement by her family, she had never repeated her first lonely and disappointing experience in London; and only went now in the specious hope that by doing so she might mitigate the wicked deception she was about to practise. On Monday, as she was having breakfast, Mrs. Sellick dramatically brought in the telegram announcing Aunt Helen's death. Hilda stared apprehensively at the orange envelope, and Mrs. Sellick, her curiosity getting the better of her manners, hung about the door and said she did hope it wasn't bad news coming on her holiday like this.

Hilda opened it slowly, and sat as one stunned. Mrs. Sellick, now nearly frantic, advanced to the table, and Hilda, who was trying vainly to squeeze out a few tears, handed it to her without a word.

'Oh, Miss Winstanley, I am sorry! Poor lady! And so sudden. It's terrible. Cry, my dear! You'll feel better for it. It's not good for you to be all strung up without something coming out. Poor lady! Have some more tea. There, drink up! Fancy, and right at the start of your holiday.'

Hilda, endeavouring to look as stricken as the occasion demanded, obediently drank the tea, and wearily pushed away the fragmentary remains of her substantial breakfast. She would have liked to finish the bread and butter, but of course it was common knowledge that grief took away the appetite. Looking distractedly at Mrs. Sellick, she said that naturally she would have to go home at once to comfort her remaining aunt.

'Of course, my dear. Of course you will. There's plenty of trains. There's a fast one in half an hour. If you hurry a bit you'll catch it.'

'Thank you, Mrs. Sellick,' Hilda said. 'Thank you very much. How kind you are! But I must settle up

with you first,' and reaching to the sofa for her hand-bag, she produced the guinea for her week's lodging.

'No, Miss. That's too much. I'm not one to trade on trouble. It's not your fault you have to go before you've come, so to speak. We'll say five shillings for the week-end — that's fair and suits me all right. Don't you fret. I'm comfortable enough. And I hope you'll be able to come down later on. It's pleasant having young company about.'

Hilda, feeling excessively mean, protested, but Mrs. Sellick was firm, and Hilda, the richer by sixteen shillings, set her face towards Lancashire as eagerly as she had left it nearly three years before.

CHAPTER XIII

RETURN TO MOSS FERRY

SHE arrived in Manchester late that evening with a
good hour to wait for her train to Kilnbrook, the
station for Moss Ferry. Having eaten nothing but a
slab of chocolate since breakfast, she treated herself to a
meal in the nearest restaurant. Though proud of the
fact that she herself now had no trace of a Lancashire
accent, she was nevertheless surprised to find how much
she enjoyed listening to the conversation of her fellow
diners, which fell like music on her ears. After the meal
there was just time for a walk to St. Ann's Square and a
peep at the handsome windows of Messrs. Hankinson &
Sankey, its most distinguished ladies' shop. She glanced
upwards towards the workroom, from which she had
once hoped to emerge an exemplary and original court
dressmaker, and wondered whether everyone she had
known during her brief apprenticeship was still there.
She recalled the fair and elegant Miss Jackson, the
buyer, and Violet, the workgirl who had been so kind to
her. If they were to see her now they would not recognize
her, so different was she from the shy country girl who
had deemed it an honour to run their errands and pick
up pins and snippings for them. Now that she was a real
Londoner, she would have loved to talk with Miss Jackson,
as one lady to another; to be kind in her turn to Violet,
and to deal graciously with all the other workgirls.
These pleasant reflections were interrupted by a nearby
clock striking the quarter, and she hurried for her train.
A mere fourteen miles and she would be there, in Moss
Ferry! How slowly the train seemed to be moving, as if
it had to fight every yard of its way through the drab

and grimy landscape; and it stopped at every station, too. It was lucky that she had the compartment to herself, for she was in no state to be seen by strangers, so agitated did she both look and feel. Kilnbrook at last, seeming strangely smaller than when she had left it a few years before. She was the only passenger to alight there, and she stood still for a moment or two, looking about her at the familiar scene. She could see Mr. Partington, the station-master, working in his garden by the last dim light, and he did not even turn round to see if anyone had left the train. Although nobody as yet knew of her visit, Hilda felt queerly disappointed at her solitary and unnoticed arrival. She would, at any rate, she thought, surprise George Partington, and walking slowly towards him she called out pleasantly: 'Good evening, Mr. Partington! Aren't you going to collect my ticket?'

Mr. Partington, startled by the non-Lancastrian accent, straightened himself up and peered through the gloom, wondering who the tall young lady, who addressed him so familiarly, could be. He came to the fence, looked into her face, and exclaimed with a welcoming smile: 'Well, if it isna young Hilda Winstanley! Well! This *is* a go! Us hasna heard tell o' you for years. Joe and Lizzie will be that glad. Didst tell 'em you were coming?'

'No. I want to surprise them, and I didn't know myself until this morning whether I should be able to come or not. It's nice to be home again, though I can only stop for a day or two. I must be back in London by Saturday. And I must be off now, or they'll all be in bed before I get to Moss Ferry.'

'They will that, if you dunna make haste. Ah didna know you at first, lass, you've shot up so. Moss Ferry'll 'ave summat to clack about now for months, Ah'm thinking!'

'Well, good night, Mr. Partington,' said Hilda, warmed by his friendliness, and eager to be on her way.

'Good neet, lass. See you when you goes back, if not afore,' he replied sociably, burning to impart the staggering news to his wife that young Hilda had come home grown out of all knowledge, and that he for one wouldn't be taken aback if they heard as summat was up.

Though it was now almost dark, and, as each stile and bush took on a menacing shape, her old fear of boggarts rose from its long slumber, Hilda bravely chose the short cut to Moss Ferry along Lovers Lane and through the silent fields. In spite of her abounding vitality, she was exceedingly tired, and her bag, though not heavy, began to seem enormous. But when finally she was through the fields and saw just ahead the church spire and the lamp-lit windows of the village, her fatigue vanished in an instant. No longer afraid, she walked more slowly, and by the time she reached the gate of her old home she was trembling with emotion. There was a light still in the kitchen, and the blind was undrawn. She tiptoed up the side path and looked in. Her foster-mother was sitting at the table, mending. Her foster-father was in his rocking-chair, asleep; and Lily, her foster-sister, sat on the horse-hair sofa, knitting. Neither of the boys was there. With her heart thumping madly, she crept round to the back door, unable to make up her mind whether to knock, or to make a dramatic entry unannounced. Incapable for the moment of doing either, she stayed there wrought up to the very edge of hysteria. Then she gave three clear raps with her knuckles, for there was no knocker. She could feel the shock of surprise that went through the kitchen, and she heard Mrs. Winstanley cry sharply and apprehensively: 'Whatever's that? Joe, wake up! Summat's amiss! See who's at t'door.'

The door opened and her foster-father stood there in

his stockinged feet. The light from the lamp streamed out, silhouetting her in its rays. Joe stared at her blankly for a second, then turned towards his wife and gulped out: 'It's 'er, Mother! It's our 'Ilda!'

Hilda entered the kitchen and Mrs. Winstanley rose to greet her. They gazed at each other, neither at first able to speak. And then her foster-mother said quietly: 'It's bin a long time, 'Ilda! You should 'a wrote,' and cried as if her heart would break. Hilda cried too, and Joe looked miserably at Lily, who remained motionless on the couch, full of bitterness towards Hilda for having made her mother cry. Mrs. Winstanley, becoming aware that the two girls had not yet spoken to each other, wiped her eyes, with a possessive gesture took off Hilda's hat, and pushed her down beside her foster-sister with the remark: 'You're forgetting our Lily, 'Ilda. She's grown too. And she's left school now and works at Morgan's farm.'

Hilda magnanimously kissed her old enemy, and politely inquired how she liked farm work, admiring her, against her will, for being so plucky. But she got small thanks for her trouble. Lily, always jealous of her, eyed her sourly and replied sulkily that she liked it well enough, and that any road, not being as lucky as some folk, it was Hobson's choice. She was not pleased at the return of the prodigal with her smart London clothes, and la-di-da speech, and hands that were an affront to honest work. Her own hands, never pretty, were now roughened and broadened by the farm work, and appeared like tools when compared with her foster-sister's.

Hilda asked how long it would be before John, the eldest son, came home, for by this time she was really tired and longing for bed.

'Our Jack!' Mrs. Winstanley exclaimed. 'Why, him and Edie's bin wed this twelve-month. I axed your Grandma Stringer to be sure and let them at London know, for

I mind as how you was allus one for Jack. By t'same token reckon you hanna heard about our Jim, neither, poor lad. He's lain in t'church-yard for nigh on two year. It was that chest of his betrayed him. Pneumonia. Wi' you lost to us i' London, us only 'as Jack and Lily now. Fancy your Grandma saying nowt! It's not like 'er.'

She surveyed her foster-child, debating whether to ask a question which, in view of Hilda's whole appearance, seemed unnecessary. But at last it came out: 'Them as you live wi' at London, 'Ilda. Are they good to you?'

'Aye,' Joe put in quietly. 'Are they good folks? The lady as took you away said as 'ow you would be sartain to write, but us never 'eard but the once telling us you was settling down. But Ah mun own you look gradely enough.'

'Oh, yes,' said Hilda loyally, 'they're all very kind, except about letting me write to you. But just think of Jack being married, and Jim dead. Where does Jack live now?'

'In Daneshead,' her mother answered, 'in t'next road to Edie's folk. Us'll go over there one neet. But whatever can Ah be thinking on! You mun be clemmed coming all that road from London.'

'No, no. I'm not hungry. I had something to eat in Manchester,' Hilda protested as her mother bustled to the pantry, 'but I *am* tired.'

'Reckon you'd best be off to bed, then. Our Lily'll find it queer 'aving somebody to sleep wi' 'er again, eh Lily?'

Lily frowned. She was dead tired too, having stayed up far beyond her usual time, and she had to be about again by seven in the morning.

It seemed very strange to Hilda to be following Lily, candle in hand, up the steep, uncarpeted stairs, and

stranger still to be again sharing the same bed with her. Roused by the business of undressing, she now wanted to talk a little, to inquire for old friends and playmates, but Lily fell asleep even before Hilda was half-undressed. She lay awake for a little while, overwhelmed, now that she was actually here, by the enormity of her deceit. In the bedroom next door her foster-mother and father were talking quietly, about her she was sure. They were just the same, she reflected: her mother sharp and possessive; her father a solid rock of affection. The adventure was worth it, let Aunt Helen storm as she would; and, with this reassurance, Hilda too slept, to be wakened by a vicious poke from Lily, who, dressed except for her frock, was inquiring sarcastically whether she would like her breakfast in bed.

'Oh, go away,' laughed Hilda. 'Of course I wouldn't, even though this is a holiday.'

Lily scowled and flounced downstairs, but presently, to Hilda's surprise, brought her up a cup of tea. 'Thank you, Lily. That *is* nice of you. When I'm married you must come and stay with me in London,' she said graciously. 'I'll show you everything. It's such a big place. Twenty times bigger than Manchester.'

Lily regarded her doubtfully. 'Us'll see about that, our 'Ilda. Reckon you winna want us showing you up at London. You're too grand for us now. "That *is* nice of you",' she mimicked spitefully. 'Ah dunna know what you've come back for. They was getting o'er you' — she jerked her head towards her mother's room — 'and now they'll be all onsettled again. There's allus trouble wi' you. But Ah mun go. And don't you go upsetting mi mother wi' your finicky ways,' she commanded sharply.

'Oh, go away, you great *pig*,' shouted the exasperated Hilda, in most unfinicky tones. '*I* don't care if you work till you drop. And I shan't invite you to come and stay

with me either. I wouldn't be seen *dead* in your company.'

'And Ah wouldna be seen i' yourn quick or dead,' retorted the outraged Lily, 'and you mind what Ah said about not upsetting mi mother.'

'Now then, what's to do?' Mrs. Winstanley called out.

'It's all right,' Hilda shouted back. 'Only Lily being funny.'

The kitchen door banged, and Lily was gone, leaving Hilda to meditate snobbishly upon the charms of her own life in comparison with her foster-sister's hard and humdrum existence, all Lily Winstanley was fit for anyway, she thought callously.

Hilda and her foster-mother breakfasted together very comfortably, and it was gratifying to hear Mrs. Winstanley's shocked 'Oh Hilda!' when it transpired that this visit was entirely unofficial, and that, if her Aunt Helen ever came to hear of it, she would find herself in serious trouble. She dilated at some length on the discomforts she had so nobly endured, and for so long, to accomplish it; and when she casually mentioned that she had even denied herself food to acquire an extra sixpence here and there, Mrs. Winstanley protested: 'You shouldn't ha done that, 'Ilda, just to come and see us. A growing girl like you needs all your strength to keep pace. Make a good breakfast now,' and she proceeded to cut more bread and butter, regardless of the fact that the growing girl was the very picture of exuberant health.

In answer to her mother's eager questions, Hilda described her life in London as truthfully as she thought politic. She dwelt upon the flat in great detail, her own room in particular, and, when questioned about her neighbours, had to admit that they did not exist.

'People who live in flats,' she explained gravely, 'don't have neighbours. Everybody minds their own business.

Aunt Helen and Uncle Phillip have lived in their flat for over ten years, and they never talk to anybody, not even to Mr. Tomashi, who lives next door. People in London are like that, at least people who live in flats are. Aunt Helen says it's one of the great advantages of living in a flat.'

Mrs. Winstanley looked puzzled. 'Ah dunna follow you, 'Ilda. Dost mean to say your relations is that stand-offish they dunna like nobody but theirsen?'

'Oh, no! They like a lot of people. There's always somebody coming to see us, or somebody for us to go and visit. And there are lots of parties and meetings and lectures. Aunt Helen is a suffragette and walks in pro-cessions. I've walked in one with her, too. We went to the Prime Minister's house in Downing Street one Satur-day, but he wouldn't see us.'

'Ah shouldna think so,' said Mrs. Winstanley indig-nantly, 'making a show o' yoursen in t'streets! Ah've 'eard summat about this Votes for Women. Our Lily reads to us about it. It all seems kind o' mad to me, and Ah don't hold wi' your relations mixing you up wi' it. Still, it's got nowt to do wi' me now,' she said wistfully; and then: 'But you've not said yet about going to t'chapel.'

Hilda hesitated. If she told the truth her mother would never understand it. 'We go to church,' she lied. 'To St. Nicholas's church. Aunt Helen says it's too far to attend chapel. There isn't one near enough.'

'Well, Ah suppose t'church is better than nowt, though to my way o' thinking it canna be so wholesome as chapel, whatever some folks han to say. And your relations does their best by you?' she asked again.

'Yes, yes. I'm very happy with them, but I like Uncle Phillip and Aunt Mildred best. Aunt Helen is very kind too, but she likes to interfere, and she doesn't think any-body knows as much as she does.'

Mrs. Winstanley looked pleased. She had suffered many stabs of jealousy throughout Hilda's narrative, and grasped eagerly at this implication that at least one of the London relations was not an angel from heaven. She pressed for further details, and Hilda, delighted to have such a staunch ally, dilated with relish on Aunt Helen's numerous shortcomings. It was an absorbing topic, and the more Mrs. Winstanley ejaculated 'Eh! Ah never!' the more lavishly the ungrateful Hilda embroidered, ending up with the solemn accusation that, by commanding her to forget her foster-parents, Aunt Helen had shown herself to be both cruel and unnatural, an accusation with which Mrs. Winstanley fervently agreed.

Looking fondly at her injured foster-child, she observed reasonably: 'Well, 'Ilda, us knows now as it's none o' your doing not writing, and we shanna worrit t'same as afore. But we took it hard getting only the one letter, and no proper news either from your Grandma at Bridge Farm, though she allus said as you was in a good 'ome and doing well. But one 'ears tell o' such wickedness. Ah canna see what 'arm there is i' sending us a letter every now and then, but you mun do as they bid you. It's not for us to interfere. I only hopes as they winna get to hear o' your coming back. You'd best go and see your Grandma Stringer and ax 'er to say nowt. She'll not hold wi' your venturesomeness, but Ah wouldna put it past 'er to keep quiet unless them at London axes 'er plain. You go on and see 'er wi'out more ado.'

Hilda went, and her legs felt like wax beneath her as she turned in at the gate of the pleasant old farmhouse where she had been born. Her grandmother, who was making cakes, received her grimly, pointing silently to a chair and leaving her to open the conversation. In spite of the open door and windows, the big kitchen, with its

spotless, flagged floor, was very hot, and Hilda, already warm with guilt, felt so nervous that at first she could not speak at all. Mrs. Stringer relentlessly continued to beat eggs, and finally Hilda, taking a deep breath, said feebly: 'I couldn't help it, Grandma. I had to come.'

Mrs. Stringer put down her basin, and looked at her shrewdly. 'That's only natural, Hilda. But nobody's written a word to me about it, so Ah reckon you've no business to be here.'

'Yes. They've all gone for their holiday, and they sent me somewhere else. Aunt Helen doesn't like me to remember Moss Ferry. She say's its gone right out of my life now, so I know she wouldn't have let me come even if I'd asked her.'

'Reckon she knows what's best for you, and Ah don't hold wi' your setting her at naught i' this road. You was allus headstrong and self-willed, but it canna be mended now, so let's have a proper look at you.'

She sat down opposite to Hilda, reflecting, in spite of her disapproval, that it was flying in the face of Providence for them at London to expect the girl to put clean out of her head those who had reared her and faithfully done their best by her until she had gone away. She had never been able to make sense of the secrecy which Helen had imposed upon herself, and would not easily forget the day when, some months after Hilda's departure, Mrs. Winstanley, desperate for news, had come to her and asked for it. She had, of course, been able to assure her that Hilda was well and had settled down happily in her new home, hoping that her visitor would be satisfied with this. But she had not been satisfied. She had asked, with an urgency which filled Mrs. Stringer with shame, for Hilda's address, and her face had hardened when it was explained to her that this could not be divulged. The two

women had looked at each other steadily, and then Mrs. Winstanley had observed: 'Ah can see as how you canna help it, Mrs. Stringer, but us never did nowt but our best by 'Ilda, same as if she was our own, and it's treating us like dirt for them as is mindful of 'er now to stop 'er from sending us a letter now and then. For they *mun* be stopping 'er. 'Ilda was never one to be at a loss wi' pencil and paper. And us 'as 'ad only the one letter since she went.'

Remembering again that distressing interview, Mrs. Stringer, against all her principles, was in her heart not displeased at Hilda's boldness, and was surprised to hear herself saying: 'You shouldn't ha' done it. It's deceiving them as trusts you, but Ah shall say nowt unless they ask me. But hark you, if your Aunt Helen does ferret it out, Ah shall have to speak up. So Ah'm warning you. Reckon London's not damaged your appetite, if looks is owt to go by. You try some o' this.' She cut a large wedge of her famous fruit cake, and fetched a mug of new milk. And while Hilda ate and drank, her Grandmother surveyed her sternly but affectionately, and plied her with questions about her life in London.

When Hilda said she must go, Mrs. Stringer walked with her to the gate, all the time stressing that her first loyalties now lay with her folk in London; but she counselled her never to forget her foster-parents in Moss Ferry and all the care they had lavished upon her. She remained at the gate until, by the damson trees at the turn of the lane, Hilda looked round and waved. Then Mrs. Stringer returned to her baking, ruminating on what a queer place that flat in London seemed to be, but thankful to know that the girl was happy and was making her way in life as she could never have done had she stayed in Moss Ferry. As for running away for a few days, this, though reprehensible, showed that she had gumption. She

weighed this useful asset against the sinfulness of deceit; her natural sympathies were all with her grandchild; and she finally concluded that it served 'them' at London right for being so 'snubbish' in their desire to stamp out in the girl all traces of her lowly beginnings.

CHAPTER XIV

OLD ACQUAINTANCE

FOR the next day or two there was only one topic of conversation throughout Moss Ferry, and the object of it went complacently among her fellows in full knowledge of the fact. Mrs. Winstanley, too, rose in the esteem of her neighbours for having nurtured the visitor from London. There was a constant procession of callers who came in to enjoy, over a cup of tea, Hilda's unending discourse on the charms of London, and the superior intelligence of its inhabitants. Manchester, they were startled to learn, was quite a small place by comparison, of no importance whatever; while Warrington, until now revered by everyone in the village as second only in fashion and worldliness to glorious and mighty Manchester, had no reasonable claim at all to urbanity. It could be dropped in Richmond Park — soap works, market and all — said Hilda scornfully, and be utterly lost.

She was having the time of her life, and enjoying it all the more because she really believed every single wonder that she related to them. With the exception of the Vicar and herself, nobody in Moss Ferry had ever been to London, though many of the young men nourished the fond hope of one day seeing a Lancashire side win the Cup Final there. Mrs. Winstanley, hospitably dispensing relays of tea, shone with pride in her foster-daughter, and embarrassed even that self-satisfied young person by inviting the 'company' to observe how differently she spoke from the rest of Moss Ferry. 'To 'earken to 'er now nobody'd ever think us 'ad brought 'er up. She speaks like t'Vicar,' she told them impressively. 'Our

Lily doesna like it. She says it's put on, but you can see it comes natural.'

The precious days flew by, every moment of them packed with interest, for, when her foster-mother was not showing her off at home, the pair of them were being entertained, as very special and distinguished company indeed, by one or other of Mrs. Winstanley's relatives, all of whom were anxious to have a good long crack with the lucky girl who had made history in Moss Ferry by the simple process of leaving it. They observed her as closely as good manners permitted, and, discussing her afterwards amongst themselves, agreed that the cataclysmic experience of living at London had graven no obvious marks of degradation upon her face and character. For this, they said, she had the wholesome, God-fearing atmosphere of Moss Ferry to thank, the precepts instilled in childhood proving now, amidst the shimmering pitfalls of darkest London, a very tower of strength. They were proud of her, and, as for London itself, it sounded a grand place for a trip in spite of, indeed because of, its temptations; some day, they bravely promised themselves, when their ships came home, they would give young Hilda the surprise of her life by popping in on her out of the blue.

To please her foster-mother, and not unwilling to be the focus of attention wherever she went, Hilda accompanied her to the mid-weekly Prayer Meeting in the United Methodist Chapel at Kilnbrook, where the fear of both God and the Devil had been impartially drilled into her as a child. James Turner, the Superintendent of the Sunday School, received her with grave courtesy, and ceremoniously presented her to the Meeting as a lamb that had returned to the fold, to draw strength anew after a long sojourn in a weary and waterless land. Hilda, the embodiment of springing health, felt this to

be rather extreme, and blushed. But worse was to follow.
In his opening prayer, Mr. Turner prayed for her as
passionately as he had done when, a few years before,
she had attended Sunday School for the last time prior
to leaving for London. It was too much, and thoughtlessly, vulgarly, unable to help herself, she giggled. Mr.
Turner stopped. Mrs. Winstanley, a bright scarlet,
besought her in an anxious whisper to go into the vestry,
advice which Hilda would have given much to act upon,
if she could have moved. In a desperate effort to regain
her self-control, she stuffed her handkerchief into her
mouth, but the giggles surged up and forced their way
through. Then Mrs. Winstanley, almost in tears, was
inspired. Raising her head, and with an arm round the
choking offender, she looked appealingly at Mr. Turner,
and then at her shocked and curious fellow-worshippers.
'None o' you tak' heed,' she pleaded. ''Ilda's all wrought
up wi' coming back, and doesna know what she's about.
It'll pass. At yon London they sends 'er to church, so
reckon t'strain o' being in a proper place o' worship
again 'as bin too much for 'er.'

There was a sympathetic stir amongst the kneelers,
and Mr. Turner, grateful for his cue, resumed the prayer,
tactfully avoiding any further reference to the restored
lamb. When the Meeting was over, they crowded about
her, regarding her compassionately as the unwilling
victim of a fashionable but comfortless faith, to whose
alien influence they were but too ready to attribute her
heinous behaviour. Bidding her farewell, Mr. Turner
begged her never to forget that she had been reared in
the tenets of United Methodism; let her, he said, but hold
fast by those tenets, and she might stand foursquare,
solitary but undismayed, against all the Hosts of
Midian.

Hilda, profoundly relieved that the ordeal was over,

thanked him for this friendly advice, but was convinced, nevertheless, that there was a good deal to be said for the Hosts of Midian. As the shameful fit of giggling subsided, she seemed suddenly to see her neighbours with quite a different eye. She forgot that they were poor, decent, hard-working, God-fearing men and women, the very salt of the earth, to be counted on, in adversity, to the death. She only saw them now as dull, narrow, ignorant and old-fashioned, their poverty a shameful embarrassment, their contentment with the life they led merely stupid. At supper that night she surveyed with snobbish distaste the home in which she had received so much of care and affection. How ugly the kitchen was with its hard chairs, uncarpeted floor, and American-cloth-covered table! She had longed to return, and now, having seen her foster-parents again, she longed equally to depart. There was no grace or charm anywhere. Nothing on which her eyes rested was satisfying. There were no flowers, save the dusty geraniums blocking up the window; no cushions; no books; no lightness or prettiness anywhere. Nobody talked about anything but their immediate material needs, or the comings and goings of their neighbours. Her thoughts turned tenderly to the splendours of London: to the museums and picture-galleries; the parks and libraries and theatres: and she felt at last a genuine surge of deep gratitude to her Aunt Helen for taking her out of this slow, flat, ugly, ingrowing little world of Moss Ferry. She saw, too, how impossible it would be to have any of her foster-family to visit her in London, standing out a mile, as she herself had once stood out, to the sharp-eyed, sharp-eared Londoners as 'up from the country'. Aunt Helen, she conceded, had been perfectly justified in commanding her to forget them. And, she vowed, she *would* forget them, soothing her exacerbated conscience by the specious argument that,

as visitors to London, they would be just as miserable and self-conscious as she would be in showing them round. Gone now were all the generous plans she had once made for giving them marvellous holidays. She was ashamed of them, ashamed of having been brought up by them. Only one more day and she would be off; and it could not pass too quickly.

Her foster-mother, anxious that this last precious day should be especially memorable, made one of her feathery sponge cakes for tea, and another one for Hilda to take back to London; and in the evening she took her to Daneshead to see her son Jack and his wife. Hilda had looked forward to this visit above all others, for Jack was her favourite, and he was the only member of her foster-family capable not only of reading a newspaper properly, but of expounding its political opinions into the bargain. When they reached Cobbett Road he was not yet home from work, but, almost before they had taken off their outdoor things, they heard him come whistling up the path. Hilda, her heart beating quickly, rushed impetuously forward to greet him, covered with foundry black though he was, but he drew back confusedly, muttering that he must go and take off his dirt.

Mrs. Winstanley laughed. 'Get away, lad! Fancy heeding our 'Ilda! Hanna she shot up? She's higher than thysen now. Wouldst 'a known her?'

'Dunna talk so daft, Mother! Ah'd know 'er anywhere. But Ah mun clean mysel up. It's not every day us 'as such company,' and, taking an iron saucepan of scalding water from the hob, he disappeared into the scullery while Edie set out his meal.

Quite unconsciously, Hilda set herself to charm and please him, succeeding so well that his wife jokingly remarked that she was glad she had him safely wed, even though Hilda had been reared with him. They talked,

of course, about London, and Mr. Asquith and Mr. Lloyd George, and Jack envied Hilda her luck in actually having beheld these great ones with her own eyes. Years before, when she had been a school-girl, she recalled that Jack, like every other male in Moss Ferry, had been a Tory, fervently supporting Mr. Joynson-Hicks; and she now reminded him of this.

'True enough! Ah was allus for t'Tories till they kicked up such a shindy o'er this Insurance benefit. Times is changing, and us wi' 'em. Ah'm for Asquith and Lloyd George now. And some of t'chaps at t'foundry is Socialists, and not afeard to own it either. Ah'm none so sure Ah'll not be thinking that road mysel one o' these days. But Mr. Asquith's good enough for me yet, and so is Lloyd George.'

'My relations in London like Mr. Asquith too,' said Hilda, 'but my Aunt Helen thinks he's not behaving properly about Votes for Women. She's a suffragette. She says it's outrageous that we women haven't got a vote.'

Mrs. Winstanley and Edie exchanged looks of mutual horror, and Jack, visibly shaken, advised Hilda, provided she could do so without causing ructions, not to meddle in such forwardness until she was older and could think things out clearly for herself.

'Well, I fancy I'm old enough to do that now,' she answered, rather sharply.

'Nay — Jack didna mean no harm, 'Ilda,' Mrs. Winstanley interrupted, 'and any road it's not for us to say what's for your good. That mun be left to others. But reckon we'd best be going. As it's your last neet, Joe'll be sitting up, and you mun be about betimes in t'morning.'

They said good night, and this time Jack did not draw back when Hilda went to kiss him. She held his hand affectionately. Dear Jack! There was something about him, something his father had, a gentleness and sweetness

which caught at her throat, and impelled her to run back from the gate and kiss him once again.

On this, the second occasion that she had left Moss Ferry, Hilda was accompanied by her foster-mother as far as Manchester, where they were to look in on Susannah, Mrs. Winstanley's eldest sister, who lived in Ancoats. Susannah would take it hard, Mrs. Winstanley pointed out, if Hilda returned to London without seeing her. On the way to the station, on the Manchester-Warrington Road, they came upon Joe Winstanley, who was working there with the road gang, all of whom had known Hilda since she was born. They gave her a cheerful good morning, wished her well, and with simple good manners moved out of earshot. Joe, leaning on his heavy broom, regarded Hilda sadly, unable to think of anything suitable to say. Then, feeling in his pockets, he asked anxiously: 'Han you enough money, 'Ilda? Best be on t'safe side and tak' this,' and he held out a florin. Forgetting how competently she had planned and carried out this stolen visit, he was beset by nameless fears lest her journey back, all alone, to far-off London, should be fraught with perils, in which the florin, all he possessed until his next wage day, might stand her in good stead.

Hilda waved it away. 'No thank you, Father, I've got as much as I shall need, and I promised to say goodbye to Grandma Stringer, so we must be getting along. Goodbye, and don't worry about me. I shall come and see you all again some day.'

'Tha'll be welcome, and us'll feel easier in our minds after this. But Ah hopes they winna tak' on at London if they gets to 'ear on it.'

'I shall be all right, and nobody can undo it again anyway,' said Hilda defiantly. She kissed him, and taking Mrs. Winstanley's arm hurried away. At the signpost

which said Manchester Fourteen Miles, she turned round for a last look at him. He was still leaning on his broom, gazing after them. She waved, including in the gesture Moss Ferry itself. From where she stood it looked as though it had grown quite naturally out of its level, limitless fields, a quiet, self-contained, unremarkable village, where nothing, she thought, completely forgetting her childhood, had ever happened; where nothing ever would happen.

Mrs. Winstanley, usually so talkative, was strangely silent as they walked on towards Bridge Farm. She was thinking of her husband, recalling the look in his eyes as Hilda had said goodbye to him so lightly. Although, having fostered her, she too looked upon the girl as 'one of their own', her own three children, strive as she would to hide the fact even from herself, had always come first in her thoughts. She had frequently been jealous when her husband, against all the evidence, had taken Hilda's part in any mischief she had got up to, and she had accused him of 'favouring' Hilda more than his own flesh and blood. She thought of Lily, her own daughter, and was resentful that no golden opportunities had come, or ever could come, to her as they had to Hilda. For Lily, in spite of her ill-natured mimicry of Hilda's new way of speaking, did not deceive her mother, who knew very well that she was envious and that Hilda's future visits to Moss Ferry, so far as Lily was concerned, could not lie too far ahead.

As they turned in at the farm, Mrs. Winstanley, remembering again that look of Joe's, Lily's jealousy, her own misery at the long absence of news, noted with bitter feelings Hilda's ill-concealed relief to be leaving them all again. Pointing to the farmhouse, she said coldly: 'Here you come into the world, and here, mony's the time, Ah've wished you'd 'a stopped. To look at you, none would ever

credit what us 'as done by you, you look that thankful
to be away.'

Hilda, severely shaken by this astonishing accusation,
showed her surprise, but was saved from the necessity of
making an injured retort by the appearance of her
Grandmother.

'Come you in! Ah'm glad to see you, Mrs. Winstanley.
Reckon you've 'ad your 'ands full wi' Hilda these last
few days. Han you time for a drink o' tea?'

'No thank you, Grandma. We can only stop a few
minutes,' said Hilda.

'Ah'm sorry for that, but sit down any road.'

She saw that Mrs. Winstanley was upset; naturally
enough, she concluded, with Hilda going away again so
soon. She too felt constrained, and Mrs. Winstanley did
not help matters by remaining, at first, completely silent,
dabbing at her eyes.

'Nay, dunna take on so. We canna keep t'young ones
wi' us for ever; and reckon you and Joe are satisfied now
that Hilda's making her way,' Mrs. Stringer said com-
fortingly.

'It isna that, Mrs. Stringer. Us'd got used to 'er being
gone. It's 'er thanklessness what's cutting me and Joe up.
He hasna said nowt, it's not 'is way, but 'e feels it. Hilda
doesna belong to us any more. It hasna taken 'er long to
forget as we reared 'er, doing by 'er as we did for our own.
She's too high for us now.'

Hilda, red with anger, defended herself, stressing the sac-
rifices she had made to come at all, and reminding them how
unpleasant the consequences would be for her should her
duplicity ever be discovered. And of course she did want
to get back to London, to forget these simple, ignorant
people with their coarse ways and ludicrous speech and
unlovely homes; and she was furious at being talked about
in this way before her Grandmother. Turning to her

foster-mother, she said wickedly: 'If it comes to that I never did belong to you. And I shall never come to see you again!'

Mrs. Winstanley cried out: 'Oh Hilda! Dunna talk that road! Us knows we ha' no call on you now, but me and Joe'll allus want to see you. It's only that Ah'm all wrought up.'

Hilda, wishing to leave a good impression on her Grandmother, and ashamed too of her cruel remark, said that of course she didn't mean it, and that she would certainly come to see them again. And perhaps next time, she added grandly, she need not come alone, since she had decided to get married at the earliest opportunity.

Admonishing her for being so forward, and unable any longer to restrain her hospitable propensities, Mrs. Stringer insisted that they should have 'summat' before they left, and produced a bottle of her own blackberry wine. Thus cheered, and with a stern reminder from Grandma that, if asked by Aunt Helen, she would have to speak up about Hilda's deceitfulness, they took their leave.

Her depression partly vanquished by the blackberry wine, Mrs. Winstanley listened cheerfully enough to further glowing accounts of the stimulating and sensational life enjoyed by all who dwelt in London, occasionally interrupting with an admiring 'Well! Ah never did!' And after an especially vivid description of a sunny afternoon in Kensington Gardens, she remarked simply that everybody in London appeared to be both rich and idle, an agreeable state of affairs for some, she conceded, but one which she herself did not unduly hanker after.

'Oh,' Hilda explained airily, 'people work, of course. The Underground trains are chock-a-block with people, like me for instance, going to their offices. But nobody seems to do *hard* work, and when they do leave the city

they've finished until next day. But in the country people never seem to do anything *but* work, except on Sundays and Bank Holidays.'

When they reached Ancoats, Aunt Susannah, more consumptive-looking than ever, welcomed them with delighted surprise. It was always an event for one of her Moss Ferry relations to come fourteen miles to see her, and when a visitor from London was included in the visit it was something really extraordinary.

'Fancy seeing who you've brought!' she greeted her sister. 'Didn't I always say as Hilda would turn up one day looking as smart as new paint. How are you, Hilda? Come right in and let me take a good look at you. I wouldn't have believed London could make such a difference. Quite a lady now, isn't she, Lizzie?'

Mrs. Winstanley, who had always looked up to 'our Susannah', beamed at this appreciation of Hilda, and dramatically related her arrival in Moss Ferry. 'You might ha' knocked us down wi' a feather when us took in who it was. Not a word from 'er for three year, and us fretting, as you knows. And 'er relations at London kept i' the dark too about 'er trip. Hilda fixed it all up by 'erself to come back,' she said proudly.

'I'm not surprised. Hilda was always venturesome and able to look after herself,' replied Susannah approvingly. 'Well, we'll have a bite of something. I pack up for Georgie and his father, so we've got the house to ourselves.' She moved about quickly, and soon had a cold but appetizing meal on the table. And all the time she darted questions at Hilda about London and its diverting ways. During a brief lull, Mrs. Winstanley, with sisterly candour, inquired how her husband was behaving himself these days. Hilda remembered that as a child she and Lily used to be sent out of the room whenever Aunt Susannah paid their mother a visit. Uncle George, they had been

given to understand, had failings which could not be mentioned in the presence of children. And in her capacity as hostess, Aunt Susannah was not now willing to mention those failings. 'We can have a crack about George's doings when Hilda's gone,' she reproved her sister. 'It's Hilda and her relations in London I want to talk about. What did it feel like to see Moss Ferry again, Hilda? And how have you and Lily been getting on? I never saw such a pair for upsets as you and her. And I never knew two girls so different in their ways, either.'

'There's nowt wrong wi' our Lily,' Mrs. Winstanley exclaimed truculently, suspecting that Susannah, with her clever Manchester ways, was comparing her child unfavourably with Hilda. 'They had a bit of a flare-up, but Hilda egged her on. She was allus that road wi' Lily.'

Hilda and Susannah exchanged an understanding smile, and changed the subject. For her part Hilda didn't care a rap if she never saw Lily again. She never had loved her, and she never would, and it looked as though Aunt Susannah didn't love her either, even though she was her own kin. With the dismissal of Lily from the conversation, the meal proceeded in amity, and, when they had wound up with the inevitable cup of tea, Hilda announced that she must be going. She had enjoyed meeting Aunt Susannah again, though the white, gaunt face made her feel sad, and she marvelled at the cheerfulness which enabled her to live in this mean little back-to-back house in Ancoats, continually worried by the unmentionable 'goings-on' of her husband, George Hankinson. Susannah, very smart in her Manchester-bought clothes, accompanied them to the station, and promised Hilda that she would put her foster-mother safely in the train for Moss Ferry. Being unable to read, Mrs. Winstanley, all alone on the great station, would

have been in a sad plight otherwise, for she was pathetically ashamed of her illiteracy, and hated drawing attention to it by asking even the friendly porters for help.

Having disposed her luggage, Hilda leant out of the train and kissed them both, promising to write, and to come again as soon as she possibly could. The whistle shrilled, the green flag waved, and for the second time young Hilda Winstanley left Manchester, thrilling with joy at the prospect of London. As the depressing outskirts of the city glided past, she experienced once more a rare uprush of affection for the aunt who had taken her away from this grim, work-compelling county; and she assured herself with a callousness which did her little credit that she was now completely cured of all further hankering after the scenes among which she had passed, so happily and so vitally, her early years.

CHAPTER XV

ONSLAUGHT OF THE HOSTS OF MIDIAN

HILDA, now nearing her seventeenth birthday, was as radiant and contented as any girl in London. With Aunt Helen so frequently away, lecturing on the Cause up and down the country, such evenings as she spent at home with Mildred and Phillip were wholly delightful; and, even when Aunt Helen was at home, life was still full of pleasurable activities. Her secret passion for Mr. Henry Ainley, which only a few short months ago had coloured all her waking hours, waxed fainter and fainter, and was succeeded by equally ardent raptures for other noble creatures, some real, some in books, and some, the most satisfying of all, created entirely out of her dreams. Invariably older by many years than herself, grave, careworn men unjustly battered by the storms of life, they sought her out humbly, devoting themselves utterly to her in return for the safety and warmth which she alone of her sex could bestow upon them. Amongst these suppliants, for a brief, enchanted spell, was Mr. Sherlock Holmes. Encouraged by her uncle, whose passion for the great detective was equal in intensity to her own, Hilda, pursuing avidly his energetic career, would imagine herself as Mrs. Sherlock Holmes, waiting for him to return from unimaginable dangers, the mere sight of her smoothing out those haggard lines, softening those piercing eyes, and causing that stern voice to tremble with ineffable tenderness as he thanked his God for this pearl among women.

She was never out of love. Authors, journalists, scientists, politicians, artists and merchant-princes, all elderly,

all distinguished to look upon, all leaders of their respective professions, captured in succession her abundant but transient affections. For each one, she convinced herself easily, she would, when the time for marriage came, make the perfect wife. When Mr. Talbot, one of her uncle's partners, was stricken by the violent death of his only brother, Hilda, filled with compassion for him, decided that he was the man of her dreams. Mr. Talbot, a person of unblemished character, devoted to his wife and adored by his children, eventually became so embarrassed by the compassion in Miss Winstanley's eyes and voice, that he spoke to Phillip about it. Phillip, astounded, talked to his niece very seriously, and said that she really must not gaze at Mr. Talbot so earnestly in future. He had suffered a grievous loss, and did not like to be stared at, no matter how sympathetically, every time he came into the office.

'Now I come to think of it, you do gaze at people for rather a long time, Hilda. Of course I know you don't realize it, but don't do it again to Mr. Talbot. Do it to me instead,' he said jokingly.

Hilda was very hurt that a nice man like Mr. Talbot should complain about her. After all, the way she regarded him was a mere fleeting glance in comparison with the way Phillip sometimes looked at her when no one was about. Her compassion for Mr. Talbot thus dispelled, she substituted for it a frigid and business-like nonchalance which, to her chagrin, did not appear to incommode him at all; indeed he seemed to like it. As for younger men, she gave them scarcely a thought. Occasionally Phillip took her with him to see a journalist friend of his, a widower with two student sons, both at Oxford and both there by their own industry. Their father, justly proud of them, used to boast a little that their education had cost him practically nothing, and that a

brilliant future lay before them; but Hilda found that their grave courtesy made her feel self-conscious and tongue-tied. She enjoyed herself far more with their father, whose bereaved condition so kindled her ever-ready compassion that it again burst forth, though this time with results less embarrassing than in the case of the wretched Mr. Talbot, because Mr. Clifton, being more adaptable, seemed rather to appreciate it.

In the counting-house and shop there were young men also, and Miss Preager, typewriting for her solitary lawyer next door, frankly envied Miss Winstanley's good fortune in working in the midst of so much masculinity.

'You're welcome to any of them as far as I am concerned,' said Hilda loftily. 'They're much too young to be interesting. They never talk about anything important like books or pictures or concerts, and they don't know one single thing about women. All they seem to think about is getting on in the world. My friend, Mrs. Ashton, who knows all about men, says they don't begin to be interesting until they're at least thirty or over. She says they can't possibly appreciate and understand us till then. *I* shall never marry a young man, and I hope you won't either, Miss Preager.'

With her head full of romantic thoughts about the golden future so indubitably awaiting her, Hilda's indifferent gaze rested for an instant upon her friend. Poor Miss Preager! With that blotchy skin and those gooseberry eyes how could she hope to marry any man at all, nice girl as she was. Hilda felt so sorry for Miss Preager's arid destiny that she suggested they might treat themselves to a matinée and tea afterwards one Saturday, a suggestion which Miss Preager, to her immense surprise, turned down.

Completely absorbed with herself though she was, as she solemnly awaited her wedding day, Hilda still found

plenty of time to indulge her passion for reading. And, at this period, influenced chiefly by Phillip, she read a great deal of verse, copying into a small notebook any poem that especially appealed to her romantic disposition. Listening one evening to a conversation between Mr. McGilray, who was a Roman Catholic, and Aunt Helen, who proclaimed with the licence of an old friend that she thought the ritual of his church altogether *too* beautiful, Hilda was impressed by the strangeness of his reply.

'I never heard such bunkum,' he said with equal frankness. 'You don't know anything about it, benighted protestant that you are. But I'll grant you descendants of that ... well ... of that fellow Henry VIII one thing where you score over the true Church, and that's the ritual of your Burial Service. We can't touch it, though as a good catholic I oughtn't to say so.'

'Ah!' exclaimed her aunt. 'Man that is born of a woman hath but a short time to live, and is full of misery. He cometh up, and is cut down, like a flower; he fleeth as it were a shadow, and never continueth in one stay.' 'I know that my Redeemer liveth,' she continued with brimming eyes. 'Oh Hilda, isn't that glorious? It almost reconciles one to the prospect of death!'

Hilda, quite sure that no mere glory of prose would ever reconcile her to this so final calamity, thought her aunt was being rather silly. Nevertheless, she was deeply stirred by the haunting phrases, and recorded them at once in her notebook, learning them by heart as she learnt other poetry. Into this same book she also wrote poems of her own — facile rhapsodies about nature, and bleak tragedies of limitless and unrequited love. After Wordsworth, and Keats, and Shelley, and the Burial Service, she had to admit that, on paper, they looked somewhat one-dimensional; but when she recited them softly, in the privacy of her own room, they took on

an astonishing amount of colour and body, and she was not displeased with them.

And so the happy, busy days followed one upon another, and there was no cloud on her horizon as she waited for the years to pass. But since she had become what Aunt Helen described grandiloquently as 'one of the world's workers,' Hilda began to develop various characteristics which profoundly irritated her aunt. She took an even more absorbing interest in her appearance than before, and when at home, was for ever admiring herself in the mirror, pretending artlessly to be arranging her hair if Helen caught her unawares. Her aunt, however, was not deceived, and reproved her continually for such vanity. Once or twice, with fearful daring, Hilda ventured to 'answer back', which shocked and surprised her aunt so much that she did not even remonstrate, but contemptuously turned away, thus effectually silencing the offender. Also, more and more, she went to parties at Mr. McGilray's, where, because she was the niece of his friends, Dermot made much of her, and his numerous women friends treated her with condescension when they discovered that she did not 'do' any of the things they considered worth doing. It transpired that all these ladies, with the exception of one or two older women, 'did' something, which formed the whole staple of their conversation. Some of them were journalists; some were artists' models; one or two, and these were regarded by Hilda with a veneration which they accepted as a matter of course, had even written books. One small, undistinguished-looking but charming woman, one of the few who troubled to be nice to Hilda, was an acknowledged authority on the works of Charles Dickens, though Hilda never heard her refer to the fact. Most of the younger set wore flowing, brightly-coloured dresses and barbaric jewellery of hammered silver set with

Cornish stones. Hilda listened respectfully to their gay, free chatter, and despised herself for being so ordinary, such a nobody, in this vivid galaxy of talent and charm. She did her best to create interest in herself by making up her face outrageously, thereby intimating that she was not unfamiliar with the less respectable aspects of existence; and to give colour to this suggestion she wore a black velvet beauty patch beneath one eye.

One night she sat next to a tall, slim young woman who surprised and delighted her by asking if she would come along to her studio and pose for a painting of her head and shoulders. Hilda was savouring to the full the distinction which Miss Nina Hamnett had so gloriously conferred upon her, when, with a sinking heart, she perceived Aunt Helen enter the room with Mrs. Ashton. She immediately stubbed out her cigarette, snatched off the ridiculous beauty spot, and wondered desperately whether, unnoticed by her aunt, she could get out of the room to wash her face. But there was no possibility of escape. The room was packed, and she was at the far end, immediately facing the door. There was nothing for it but to face it out and hope for the best. Surely Aunt Helen would never disgrace her by a reproof in this crowded place. Helen looked about in search of her niece, and, as her eyes took in the rouge, the lipstick and the mascara which Hilda had applied so unsparingly in the cloakroom at Sloane Square Station, she said slowly and distinctly: 'So it really is you, Hilda! At first I wasn't at all sure. Go and wash that stuff off your face immediately.'

There was a hideous silence, and all eyes save her aunt's were turned away from the wretched girl, whose cheeks flamed even through the rouge. She made no attempt to move, could not have done so had she tried. It was Mrs. Ashton who saved her from the humiliation of

tears before all these people. She laughed at Helen, and reminded her that this was a party and not a suffragette meeting; and she managed to convey to her friend that not only had she mortified her niece, guilty of nothing worse than silliness, but had embarrassed their host and his guests, and made a fool of herself into the bargain. Helen, now fully aware of her blunder, took refuge in Shakespeare, muttering something about gilding the lily, and for the rest of the evening she ignored Hilda completely.

As they were taking their leave, Dermot, anxious to do all he could for Hilda, complimented Helen upon having such an attractive 'second edition' in the family, and pressed them both to come along as often as they could, for he held his 'evenings' every Sunday throughout the winter. When Mrs. Ashton had left them, and they were walking in unfriendly silence towards home, Hilda, hoping to mollify her aunt, told her about Miss Hamnett and the suggested portrait, but this interesting news was received so frostily that she dared not utter another word. As soon as they were indoors, she darted towards the bathroom to remove the offending make-up, but Helen stopped her with a peremptory: 'No, Hilda. Come into the sitting-room first. I want Phillip and Mildred to see what an exhibition you have contrived to make of yourself. Come along!'

She took her by the arm, and startled her husband and sister, who were both reading, by inviting them to look well at this travesty of girlhood. Phillip immediately went into peals of laughter, but Mildred, who felt sorry for her unfortunate niece, did not even smile.

Furious with her husband, Helen asked witheringly: 'What does she look like! I ask you both, what *does* she look like? I tell you, Hilda, that if this is the way you mean to behave you are heading straight for perdition. Dermot

McGilray is one of my oldest friends, and there's no one for whom I have a higher regard, but if you want to go to his parties there's no need to make yourself look like a prostitute. I hoped, when you first came to us, that you would have ambition — want to make something worthwhile of yourself — and now all you seem to think about is what you look like, and having a gay time. You're a fool! Nothing but a light-minded, self-centred fool!'

Hilda, outraged for the second time that night, looked with hatred at her aunt. Phillip glanced at Mildred, who was apparently examining the carpet. Feeling that she had gone too far, Helen made an effort and laughed. 'Oh well, as I've said before, I suppose you can't put old heads on young shoulders, though you seem to have managed it pretty well tonight, Hilda. Now you can go and wash your face clean again. Good night.'

Hilda regarded her steadily, and, without realizing what she was doing, spoke aloud what she was thinking: 'Aunt Helen, you are cocooned in conceit, and I'm glad Uncle Phillip thinks I'm not in the least like you. Good night!'

It sounded grand, and it was grand too to observe Helen's incredulous stare. Hilda turned away, but before she reached the door Helen had sprung at her and smartly boxed her ears. Hilda's self-control snapped, her face crumpled up, and, in a passion of self-pity, she rushed to her room, where she was followed instantly by Helen, who looked exceedingly grim. Hilda, a pitiful sight with her streaming eyes and mascara-streaked cheeks, shook with fear as her aunt again confronted her, and gulped out that she was sorry for her rudeness.

'That's all right, Hilda. We'll forget about it. But now look at me,' she commanded sternly, 'and answer me truthfully. Why did you make that remark about your uncle? When has he said that you are not like me?'

Hilda, relieved that this was all, answered brightly: 'Oh! Uncle Phillip's always saying that to me. He likes to stare at me and kiss me and I wish he wouldn't because . . .' She paused, seeking for words.

'Because what?' Helen prompted quietly.

'Because I don't really like him to. What I mean is that I should like Uncle Phillip just the same if he didn't kiss me.'

'I expect you would, Hilda,' her aunt replied; then, regarding her niece thoughtfully, she asked very slowly: 'Is there anything else, Hilda, you would like to tell me about Phillip? If there is, don't be afraid to do so.'

Hilda, confused by the question, shook her head. Apart from his affectionate caresses, Phillip had only once actually frightened and puzzled her by pressing her hard against him and letting his hands wander over her breasts. 'Such little things,' he had said under his breath and with tears in his eyes. Hilda, brooding over this observation, had concluded that it was a masculine criticism on the inadequacy of her bosom, which she remedied at once by the purchase of a black velvet boot-polishing pad to stuff into the top of her stays. The effect was most gratifying for, from an immature, almost boyish figure, she suddenly blossomed forth with a stately bust which would have done credit to a Rubens goddess. She was very proud of this new allurement, and wore the pad rigorously for several weeks. But it made her feel uncomfortably warm and, as the day wore on, developed an inconvenient knack of riding upwards so that she had to shove it firmly down again. Presently, reading in a feminine magazine of a simple exercise guaranteed to give all slender women an irresistible outline, she took the polishing pad for its proper purpose, and rose a few minutes earlier each morning to do the exercise. Some instinct now warned her not to mention this incident to

her aunt, and indeed, now that she had been forgiven
for her recent pertness, all she wanted was for Aunt Helen
to go away instead of standing there looking so serious.

'Well, Hilda,' she said very gravely, 'don't go to bed for
a few minutes. I may want to talk to you again. Meanwhile do go and wash your face. You've no idea how silly
you look.'

Hilda, vaguely uneasy, obeyed. She had never seen
her Aunt Helen look so strange before. Back in her room,
clean and subdued, she waited nervously, a sick little fear
creeping through her that she had in some way blundered
by telling tales about Uncle Phillip, even though there
had been no harm in them. Presently she heard Helen
call, and shaking from head to foot she went slowly into
the sitting-room. Her uncle, his face a complete mask,
was standing before the fire. Hilda moved timidly to
join her aunt on the chesterfield, but stopped dead, absolutely terrified, as Phillip rapped out sharply: 'Stand
where you are, Hilda!' She felt his eyes boring through
her, and unable to meet them she gazed fixedly at a
small statuette of the Venus de Milo on the mantelpiece
behind him.

'What's this nonsense about my staring at you and kissing you, you romantic little fool? How dare you invent
such a mischievous tale? Luckily, I had told your Aunt
Helen about Talbot's complaint of how you embarrassed
him, so she knows you're quite capable of any histrionic
silliness. Why?' he asked, suddenly changing his tone
to one of paternal benevolence, 'why did you decide to
embark on such melodramatics? Now let me hear you
tell us you're sorry, and we'll say no more.'

Hilda, her wits temporarily deserting her at the extreme
injustice of his attack, remained silent, looking, in her
bewilderment, quite as guilty as Phillip had pronounced
her,

'Be sensible, Hilda, and apologize to your uncle,' her Aunt Helen said kindly.

Hilda, unfamiliar with the devices of expediency, shook her head, for she could not trust her voice. She looked unhappily at Mildred, but found no comfort there. Mildred was certain that Hilda had not lied, but her first loyalty was to her sister, so apparently satisfied with her husband's injured explanation that he was the victim of an adolescent girl's romantic imagination. They were all looking at her, Mildred appealingly, Helen kindly, and Phillip in a cold fury.

'Very well, Hilda,' he said at last. 'Go to your room and stop there until you do apologize.'

At the door, Hilda hesitated. Then, on a sudden wave of courage, she said accusingly: 'It's *you* who are telling lies, Uncle Phillip; not me! And I don't understand why it matters anyway. I haven't done anything wrong except make up my face.'

She went back to her room, and the more she thought of her uncle's cowardly behaviour, the more bewildered she became. All she had done was to answer Aunt Helen's questions truthfully, and for that she was now expected to brand herself a liar. What would happen to her? she wondered. She pictured herself friendless, homeless, cast out upon the world like a criminal, all her bright dreams shrivelled as by a frost. The prospect fascinated her. Other girls, no older than herself, had battled with the world before now and had carved out a shining path for themselves. And so would she. It was an exhilarating thought, and, chanting snatches from the Burial Service, she began to get her things together, determined to leave home that very night. As she was sorting out her little store of books, holding in one hand the Bible which had been Moss Ferry's parting gift to her, Mildred came in, and, seeing what she was about, said: 'Don't be such an

idiot, Hilda! Go and tell Phillip you are sorry. It's the best thing to do, and when you are older you'll understand why. Now go along, to please me.'

Hilda, revelling in her martyrdom, said sadly: 'No, Aunt Mildred. I haven't told any lies, and I won't spend another night under Uncle Phillip's roof. I shall go to the Ashtons until I've made my plans.'

Mildred stiffened at this reference to the Ashtons, and said sharply: 'Stop being melodramatic, Hilda. Of course you are not to go to the Ashtons. And stop thinking of yourself for a little. Think of your Aunt Helen for a change. Surely you owe her some gratitude for taking you out of Moss Ferry. Anyway, you can't support yourself properly yet, so go and see Phillip and do the sensible thing.'

'No, Aunt Mildred,' said Hilda yet again. 'How can I be sorry for what I haven't done? — But I won't go away until I'm older,' she conceded magnanimously.

'It isn't quite as simple as you think, Hilda, I'm afraid. Phillip says that if you won't beg his pardon he cannot have you here any longer, nor at his office. But go to bed now, and you and Helen can have a talk in the morning. Don't get up until your uncle has left for the City. I'll bring in your breakfast.'

Hilda undressed slowly, great tears welling up as the significance of Mildred's words sank in. She watched herself crying in the mirror, fascinated by the pathos of the sight. So, through no fault of her own, she was to be turned adrift, a very different matter from leaving, in quiet, proud dignity, of her own accord. And this monstrous injustice had been inflicted upon her by Uncle Phillip, who had always been her friend, and to whom she had done nothing at all. She searched through her secret notebook for lines befitting the tragic occasion, and with great feeling chanted aloud:

> From too much love of living
> From hope and fear set free,
> We praise with brief thanksgiving
> Whatever Gods may be! . . .

'That even the weariest river flows somewhere safe to sea!' How aptly the words applied to herself, standing on the brink of dark, uncharted seas. Hilda, eager now for her great adventure to begin, switched out the light; concentrated hard on the desire for one of her flying dreams, and fell asleep.

CHAPTER XVI

A YOUNG GIRL OUT IN THE
WORLD

IT was Aunt Helen who brought in her breakfast next morning. She looked closely at her niece, who, her eyes bright and her cheeks flushed, showed no traces whatever of unhappiness. Hilda, indeed, was the only one of them that had slept long and well, waking up, as she always did, full of joy in the miracle of another day. Years before, when a child in Moss Ferry, she had awakened very early one May morning to finish a book she was reading. The little room she shared with her foster-sister was alive with sunlight, and, as she lay there, half-awake, a queer certitude swept through her that outside a great mystery walked abroad. Leaning as far out of the rickety window as she dared, she looked down on an immense orchard of apple trees which surged, a foaming sea of blossom, further than her eyes could see. And beneath the trees were narcissi, thousands of them. Forgetting her book, she stayed at the window for several minutes, breathing in the fragrance, as elated as if she had discovered some rare treasure. She saw the orchard every day of her life, but seeing and smelling it then, drenched with dew, was like coming upon it, round a corner, for the first time. Eager to share her pleasure, she had prodded her sleeping foster-sister, whispering dramatically: 'Come and see what I can see, Lily Winstanley! Come and smell what I can smell! Cut my throat and pierce my heart if I don't speak true. Come on, slowcoach!'

Lily, her curiosity aroused by Hilda's excitement, had poked her head out and stared drowsily around; then she

had gone straight back to bed, exclaiming peevishly: 'What's come o'er you now, our 'Ilda? Fancy waking me up to look at the orchard! You must 'a gone clean daft.'

But Hilda, snuggling down to her story, knew that something quite tremendous had happened to her. Here was another lovely day. Something wonderful was always happening. Something would always happen. There was no dullness anywhere, except in Lily Winstanley. And that was how she was feeling now. It was another day, and something marvellous was bound to happen. It was a comforting reflection, which enabled her to eat a hearty breakfast in spite of her Aunt Helen's grave demeanour. When she had finished, however, Helen, without preamble, announced: 'Mildred and I have been talking, Hilda, and we have decided that it would be better for you not to live with us, for a time at any rate. There's a Residential Club for Young Girls quite near, and we think you'll be happier among people of your own age. And we must find another post for you. You've had a useful training in Phillip's office, and can now aim for something better. We shall look after you, of course, until you're self-supporting, as you will be in a year or two. I know you will think me tedious and old-fashioned, but you'll never achieve anything worth while until you stop thinking so much about yourself. Ah youth — youth! — how sad it is!'

Hilda, reflecting that she had never known anybody so capable of thinking about herself as her Aunt Helen, listened with a serious face; but her heart was undismayed. There rose before her an inviting vista of absolute, sovereign freedom. It would be like leaving Moss Ferry all over again. She would be free to make up her face exactly like Mrs. Ashton, but even so she would not neglect her mind. She would work harder at languages, and would take a proper interest in politics, in

spite of Mrs. Ashton's belief that men did not really like attractive women to be politically-minded. And finally, of course, she would be at liberty to choose a husband. With the waning of her passion for Mr. Henry Ainley, Hilda had ceased to be interested in actors and had decided to marry a writer, a painter, or a poet; failing these a harassed doctor, a Member of Parliament, or an unhappy millionaire might prove suitable. The prospect was so pleasing that her face betrayed her, and Helen broke off to say sharply: 'Hilda, you're not paying attention! What were you thinking about?'

'My husband,' said Hilda simply, taken off her guard.

Helen sighed, and said fiercely: 'Will you please listen! What do you think about this Girls' Club? Would you like it?' She did not think it worth while to mention that, whether her niece liked it or not, it was the only solution that she and Mildred could find to the present embarrassing situation.

'Yes, I think I should like it, Aunt Helen,' Hilda agreed, making a creditable effort to look a martyr. 'When do you want me to go?'

Helen flushed. 'We'll go this morning and make arrangements. And if I were you, Hilda, I shouldn't go quite so often to the Ashtons, dears though they are. You must try to make younger friends. Besides, you may find that, as you grow up, Mrs. Ashton may not care as much for your society as she does now. You have only, by your youth, to deflect one single glance from one of her admirers, and you'll see a very different Nora. So 'ware shoal, my dear, 'ware shoal!'

When her aunt had gone, Hilda pondered deeply upon what she had said about Mrs. Ashton. Was it really possible that she, Hilda Winstanley, possessed something which the incomparable Mrs. Ashton might one day come to envy? She sprang out of bed and gazed earnestly

into the mirror. 'I am young!' she exclaimed, as though making a profound discovery. 'Young!' That was what Uncle Phillip was always telling her, and until now she had thought he said it reproachfully, almost accusingly. But Aunt Helen had flung wide a door through which Hilda now passed into an even more intoxicating world, a world in which it was an advantage for a woman to be as young as she was. Still before the mirror, she combed out her hair, and decided that a touch of bright henna would improve its dark brown plainness out of all knowledge. She stroked and patted her cheeks, and turned sideways to get a good view of her lashes. She remembered a picture Phillip had pointed out to her in the National Gallery. It was the head of a girl by Greuze, and, with her chin upon one hand, Hilda fondly imagined that she bore a striking resemblance to that melancholy young girl. Unsmiling, like the painting, she mused upon herself very tenderly. Propping her chin more comfortably, she remained for some minutes completely self-absorbed, wondering whether she looked interesting as well as young and attractive. She assumed in turn various expressions — smiling — wistful — serious — grave, and concluded that it became her best to look grave, as if wrestling with some deep spiritual problem.

Having settled this important point, she thought again of her aunt's suggestion that Mrs. Ashton might one day be jealous of her. She did not believe it. She had heard Mrs. Ashton many times being wittily feline at the expense of other women, even at the expense of Aunt Helen, who was her friend; but it was quite unthinkable, Hilda told herself, that Mrs. Ashton would ever treat her in such a way. Even so, it would be fun to detach just one of those many admirers for herself. Mr. McGilray, for instance, who was always so nice to her, and for whom, in consequence, she felt a most grateful affection. Yes, Mr.

McGilray, an avowed bachelor, full of charm and gaiety, would do to be going on with. He might even, she thought hopefully, find a perfect husband for her, for he was as popular with men as he was with women, and Aunt Helen could not object to her going about with such an old family friend.

Delighted with these agreeable plans, Hilda duly accompanied her aunt to the Residential Club for Young Girls. They were received by a cheerful matron, who assured them that this was a real 'home from home', and that all her girls were completely happy and comfortable. She looked curiously at Hilda, thinking it a little odd that a girl of her tender years, with a family in London, should wish to leave home; but she asked no questions, and Helen volunteered no information. She showed them the dining- and sitting-rooms, which struck Hilda as being rather dark and depressing; but it was not until she saw where she was to sleep that her self-assurance oozed away and her spirits slumped. For it seemed that she was not to have a room of her own but a cubicle, a narrow, miserable space containing a heavy iron bedstead, a small bedside table, a tiny chest of drawers, and an arrangement of pegs for her clothes. There were curtains on three sides of this space, and on the only stretch of wall was a notice to the effect that all lights must be out by eleven o'clock. The contrast between this rigidly mapped-out space and her own lovely room in Glynne Mansions was dreary in the extreme. There would be no flying dreams from here, no reading in bed, no play-acting before the mirror, no chanting aloud, in respected privacy, of stirring ballads and heart-rending poems. And how, Hilda asked herself grimly, could she wake up in here and leap out of bed to the sunshine and music of another day? This was a bed she would have to leave in a gingerly manner, circumspectly. She turned appealingly

to her aunt and begged that she might have a room to herself.

The matron, wondering more than ever, said brightly that there were, of course, private bedrooms, and she had one vacant, but that naturally it was more expensive than a cubicle. Would they like to see it?

'No, no,' said Helen firmly. 'Don't be unreasonable, Hilda. What more can you want than this? There's that fine, big sitting-room downstairs. That's where you'll want to be, with the other girls. A healthy girl comes to bed to sleep. What can it matter where, so long as she has a comfortable bed to herself. Oh, for goodness sake, do stop looking so aggrieved!'

Hilda, feeling unspeakably desolate, said nothing further, but determined, as soon as she should achieve financial independence, to contrive her own domestic arrangements. She would have a room of her own again, no matter what the sacrifice; she knew that she could never lie here, wide awake, dreaming of a future more beautiful than any other girl had dared to hope for. Not here would come, unbidden, the sight and smell of that dew-drenched apple orchard in Moss Ferry; here she would never, by merely closing her eyes, be able to conjure up the enchanting vision of those three riders in Rotten Row that her first visit to Hyde Park had given her. She would never feel alone here, free to float away into the night, as she had been free in her own room. It would be like being in prison, barred and bolted in so securely that even in her dreams she could not escape into the lovely, secret world of her imagination.

Helen, who suffered many twinges of conscience over sending her niece away, sought to make amends by promising to buy something rather special for Hilda to wear when Nina Hamnett painted her portrait, and, as a further sop, said that she should choose it absolutely for herself. And

so, a few days later, Hilda, arrayed in a blouse of flame-coloured ninon, trimmed round the neck with a narrow edging of black fur, made her radiant way to Miss Hamnett's studio in Camden Town. The flame colour did not suit her, but Helen, though it caused her real distress to pay for something of which she did not approve, kept her word and did not interfere by so much as a glance with Hilda's unfortunate choice. In fact, she was secretly proud of the compliment that had been paid to her niece, for people who knew about such things said that Nina Hamnett was one of the most brilliant of the younger painters and had a great future before her.

Having arrived at the studio, Hilda received a most friendly welcome from the artist, who talked away gaily to put her at her ease. This was a new and mysterious world to Hilda, and she felt bewildered as she looked about the big room, bare of nearly everything but pictures, and not one of them, she noticed with interest, framed. But, responsive to Miss Hamnett's charm, she soon felt perfectly at home, and thrilled with self-importance as the work began. The sittings continued for some little time, and occasionally a visitor dropped in, when there was much fascinating and technical talk in which Hilda, who did not understand it, was wise enough not to join. There was a warm friendliness about most of these callers which was very agreeable, but one Saturday a young woman of quite a different stamp came in. The sitting was over for that day and, while Miss Hamnett had disappeared to make tea, the visitor, assuming doubtless that Hilda was a professional model, patronized her with extreme arrogance, causing her to feel both uncomfortable and resentful. When Miss Hamnett came back with the tea-tray, however, she at once perceived the lie of the land and quietly told her visitor how indebted she was to Miss Winstanley for consenting to sit for her.

Hilda looked her gratitude and was content to be herself again, an interested and appreciative listener to a conversation that was far above her head. Her embarrassment was profound when the caller, speaking now as one social equal to another, politely inquired who were her favourite painters. Blushing, Hilda mentioned Rembrandt, Botticelli, Raphael and others whose pictures her Uncle Phillip had shown her in the National Gallery; and she was congratulating herself on not having appeared an utter ignoramus when her tormentor exclaimed contemptuously: 'Good God! They're a thousand years old at least,' and thereafter, to Miss Hamnett's obvious annoyance, expended no further conversational favours upon the wretched Philistine.

In addition to the portrait, Miss Hamnett made some drawings of her hands, and then, feeling her way cautiously, asked if she might also make some studies of her figure. Hilda, who thought that Miss Nina Hamnett was quite the nicest person she had ever met, and feeling too that it would be tremendously daring, and would give her a most interesting status among the bright young women at Mr. McGilray's parties, agreed. She asked, however, that no visitors should be allowed to see her undressed. It was very strange standing there upon the little dais while the artist drew her as God had made her, and she was so plainly nervous lest anybody should come in that Miss Hamnett had to reassure her. 'There's nobody up here,' she told her. 'At least, there's only Edgar in the next room, and he won't come in whilst I'm working. He never does. He's too busy with his own work.'

Hardly had she given this assurance, however, when the door opened and he did come in, but, though he gave her no more than the briefest and most casual glance, Hilda screamed out at once: 'Send him away! Send him away!' and, instinctively folding her hands over her

breasts in a futile attempt to conceal herself, shrank back against the wall in a frenzy of embarrassment. Her immediate misery was short, for Miss Hamnett whispered something to her visitor, and he went out at once.

'I'm so sorry, Miss Winstanley. There's nothing to be upset about. I doubt if he even saw you,' the artist apologized, probably thinking her model little better than a squeamish young idiot. But this experience shook Hilda considerably, for, in spite of all her attempts to pose as a sophisticated young woman, her rigid Methodist upbringing kept breaking in, and at such times her thoughts returned naturally to Moss Ferry and to her foster-mother. What would she think if she could see her now! In Mrs. Winstanley's eyes for her to be seen naked, even by one of her own sex, would brand her as the most shameless and abandoned of all God's creatures, while for a man to see her so would damn her for ever without hope of redress. Hilda did not think either that her aunts, in spite of their advanced ideas, would approve, and wisely kept the incident to herself. She never knew what became of the portrait or the drawings, but for many years she retained a happy memory of Miss Hamnett's delicate charm, and blushed whenever she recalled her own prudish behaviour on the dais.

CHAPTER XVII

ENCOUNTER WITH A
REAL AUTHOR

BECAUSE it gave her immediate freedom from
Aunt Helen's dominance, Hilda adapted herself
reasonably well to the depressing 'home from home'
atmosphere of the Club for Young Girls, and observed
with curiosity her fellow-residents. Including herself,
there were about a dozen, mostly her contemporaries,
and all, she was sure, far cleverer than herself. They came
from Scotland, from Ireland and from Wales, and seemed
to be studying either for the Civil Service or for the teaching profession. Hilda was the only one to work in an
office, which they thought a foolish career to have chosen,
since it offered no security whatever. During breakfast,
which invariably consisted of cold boiled ham on week-
days, and a boiled egg on Sundays, they were silent and
pre-occupied, always in a hurry to get to their respective
classes; but at the evening meal they were talkative
enough. Afterwards, however, in the vast and melancholy
sitting-room, a deep silence reigned. In shabby basket
chairs, or sitting stiffly at the table, they pored sombrely
over their text books, and, if Hilda so much as ventured
an occasional remark, they glared at her. She was quite
as eager to improve her mind as they were, but none of
them gave her credit in this respect, choosing rather to
regard her as a flighty young person exclusively concerned with her personal appearance. Not even the
prettiest of them appeared to take any interest in love, at
least they certainly never talked as if they did; and when
one night during supper a Scotch girl sitting opposite
Hilda asked her gravely what she desired most out of

life, Hilda reduced the whole table to shocked silence by
replying, with an equal gravity: 'A perfect marriage.'
After that they left her more or less alone, and contrived
to make her aware that they despised her for her un-
scholarly aspirations. For her part, she did not care,
but decided that they were, for all their cleverness,
stupid in their refusal to make the most of such feminine
charms as they possessed.

Armed with an admirable reference from Messrs.
Talbot, Reed & Shepheard, Hilda put up her hair,
added a couple of years to her age, and set herself in
earnest to find a new post. She had never relinquished
her hopes of ministering one day to an author, and each
morning she searched the advertisement columns of three
substantial newspapers with this object in view. But there
were, apparently, no authors in London in need of her
services, or, if there were, they preferred not to make
their requirements public. An author, she supposed sadly
at last, would always be able to secure a secretary by
merely intimating as much to one of his numerous
admirers. She took counsel with Aunt Helen on the
matter, and her aunt, who loved an author as some people
in their time have loved a lord, undertook to advertise
her niece's aspirations in *The Times* and *The Morning Post*.
The result of these advertisements was most interesting, for
London suddenly overflowed with hard-working authors
all anxious to secure Miss Winstanley's services. It was
evident that they were also in far greater need of pay-
ment for their work than Hilda was for hers, inasmuch as
the salaries they offered would scarcely have supported
life in a self-respecting sparrow. And they were, with
one exception, totally unknown even to Aunt Helen,
who prided herself on being extremely well-versed in
current literary matters. But the exception was sufficiently interesting to rouse the brightest hopes in Hilda's

breast. For Mr. Walter Grainger was a *real* author, whose last daring and highly successful novel she had read with deep enjoyment. Aunt Helen, perceiving that her foolish niece intended to go and see him, threw cold water on the idea, pointing out drily that, although it would doubtless be a great honour to work for Mr. Walter Grainger, the salary he proposed was incommensurate with his renown. Hilda reluctantly conceded this, but decided all the same, unknown to her aunt, to keep the appointment he had suggested. She nourished a sweet, wild hope that her capabilities, aided by her personal attractions, would so impress Mr. Grainger that, rather than lose such a treasure, he would be impelled to offer her an increase in salary.

As she mounted the steps of the Georgian house in Bayswater where he lived, her hopes rose. It was obvious, from the spotless, neatly-curtained windows, and shining brass knocker, that here, at any rate, there lived an author who was not ostentatiously poor. The smart young parlourmaid who answered her timid knock was a further evidence of Mr. Grainger's substantiality, and so was the austere but elegantly furnished dining-room in which Hilda eagerly awaited his coming. When at last he entered, she rose, trembling with nervousness and blushing deeply. He smiled at her pleasantly, motioned her to sit down, and, himself standing, asked her various questions. Finally he suggested that she should type something from his dictation, and led the way to his study across the hall. This was going to be something of an ordeal. She knew that she would now be at her ease at any task with which she was familiar, but to sit at an entirely strange typewriter being dictated to by an entirely strange author of Mr. Grainger's distinction was quite another story.

'Yes, of course,' she agreed, 'though I know I shall be

nervous. I have to get used to things, then I'm quite all right.'

Mr. Grainger laughed at her naivety. 'Well, you're truthful, at any rate. But there's no need for you to feel nervous, and if I go too quickly you must stop me.'

Hilda, in a state of semi-paralysis, sat tensely before the typewriter, her fingers already feeling as if they were encased in lead.

'Suppose you take off your hat, Miss Winstanley. It's such a big one. I can't see you properly,' Mr. Grainger said, surprisingly.

Hilda obeyed, and with a 'Now, are we ready?' the test began. It was some kind of ghost story, not at all like the novels of his which she had read, and to her astonishment Mr. Grainger made it up as he went along. She typed a whole page, far from perfectly. She knew with horrid certainty every time she made a careless slip, but of course there was no question of rubbing out. She took out the sheet and gave it to him. He read it carefully, and put it aside, saying in the friendliest way: 'I see you know how to spell, Miss Winstanley.'

As she put on her hat, Hilda looked at him shyly. In spite of his prominent grey eyes and rather nondescript features, she thought him charming. He had a soft, caressing voice and a delightful smile. And he was an Author, and therefore not as other men. Hilda's romantic imagination clothed him with all manner of graces and distinctions which she felt he must surely possess, and, in an effort to convince him that she also, in her humbler fashion, was not as other girls, said depreciatingly: 'I'm afraid I haven't done very well, but I *know* I should be all right once I got used to you.'

'I'm sure you would, Miss Winstanley,' said Mr. Grainger kindly, 'but I have one or two other ladies to interview before I can make a decision. I'll drop

you a card. And thank you very much for coming.'

He escorted her to the front door and shook hands with her, repeating that he would let her know. As she closed the gate, Hilda saw that he was regarding her thoughtfully. She smiled, and he smiled back. The door closed softly, and she walked slowly away. Mr. Walter Grainger was a delightful man, absolutely charming. And he had liked her too. She knew it by the way he had looked at her from the doorway. Oh! why had she been so careless and nervous over that simple bit of dictation! Some other girl would get the post, a stodgy, competent girl like Miss Preager, for instance; a girl who knew nothing at all about books or poetry, and would never understand and appreciate Mr. Grainger as she would have done. She had thrown away a wonderful opportunity of ministering to a distinguished and famous man, for, though she watched feverishly for every post, she had little hope. Still, he had said he would send her a card, and her spirits leapt sky-high when, on searching the letter rack for the twentieth time, she caught sight of her own name written in a small, unfamiliar hand. It was from him! He was so sorry, he wrote, not to require her services, but he had decided to engage a much older lady. He thanked her again for going to see him, and trusted that she would soon find something more satisfactory than he had to offer. Nothing could have been more prosaic and business-like, but the impressionable Hilda, still profoundly disturbed by Mr. Grainger's charm, gazed at the postcard with reverence, full of gratitude to him for so courteously keeping his word. Inexperienced in the art of seeking employment, she decided that his card called for an answer, and, without further ado, she wrote:

Dear Mr. Grainger: Thank you very much for your postcard. It was kind of you to remember your promise.

Naturally I am very disappointed indeed, but if at any time you should require extra help perhaps you will let me know. I should like so much to work for you. Yours sincerely,   HILDA WINSTANLEY

She felt better when she had posted this note, which, she told herself, would surely please Mr. Grainger by indicating how deeply she admired him. Not expecting to hear from him again, not even hoping for such a miracle, she mused about him romantically for the next day or two. She read and re-read his postcard, every word and comma of which she knew by heart; dwelt fondly upon the magic of his smile; and wished him well. When, later in the week, she again saw his handwriting in the letter rack, she could scarcely believe her eyes. She stood for a second staring at the letter, and then tore up to her cubicle to read it. It was only a note, very short, but oh, how sweet! It had neither beginning nor end, but said simply: 'Let us meet again, Hilda. Will you lunch with me at the Café Royal on Wednesday? I will be outside at 12.45. Please don't trouble to answer, as I shall be there anyway.'

So he had not forgotten her! 'Let us meet again, Hilda.' How wonderful! How perfect! She chanted the little sentence aloud, as if it were a poem. Wednesday! And today was only Monday. How would she ever live till Wednesday! Oh, what a lovely world! 'Let us meet again, Hilda.' The cheerless walls of the 'home from home' seemed to be closing in on her. This was no place in which to gloat over such a message. Taking the precious note with her, she went to Kensington Gardens and sat for hours in the Flower Walk, thinking only of Mr. Walter Grainger, and seeing nobody but Mr. Walter Grainger. Although it was quite a long way, she walked back to the Club. She wanted all the time she could get

by herself to revel quietly in her dreams. What would her fellow-residents say if they knew that she was invited out to lunch by Mr. Walter Grainger? What would Aunt Helen say? She skimmed the unyielding pavements of Kensington, West Kensington and Hammersmith as if they had been shaven lawns, savouring deliciously that simple: 'Let us meet again, Hilda.' Already she had repeated it a thousand times, but it did not pall. She must look her very best. Passing a shop which said 'Coiffeur des Dames' she paused to admire a wig of gleaming auburn hair, attainable by any woman, the advertisement read, for only a few shillings. She made a hasty calculation of her financial resources. Yes, by raiding her post-office bank-book she had enough, and she could buy a new pair of white kid gloves also. A vision of Aunt Helen's disapproving stare rose chillingly before her, but, taking a deep breath, she went into the shop and made an appointment for the next day to have her hair 'rejuvenated' by the aid of henna. She wished her hair to look, she confided to the assistant, exactly like that on the lady in the window; than which, he assured her, nothing could be simpler.

Wednesday came at last, and Hilda found herself crossing tremulously from Swan & Edgar's corner to the Café Royal, glowing with pride at the glory of lunching, in her own right as an interesting young woman, with a well-known author. It was, too, her first visit to the Café Royal, and this in itself was thrilling beyond words, for, although her family never went there, she had heard, in one way and another, what a famous and eclectic rendezvous it was.

Mr. Grainger was there, searching gravely in her direction, and, as he caught sight of her, he hurried forward.

'I'm so glad you were able to come, Hilda. You look charming; like a lovely boy.'

Blushing and speechless, Hilda gave him a smile calculated to cover her astonishment at his strange comparison.

'Come along. I've booked a table in the balcony, and I hope you're as hungry as I am. What a perfect day!'

Unspeakably happy, she sat down at the softly-lighted table, and, entirely unable to think of anything sufficiently striking to say, confined herself to smiling at Mr. Grainger in pure ecstasy.

Walter, for he asked her to call him that, ordered some sherry, and, while they were sipping this, consulted her earnestly about the menu, and even more earnestly about the sort of wine she would like.

Hilda, anxious to give the impression that lunching at the Café Royal was an everyday occurrence with her, casually read out the menu, but became so agitated when Walter asked her to choose for them both that she finally asked him to choose instead, naively remarking that she liked everything. He ordered an exquisite meal, which the unsophisticated Hilda consumed merely because it was food. She would have been perfectly happy not eating at all, but just listening rapturously to everything that Walter said. She hoped that he would talk to her about his books, but he made no allusion to his work beyond the fact that, when he was writing, he never read contemporary novels, adding modestly that most of these were infinitely better than his own. 'But it's *you* I want to talk about, Hilda, not myself. After you had gone the other day I told my wife about you. I said you had a mouth like a wound.'

Poor Hilda! She had never felt so mortified or so bewildered in her whole life. His wife! She had not even thought about a wife. The mere fact that he had asked her to lunch with him had precluded so insurmountable an obstacle. She looked at him blankly, not knowing

how to cope with the situation, and strained every nerve to keep her mouth from trembling.

'You seem surprised, Hilda. It's no secret that I am married. I adore my wife. She's very beautiful.'

He looked at her so curiously after this remark that, in a flash of wisdom which owed nothing to experience, Hilda realized clearly that he had mentioned his wife deliberately, because, in her usual artless fashion, she had shown too frankly how deeply she responded to his charm. She flushed to her ears, but her voice was quite steady as she asked, with tremendous dignity, why, since he was married, he had asked her to see him again.

Walter laughed, and stroked her hand.

'You interest me, Hilda. You are young, and, in your way, quite beautiful too. I told my wife that you interested me, and she wanted to meet you. She's an intelligent woman, not in the least jealous. As Pope says: "The proper study of mankind is man", which for me, as a novelist, also means woman. But all the same, I think we had better keep this friendship to ourselves. I was very tempted to give you the job as my secretary, but it wouldn't have done. You're far too disturbing.'

Hilda, grateful for this healing balm, but resolved in her newly-acquired wisdom not to meet Walter again, inquired what kind of a secretary he had chosen.

'Somebody quite different from you, my dear. She's short, and plain, and extremely efficient. Her name is Miss Crump, and I shall never speculate about her for a single instant if she stops with me for a lifetime. That pleases you, doesn't it?'

Hilda frankly admitted that it pleased her enormously, and, her self-esteem partially restored by the tribute he had paid to her attractions, said loftily that it was now time for her to be going.

Walter smilingly remonstrated; he pointed out that it

was only two o'clock, that it was a heavenly day, that he still had many, many things to say to her, and that surely they might stroll along to the Green Park and there converse quietly for an hour.

Hilda, to whom the prospect of another hour with Walter seemed like Paradise itself, hesitated. Why not? she asked herself defiantly. She knew that she was behaving foolishly in letting him see how much she liked him, but when he looked at her as he was looking now, gravely, tenderly, her resolve to appear proud and aloof weakened and so towards the Green Park they went. Walter found chairs in a secluded spot under the trees, and Hilda, entirely happy, felt that she could have stayed there with him for ever. During lunch she had been quiet, awed by the tremendous honour of lunching with Mr. Walter Grainger, but now, in the leafy sunshine, drawn out encouragingly by him, she talked freely. She told him all about Moss Ferry and her upbringing there. She described her home in Glynne Mansions, and Phillip and Helen and Mildred. She discoursed about Mr. Rumsey's Business College, and her harrowing experience with Mr. Ram Lal. She even told him of her marvellous flying dreams, which interested him so much that he asked her to describe them in the minutest detail. He said they were lovely dreams for a girl to have, and he thanked her for letting him share her secret. He was particularly curious to know why she was not still living with her family. Disconcerted, Hilda fidgeted uneasily, and made no reply. Walter regarded her intently, but respected her embarrassment by immediately passing on to other questions, asking her finally what she wanted to do with her life. Hilda even told him this, and he laughed and took her hand. Eager for him to admire her wonderful new coiffure, she casually took off her hat, and was gratified when he exclaimed: 'Why! your hair is quite

auburn. I never noticed it the other day at my house.'

'It isn't really,' said Hilda. 'It's just brown, but I had it rejuvenated with henna yesterday.'

Walter looked at her in astonishment. 'Now why on earth did you tell me that?' he asked.

'I don't know,' she blurted out, annoyed with herself for her stupidity. She had never before met anyone so frankly and inoffensively curious about herself as Walter; and he had, moreover, the knack of making her feel quite clever, which was so unusual as to be highly agreeable. The shining hour slipped away like a dream, and, when he looked at his watch and said that he would have to go, she gazed at him in silence. As they walked towards Hyde Park Corner, neither of them spoke. At length he stopped, and, taking her hands in his and regarding her very strangely, said quietly and with a finality which stung like ice: 'You are a sweet girl, Hilda, but we must not meet again. There are all sort of lovely things lying ahead for you. I am sure of it. This has been a delightful experience, and I shall not forget you. Let us say goodbye here. There's nobody near enough for us to mind.'

He kissed her, took her hands again, looked at them for a moment, and said softly: 'Take care of them. You must never let them get old. And now I really must be off. Goodbye, and thank you, my dear, for everything.'

Hilda, too stunned to reply, watched him as far as the entrance, where he turned once and waved. She waved back, and walked quickly in the same direction, hoping that by the time she reached Hyde Park Corner he might still be waiting for a bus, but of course he had gone. Blinking back the scalding tears, she crossed dejectedly into the Park, and began the long, beautiful walk up Rotten Row into Kensington Gardens, repeating to herself for comfort that enchanting: 'Let us meet again, Hilda.' There were no horses in sight, but looking back

to that October afternoon, nearly four years ago, she fancied she saw again those three exquisite riders moving up abreast. Why, thinking only of Walter, they thrust themselves before her, she could not imagine, but the vision was there, unbearably lovely, mixed up in the queerest way with the apple orchard seen and felt such years before; with enchanting Kathie in *Old Heidelberg*; and most of all with her flying dreams. Utterly miserable, she walked on through Kensington Gardens, wondering what she could have done or said to precipitate that tender but final farewell. Surely Walter would write to her again; but, though she watched every post, nothing came. She was so unhappy that for several nights, as soon as it was dim enough for her not to be recognized, she walked up and down the pavement opposite his house, watching the windows, longing to catch even a glimpse of his shadow on the blind. She read avidly all his books, and searched the daily papers for weeks in the hope of finding his name. She did not see him again for several years. Then, walking down Lancaster Gate, something impelled her to look up and scan the top of a passing bus, and there, smiling down at her, was Walter. Again, in a theatre, she saw him sitting in the stalls with his lovely wife, but looking so mortally ill that her heart contracted; and when, a few months later, she saw the announcement of his death, the memory of that brief enchantment stole over her like a perfume, and she mourned for him sincerely.

CHAPTER XVIII

THE YEAR 1914

AFTER this, Hilda abandoned all further hope of becoming indispensable to literature, and secured an interview with the manager of a concert hall and pianoforte showrooms in the West End, who had advertised for 'an intelligent young lady secretary of good appearance and pleasant manners'. Mr. Belton, a stout florid man wearing a frock coat and with a pink carnation in his lapel, was sufficiently understanding to make allowance for her nervousness, with the result that she came adequately through the simple test he gave her. The salary, though not, Hilda felt, commensurate with her abilities, was at any rate enough to make her financially independent of Aunt Helen, and she could now take leave of the gloomy 'home from home', and enjoy once more the privacy of a room of her own. Neither Helen nor Mildred approved, and they did their utmost to dissuade her from this project. Helen, indeed, went so far in her eloquence as to prophesy, most unwarrantably Hilda thought, that, by leaving the shelter of the Club for Young Girls, her niece was heading straight for perdition; at which Hilda had the bad taste merely to laugh. In self-justification she pointed out that, if she was old enough to support herself, she was undoubtedly old enough to live by herself; and added tactlessly that in so doing she was only asserting her right to a free and equal existence with men, a right for which Aunt Helen had spent all her adult life fighting. Helen flushed with annoyance, but raised no further objection beyond the familiar reference to old heads and young shoulders, and a deprecatory wave of her hands. So Hilda spent

a distracted Saturday afternoon inspecting one furnished bed-sitting room after another. Every landlady she interviewed was eager to welcome her, but the rents varied so much that it was some hours before she finally settled on a large, airy room in the Hammersmith Road, which had the merit of containing only the most essential furniture, and was spotlessly clean. It was ugly, but within a few weeks she had transformed it with books and inexpensive cretonnes into an attractive little home where, since she was seldom in it except to sleep, she never had time to feel lonely.

Her new job at Pierian Hall was both pleasant and interesting, and the frock-coated Mr. Belton, who displayed each morning a fresh carnation, treated her with a paternal friendliness which aroused in her no restless yearnings, save for the passionate hope that one day her own husband would spoil her as devotedly as Mr. Belton spoiled the apparently imbecile but charmingly pretty Mrs. Belton. Every morning, tidying Mr. Belton's massive mahogany desk, Hilda dusted an immense, silver-framed photograph of his wife, taken in evening dress; and punctually at eleven o'clock, no matter who was with him, it was one of her duties to telephone Mrs. Belton at her home in Mitcham and say that Mr. Belton wished to speak to her. Although it could not have been more than two hours since he had left home, Mr. Belton took the receiver as eagerly as if he had only been married the day before, and the following invariable conversation ensued: 'Is that you, Mum? How are you? What have you been doing with yourself since I left? What's that? Oh! Had a walk round the garden? That's a good girl. Lovely day, isn't it? Have you had your milk? That's right. Well, I must ring off now. Take care of yourself, Mum. Goodbye! Goodbye, Mum!'

Even when Mrs. Belton went to Paris for a day or two

with her sister, Mr. Belton still telephoned her at eleven o'clock. Hilda, thrilled by the wonder of actually getting through to Paris, and awed by Mr. Belton's superb disregard of the cost of it, waited expectantly for the opening question: 'Is that you, Mum? How are you? Did you sleep well? Having a good time? That's right! What's that? Walked up the Champs-Elysées! Been to the Opera! That's fine! Have you had your milk? That's a good girl. Enjoy yourself, Mum. Well, I must ring off now. Take care of yourself, Mum. Goodbye! Goodbye, Mum!'

Hilda, who thought it very singular that anybody on holiday in Paris should find it necessary to drink milk in the middle of the morning, boldly asked Mr. Drew, the Assistant Manager, if Mrs. Belton was consumptive. Mr. Drew, who evidently did not like Mrs. Belton, laughed and said coarsely: 'Not she! The old man treats her as if she was made of cotton-wool. She's never done a day's work since he married her. He's potty about her. Any one of our young ladies here is worth a dozen of her. But don't you say I said so.' Lucky, lucky Mrs. Belton, thought Hilda, wondering if she too would one day walk up the Champs-Elysées. But of course she would when she was married: when that time came nothing would be denied to her. The whole world would be hers for the asking. It was all so simple, and she had nothing to do but wait.

Since the distressing scene with Phillip, Hilda, still smarting under a deep sense of injustice, had not been back to Glynne Mansions in spite of Mildred's assurance that she might now do so without embarrassment. She saw both her aunts frequently, meeting them on Saturdays for tea, or proudly entertaining them in her bed-sitting room. But one Sunday, when meeting them at Kew, Uncle Phillip turned up as well, and greeting her with an

affectionate 'Silly old Gretchen', took her arm as if nothing
at all unusual had occurred. Hilda, who had never lost
her childish love for him, was relieved and happy, as
also were her aunts. But when, during tea, Aunt Helen
craftily introduced the subject of her niece's best interests,
and seriously suggested that she might now come home
again, she was met with such an inexorable refusal that,
with an exasperated: 'Very well, you stupid girl,' she
dropped the matter.

Hilda, happy at her work, and revelling in her domestic
freedom, now found herself welcomed by her family's
friends not merely as their niece, but as an individual
in her own right. There was always something interesting
taking place. She accompanied Mr. and Mrs. Ashton to
plays and lectures at Toynbee Hall, and shared delightful suppers with them afterwards. Sometimes she went
with Aunt Helen to meetings of the Fabian Society, and
conscientiously tried to show an intelligent interest in
Socialism. It was certainly great fun to hear the respective
speakers tearing to ribbons the tenets of all other political
creeds, but, though Hilda endeavoured to look wise after
these denunciations, they taught her very little and never
diverted her from her dreams of a blissful future in which
they had no part. Most of all she enjoyed Mr. McGilray's
'Sunday Evenings'. She was the youngest of his many
friends, and one night, surveying her with unusual
interest, he said surprisingly: 'Why, Hilda, you seem to
have blossomed all at once! Until now I've always
regarded you as a flapper, and here you are suddenly
grown up,' and he flattered her still further by asking if,
until she grew tired of him or discovered somebody more
stimulating, she would spend an occasional evening with
him, 'for decorative purposes', at the Café Royal. Hilda,
greedy for both experience and pleasure, said that she
would love to.

They made a fantastic, ill-matched pair, the cynosure of all eyes, wherever they went. Hilda, shedding around her the radiant glow of youth in spite of her silly, sophisticated clothes and ludicrous make-up, and Dermot, some twenty years her senior, an intriguing figure with his strange, dark face, huge black stock, button-hole of artificial violets perfumed with violet scent, and tall, silver-headed cane. It was the fashion for women to wear cloaks, and Hilda, fancying herself in one of these graceful garments, bought one at a sale; it was of apple-green Venetian cloth, and she wore it over a long black dress with the tightest of hobble skirts, completing the ensemble with an immense picture hat of black velvet which swept upwards at one side to reveal her 'rejuvenated' hair. Dermot, who had a passion for colour, pronounced this costume the perfect setting for her, and she consequently wore it, on their Café Royal evenings, without a tremor. Seated with him in that splendour of crimson plush and gilded mirrors, seeing LIFE for the first time, Hilda was so happy that she even lost, temporarily, the desire to fall in love. Dermot, who wrote for a substantial daily newspaper, appeared to know everyone in the place, and by midnight they had either gravitated to some other table, or friends of his had gravitated to theirs. Hilda gazed at them all, journalists, writers, painters and poets, with deep reverence, which no doubt they found gratifying. The mere fact that she was with Dermot ensured her a fair amount of attention, but she was still so self-conscious, so afraid of saying the wrong thing among these clever and important people, that for the most part she just sat smiling when the conversation was gay and general, or looking preternaturally grave and intent when it was serious and particular. And all the while she did her best, by venturing an occasional outrageous remark, to appear a thoroughly sophisticated and knowledgeable

young woman, fully conversant with the facts of life; an attempt in which she succeeded so admirably that, had anyone hinted that she was not Dermot's especial 'friend', he would have been laughed out of court.

Not all her evenings, naturally, were so feverishly social. As Mr. Belton's secretary, she was privileged to visit Pierian Hall any evening she liked, accompanied by a friend, and usually once a week she and Mildred attended a Recital; at such times, Hilda, proudly doing the honours, delighted to show herself in her green cloak and black frock as an utterly transformed Miss Winstanley from the one who worked there. It was always pleasant to be with Aunt Mildred, but Hilda would have preferred Dermot's company since this would have enhanced her importance. He, however, though much attached to her, was very far from being in love with her, so much so, indeed, that having been once persuaded to accompany her for an evening of chamber music, he had afterwards besought her, in the Café Royal, never again to inflict such torment upon him. Chamber music, he confessed frankly, was not in his line. He said it did him no good, whatever effect it might have upon others. 'At my age', he observed sombrely, 'I cannot afford to take life so seriously. One has to be young, dear girl, for such self-abnegation. So don't, for God's sake, let me in for it any more, much as I like to be with you!'

Hilda was not surprised, for she did not herself really know whether she too enjoyed it unreservedly. However, Pierian Hall, with its cool austerity, was an attractive place in which to pass an evening, and, as she became familiar with the music of Haydn and Mozart, Chopin and Beethoven, she found herself going quite frequently, sometimes even alone, though she would always gladly miss the most distinguished Recital to be with Dermot in the Café Royal.

All this social activity, she soon discovered, made great demands on her slender wardrobe, upon which she now spent every shilling she could spare. She was for ever working out how little of her salary was required for basic, necessary expenses; and the few meals she ate in her bed-sitting room would have done credit to an ascetic. She even renounced butter, and substituted the best Blue Band margarine; she budgeted with frenetic niggardliness, saving all she could for her personal adornment, for it was quite impossible for her to gaze unscathed into the Oxford Street shops. She was continually seeing something, a hat, a blouse, a dress, without which life, all glorious as it was, suddenly became insupportable. She was a natural prodigal, and many were the lectures she had to endure from Aunt Helen upon the virtues of thrift. And, for a girl whose ambition it had once been to acquire fame and riches by dressmaking for the Court, she was singularly inept at making even the simplest blouse for herself. There were girls in the big general office at Pierian Hall who seemed to find dressmaking the easiest thing in the world, though they had received no special training for it: they appeared to do it by instinct, and consequently flaunted half a dozen new blouses or frocks to Hilda's solitary one. Once, determined to master the art, she devoted an entire Sunday morning to cutting-out a simple cotton dress, but the finished garment was so ill-fitting and capacious that she wore it out as a summer nightgown, affronting with it no eyes save her own. Furthermore, her old yearning for a real tailor-made coat and skirt again took possession of her, but save and cheese-pare as she would, she still could not afford it. Dreaming of it one morning, as she glanced through her newspaper, her attention was riveted by an advertisement, by a whole wedge of advertisements, all exactly alike, and all, apparently, inspired by the purest philan-

thropy. She read aloud the enticing words: 'From £10 to £10,000 advanced without security'. Well, she did not, of course, want ten thousand pounds! Ten pounds — ten golden sovereigns — was fortune enough for any reasonable girl. Delightful visions danced before her of what she could purchase with so immense a sum — the coveted tailor-made, new hat, new blouse, new shoes and gloves and handbag — a glorious new outfit, in fact, that would make her the equal of any fashionably-dressed woman in London. On Pierian Hall's exquisite notepaper she wrote to one of these public benefactors, requesting the immediate loan of ten pounds; and waited expectantly for the money to arrive. Some days passed and nothing happened; but one morning the messenger informed her that there was a man waiting in the entrance hall to see her. A mad hope surged through her that it might, at long last, be Walter Grainger, only to vanish as she caught sight of a small, shabbily-dressed individual, peering about with shifty eyes in a most unprepossessing fashion.

'Miss Winstanley?' he inquired, surveying her with evident surprise.

'Yes,' said Hilda, wondering who he could be, and praying that Mr. Belton would not see him, for the unappetizing stranger was not only shabby but sinister, and reminded her of a grey sewer rat in search of garbage.

'I am from Messrs. Macintosh, Macintosh & Macintosh. You wrote to us about a loan,' he began accusingly. 'Would you care to answer a few questions, please?'

'Certainly,' said Hilda, feeling rather flustered. He asked her age, her position, her salary, whether she had any 'expectations' (this with a knowing leer as his eyes travelled over her slender figure), and finally, precisely why she wanted to borrow the large sum of ten pounds. Hilda, disliking him more and more, answered all but the last question truthfully. Vain and silly though she was,

she had sense enough to realize that it would never do to give her real reason for wanting ten pounds so urgently, even though Messrs. Macintosh, Macintosh & Macintosh, in their advertisement, had appeared so eager to lend it to her. Hesitating slightly, she said that she required the loan for very private and personal reasons. The individual leered at her again, and said with a horrible wink: 'Not in trouble, are you, Miss?' Hilda, as she grasped the insulting implication, flushed scarlet. 'Certainly not!' she retorted indignantly.

'Sorry, Miss. No offence intended, I'm sure. All in the way of business. Well, we'll consider the matter, and let you know.' He looked at her distastefully, bade her a cold good-morning, and left, having contrived to make her feel practically a criminal, and so contaminated with dirt that she had to go and wash her hands. She did not, of course, hear from him again, but so unpleasant was the impression he had made that she was not even disappointed. She was, however, surprised at the tireless manner in which Messrs. Macintosh, Macintosh & Macintosh continued, daily, to advertise their gold; in view of their evidently extreme reluctance to part with any of it.

CHAPTER XIX

THE PLAINS OF HEAVEN

HILDA had to wait a little longer for her tailor-made. The War, which everyone said could never happen, was suddenly upon them, and young Mr. Drew, the assistant manager, led the exodus of recruits from Pierian Hall to fight for their King and Country. Mr. Belton, renouncing his pink carnation as an unseemly luxury in such grave times, had a business-like talk with his secretary and suggested, to her delighted astonishment, that they might manage Mr. Drew's work between them for the few months that the war would last. And of course, he said, her salary would be increased accordingly. Proud of her new responsibilities, Hilda worked with a will. Everybody she knew was working, doing their bit as they called it. Aunt Helen, predicting that with the fall of Germany women all over the world would at last come into their own, worked in a canteen; and Aunt Mildred, leaving the flat entirely to Mrs. Sherman, worked with her. Uncle Phillip and Mr. Ashton, lamenting bitterly that they were too old for active service, joined the National Guard. Mrs. Ashton, saying that if she must work she would do it at home in comfort, turned out hundreds of flannel body-belts for the soldiers, a job at which Hilda, in the evenings, helped her. Dermot McGilray, extra busy for his paper, had little time for the Café Royal, though he somehow managed to keep his pleasant Sunday evenings going.

Hilda, by slow degrees, began to realize that life was now very serious indeed. At first she did not comprehend how terrible the war really was. She was busy, and excited by all the bustle going on around. Once Uncle

Phillip actually shook her and stormed at her for repeating to him a stupid joke she had heard a conscientious objector make about the 'British Expeditionary Farce'. He spoke to her very sharply, and informed her that she didn't now matter at all; that nobody mattered except the fighting men.

By day the streets were full of eager young recruits marching and singing, and their favourite song, *Tipperary*, rolled out with the haunting grandeur of an old ballad. Miss Preager, with whom Hilda had kept up a desultory friendship, suddenly flaunted a young man in khaki, and Hilda felt envious and desolate in spite of her numerous activities. Only in her flying dreams, and they were very frequent, did she become a person of any consequence. Bereft of Dermot's attentions, she began to feel alarmed at her solitary estate. Girls in the general office at Pierian Hall were getting engaged or married by the score, and the cloakroom buzzed with their gay chatter as they made wonderful plans for the future. The future! Hilda thought of it bleakly as she listened to them and admired their engagement rings. It was true what Uncle Phillip had said. She didn't matter to anybody, in spite of all her longings and her dreams. Here she was, a grown woman of eighteen, doomed to live and die an old maid, while other girls, no more attractive than herself, secured husbands or at least fiancés. She became increasingly restless and unhappy. London was teeming with possible husbands, all in khaki, but seemingly none were for her. She felt an urgent, overwhelming desire to perform some great and sacrificial act that would make her of some importance to the world. She might, for instance, go out to nurse in a leper colony, or join the Roman Catholic Church. At Dermot McGilray's she had got to know some pleasant young Irishwomen who lived at a Convent near Sloane Square, and several times she had been there

to tea with them. The Convent was a dark, romantic place, full of mystery, but a happy place too. And the Irish girls were happy and not always worrying, as she worried, about their spinsterhood. Yes, she would become a Roman Catholic, and find consolation in this ancient faith, the only satisfying substitute she could think of for a husband. But she would wait just a little longer before taking the irrevocable step. She brooded and pondered and waited. Surely something wonderful would happen. Something, until now, always had happened. But the weeks passed, and no gay, khaki-clad figure came for her. Wherever she went she saw laughing girls with their proud, military escorts, and the sight made her feel somehow ashamed. In a world full of men, she was a failure, unloved and unwanted. One Saturday, in despair at her miserable plight, she suddenly made up her mind. She would call at a Convent she had often passed in Bayswater, for she felt shy of going to that in which her Irish friends lived.

The nun who admitted her showed no surprise when Hilda stated nervously that she wished to become a Roman Catholic as rapidly as possible. With a gentle smile she ushered her into an austere and spotless waiting-room, and said that she would fetch the Reverend Mother. Hilda, feeling that she had now crossed the rubicon, began to quake, and remembered just in time to rub off her lipstick and powder, worldly assets which, as a Roman Catholic, she would no longer require. She was rubbing vigorously when the door opened softly and the Mother Superior, tall and very beautiful, came in.

'What is it, my daughter?' she asked quietly, taking Hilda's hands and holding them for a second.

Hilda, full of confusion, stammered out her wish, and explained, as clearly as she could, that she felt the time had come for her to make something real of her life,

something satisfying. The Mother Superior regarded her thoughtfully, and asked her many questions. The interview, which lasted for about a quarter of an hour, ended with the exhortation to think things over very carefully, and, if she was still of the same mind, to come again to the Convent on the following Saturday. There was one thing especially which the Reverend Mother urged her to consider well, namely, that should she embrace the Roman Faith she must be prepared to submit herself utterly to its teachings. The nun who had admitted her now came to show her out, and Hilda, considerably chastened, and by no means comforted, walked disappointedly away. She had always believed that the Church of Rome would stop at nothing to gain a convert, but here she was, though burning with desire to enter it immediately, sent away to think things over.

When she saw Dermot the next evening, she related her experience, and was astonished to find that he agreed wholeheartedly with the Mother Superior. 'You must think very hard indeed about the matter, Hilda. My faith means a lot to me, but then I was born into it. Yes, you must be absolutely sure before you commit yourself. Go to see the Reverend Mother again by all means, but don't ask me for advice, for I shan't give you any, my dear. This is something you must decide for yourself. And now I want you to meet an old friend of mine, Frank Burton. Look, over there by the window! Your family know him too, but, though he works in Fleet Street, I sometimes don't see him for months. He's a queer chap, in a way. Very moody and solitary, but the best of good company when he likes. He joined up two days after war was declared, though he needn't have done at his age. — Frank,' Dermot called, 'come and meet the niece of a friend of yours. This is Miss Hilda Winstanley, Helen Shepheard's niece.'

Hilda, when she perceived that Mr. Frank Burton was an officer, looked at him with great interest, and instinctively set herself out to please him. How absurd of Dermot to suggest that he was over military age! He was so tall and slightly built that he looked almost like a boy, in spite of the fact that his thick, fair hair was greying at the temples. He had a splendid forehead, deeply-set blue eyes, and a gentle mouth which belied his stern expression, an expression which changed to a friendly and interested smile when she mentioned that she had heard her uncle and aunt speak of him. He sat by her throughout the whole evening, having eyes, apparently, for no other woman in the room. He was like Walter, Hilda told herself happily, a real man of the world, charming, delicate and interesting. He said the loveliest things to her, and though the room was crammed and the talk buzzed like a hive of bees, the pair of them were oblivious to all but one another. Once or twice Hilda, flushed and excited, caught Dermot watching her quizzically, almost, she fancied, warningly. It was quite early, only about half past ten, when Captain Burton said that he must go. Her heart sank. The evening had gone in a flash. Hilda, once again madly in love, and no cleverer at concealing the fact than she had been with Walter, sought for a way to say goodbye in solitude to Captain Burton, but the room was so packed that there was no question of just slipping out casually after him. She wanted to ask him, desperately, foolishly, to see her again, but she knew that she must not offend so flagrantly against all the traditions of her sex. Trembling, she hoped that he would ask this of her, but he said nothing. He smiled at her gently, pressed her hand, and made his way out, followed by Dermot. In a few weeks, he had told her, he would be leaving for the Front. It seemed unthinkable that she might not see him again before then, so unthinkable that,

heedless of appearances, she was actually on the point of rushing out after him when the door opened and Dermot called to her across the crowded room: 'Hilda, can you come here for a moment. Someone wishes to speak to you.' Bright-eyed and oblivious to the curious looks thrown at her, she threaded her way through, and at the turn of the stairs found Captain Burton waiting for her. He drew her to him and said softly: 'You have youth, and health, and beauty. I have no right to say more than that to you. So much may happen, Hilda, before this war is over. Life is only just beginning for you, and you will meet other men, younger men. I want you to be happy, and whatever happens I shall always remember you as you stand here now.'

He kissed her hands and turned to go, but Hilda, throwing convention to the winds, cried passionately: 'But I don't want other men! And I don't want young men, either. I don't *like* young men. They're all so stupid and dull, not interesting like you.'

Captain Burton smiled. 'They're the only men who count just now, darling girl, and they're not all dull and stupid, as you'll discover one day. But I have a little time before my battalion leaves, and every evening shall be yours, if you want it. Give me your telephone number so that I can ring you up tomorrow.'

Hilda, suddenly shy, gave him this. He kissed her hands again, and left her without another word. She stopped where she was for a few minutes, trying to control her shaking limbs. It was all so glorious that she wanted to shout and dance and inform the whole world that she was in love with Captain Frank Burton, and that, wonder of wonders, he was in love with her. She went into Dermot's room to powder her burning face, and sat before the mirror unaware for once of her reflection, so lost was she in her dreams. Dermot presently came in and found her

there, and was not slow to guess that something had happened.

'I was beginning to think that you and Frank had eloped,' he chaffed her. 'Well, Hilda, what do you think of him? Nice chap, isn't he? But a bit irresponsible. I don't believe he'll ever settle down like other men, even if he comes through the war all right. It's no business of mine, but don't do anything rash, like getting married one day and waking up a war widow the next,' he said lightly, but with an undertone of seriousness that was lost upon the enamoured girl.

'I can't get married if nobody asks me,' Hilda answered gaily.

'I'd ask you myself, if I were ten years younger,' said Dermot gallantly. 'Let me think — Burton can't be more than a couple of years younger than me, and I'm forty. Quite an old fogy, in fact.'

'Oh! but you look years older than Captain Burton,' Hilda replied simply. 'Why, he's not an old man at all. He's in the very prime of life.'

'This is where I lie down and don't get up again.' Dermot grinned cheerfully. 'Well, well, just as you like, my dear. As I've said, it has nothing to do with me, but I shouldn't like to see you do anything silly, all the same.'

Hilda scarcely heard him, and, looking rather thoughtful, he rejoined his guests. Left to herself again, she sat on, reliving the wonderful evening, through every word and look and gesture. She could not go back to the sitting-room. She wanted to be alone, to think only of Frank, until she saw him again; and, asking the house-keeper to make her excuses to Mr. McGilray, she let herself out and went home. To think that only yesterday she had been so unhappy, such a failure, that she had wanted to join the Roman Church! And now, because of Captain Burton,

she was the happiest girl in London. He was charming, even more charming than Walter had been, and, unlike Walter, there was no beautiful wife waiting for him. Marriage! She had not consciously thought of Captain Burton as a husband until Dermot had, as it were, warned her against him. Indeed she had not thought of anything at all; it was enough just to feel, just to be alive, young, and admired, and loved. But now she did think of it. Could anything be more perfect, she asked herself breathlessly. Mrs. Frank Burton! She repeated the title lovingly. Mrs. Frank Burton! Her own home! Her own adored and adoring husband! Her own lovely children! Life going on, into the golden future, world without end, Amen. 'Please let it happen,' she said aloud, as if by praying for it solemnly and openly she could make the miracle occur. As she tried to sleep, to shut out the hours before she could see Frank again, a picture kept floating before her. It was a picture that had hung in her grandmother's parlour in Lancashire, a picture painted in misty hues of rose and palest blue and pearly white. It was called The Plains of Heaven, and she remembered how, as a child, she had gazed and gazed at it, confident that when she died she would go to the plains of Heaven and live there, freely and splendidly, for ever. The picture was still before her, glowing softly, as she fell asleep to dream that she was flying over the painted landscape. But this time she did not fly alone; Frank was with her, and side by side they flew gently, slowly, through the drifting clouds, glimpsing far below them the spreading, fertile plains of Heaven itself.

The next morning at Pierian Hall, Hilda, every time the telephone bell rang, took off the receiver with unsteady hands, and, after putting the caller through to Mr. Belton, replaced it with a sick little feeling of fear. One o'clock, her lunch hour, came, and still Frank had

not telephoned her. She was afraid to go out, lest he rang up during her absence, and she sent the messenger boy to get her some sandwiches from the neighbouring A.B.C. She was with Mr. Belton, who was dictating letters to her, when the precious call came, and her voice shook so wildly as she answered that Mr. Belton, looking at her in surprise, said that if it was a personal call perhaps she would like to take it in her own office. 'Oh, thank you, Mr. Belton,' she said gratefully, and rushed into the other room. Frank sounded just like Mr. Belton did when telephoning his wife, for he asked her how she was, and what she was doing, and whether she still remembered him. Hilda laughed for pure joy, and, when he asked what the joke was, she felt silly and constrained, and answered his question by laughing again. His voice was very gentle and intimate, as though he had known her all his life, whereas she felt nervous and shy, and unable to talk naturally. He asked if he might call for her and take her out for the evening, and he would have kept her at the telephone indefinitely had she not reminded him that her time was not her own, and that she must ring off. 'All right, Miss Winstanley, I understand,' he said teasingly. 'That's settled then, and I'll call for you at six o'clock.' 'Yes, and don't wait outside. Come in and wait in the entrance hall. Just say that you are waiting for me,' she said importantly. 'I really must ring off now. Goodbye!' 'Goodbye, Hilda! Goodbye, and roll on six o'clock; it's an eternity till then, dear girl. Goodbye!'

She went back to Mr. Belton, wondering how on earth she was going to keep her mind on her work, and away from Frank, for three interminable hours. As she typed the letters, she made such stupid mistakes, trying not to think of Captain Burton, that she had to begin most of them again, and by the time she had finished the waste paper basket was crammed full with spoiled sheets of the **Pierian**

Hall's beautiful notepaper. Mr. Belton, too, for the first time since she had worked for him, suddenly exhibited many imperfections of character; he dictated letters which she could easily have dealt with herself, while she had never known him to have so many irritating interruptions. When it was nearly time for her to leave, he was called away, and, though he was absent for only ten minutes, Hilda, waiting feverishly for him to sign some letters, privately and unjustly accused him of deliberately prolonging her agony. But six o'clock finally came, and, as she ran down the stairs there was Frank standing near the door, watching for her. How fine and distinguished he looked, quite different from anyone she had ever known! And to think that he was waiting for her, Hilda Winstanley! Thrilling from head to foot with pride, and stifling an impulse to run straight to him, she descended more slowly, at the same time looking hopefully around. Yes, there was quite a number of her colleagues standing about, and she could tell that they were observing him with interest. As he caught sight of her, and came quickly towards her, she tried to appear proud and indifferent, as if it was no more than her due to have this tall, splendid officer dancing attendance upon her; but when he smiled and took her hand, her face betrayed the tumult within her and she deceived nobody, Frank least of all.

They greeted each other with a casual 'Hello,' and he placed in her hands a small, perfect spray of tiny rosebuds and maidenhair fern, saying as he did so: 'Sweets to the sweet. You look like one of them yourself, and I wouldn't change places just now with Kitchener.' Radiantly happy, Hilda held the little gift against her face. This was one of the moments she had so often day-dreamed about, the moment when a man, *the* man, would give her flowers. She touched the cool, tight buds gently. They were red. Red roses for love! Her cheeks flushed and her heart sang

as she said shyly: 'Thank you. Oh, thank you! Nobody
has ever given me flowers before.'

'Nobody?' exclaimed Frank indignantly. 'What a world
of fools we live in. Why, if I were a rich man I'd buy you
a whole florist's shop! But tell me what you would like
to do, Hilda? Dinner and a theatre, or just dinner and a
lazy evening so that we can talk. And where would you
like to go? I know a place in Soho where we can sit and
talk and not be rushed or bothered. All I want to do is
look at you — especially when you blush like that.'

'Yes — let's go where we can talk,' Hilda assented
quickly, 'anywhere you say.' The prospect of a whole
evening just talking with Frank made her feel quite giddy
with joy, and when he took her arm, tenderly, possessively,
her cup was full and overflowing. It was too early yet
for dinner, and Frank suggested that they should go somewhere first for a glass of sherry. He stopped a cruising
taxi and told the driver to go to Shorts, in the Strand;
as he settled down beside her, and slipped an arm round
her waist, Hilda sighed contentedly. If only they might
just drive on and on, anywhere, nowhere, so long as they
were together, saying nothing, thinking nothing, but just
being happy. She caressed her flowers; and Frank, quite
as gently, caressed her, as if she too were very fragile and
very precious. Her heart was so full of love for him that
she wanted to tell him so, but words would not come.
Instead, she timidly lifted his hand and kissed it, but he
drew it back quickly and said fiercely: 'No, dearest girl,
no! You must never do that again. What a child you
are! You make me feel so humble, and so useless!'

Hilda looked at him in astonishment. Useless! Captain
Burton useless! Why, in a time so pitifully short that she
dared not dwell on it, he would be out at the Front, leading
his men, encouraging them by his own fearless example,
and shooting the Germans down like rats. In her eyes he

was a hero, more glorious, and more powerful, than the whole of the British Expeditionary Force. And he called himself humble and useless! Oh! if only she too could go to the Front. She would do anything in the world to be near him, to be a comfort to him.

As they drank their sherry, Hilda asked him if it was true that the Germans would be beaten by Christmas, confident that he would know. 'I don't think so, Hilda, though God knows I hope so. But the Boche won't go down as easily as that. No, that would be too much of a picnic. But don't you worry your charming head about the war. There won't be a Hun left by the time we're through. I didn't know I hated the Boche so much until I met a girl called Hilda Winstanley. So let's be happy while we can. Drink up your sherry, or would you rather have something else?'

'No, thank you. I like the sherry, please.'

She watched him proudly as he ordered sherry for her, and this time whisky for himself. How stern he had looked when he spoke about the Germans, as if, single-handed, he could wipe them from the face of the earth, and all for her. He wanted to make everything safe for her, he said tenderly; and if he came back, then he would have things to say to her, things that a man going into the war had no right to say to a young and charming girl with all her life in front of her.

Hilda, emboldened by the sherry, said that he had every right, that she loved him, that she would always love him, and pleaded with him to say all that he wanted to say, now, so that no matter how long the war went on nothing could ever alter between them.

Frank looked at her gravely. 'No, darling child, it wouldn't be fair. I don't want to hurt you, but, you see, I may not come back as I am now. Anything might happen. I want you to be free, to be happy. You will

meet other men who will love you, younger men, though none who will love you as I do. Let us leave it like this: if I come back all right, and you are still free, still of the same mind as you *think* you are now — then to take care of you will be the whole of life for me. And if you are not free, if you are happy in some other way, then I too shall be happy for you.' He took her hand, and Hilda, gazing at him in rapture, was content.

CHAPTER XX

PARADISE DEFERRED

. . . Paradise, so late thir happie seat,
Wav'd over by that flaming Brand, the Gate
With dreadful Faces throng'd, and fierie Armes

THE days, now all enchantment, flew on wings, and
Hilda went about looking so pleased with herself
that even Mr. Belton, who never noticed any woman
but his own pretty wife, asked her one morning who the
lucky young man was, and expressed the hope that he
was not going to lose his secretary just yet. Highly
flattered at such interest, Hilda told her employer all
about Captain Burton, and assured him that they would
not be getting married until the war was over. And she
painted, too, so heart-breaking a picture of the imminent
parting between herself and Frank that Mr. Belton, the
kindest of men, said she might take the afternoon off, and
wished them both a happy time. Frank telephoned her
continually, and Mr. Belton became so expert at divining,
from her voice, who the caller was that with a benevolent
sigh he would dismiss her to the privacy of her own little
office that she might talk freely. She never revisited the
Convent in Bayswater, for now that she had Frank her
restlessness had vanished, and she experienced no further
urge towards the Church of Rome. Every evening, Frank
came to Pierian Hall for her, and they dined at the same
restaurant in Soho so frequently that Guiseppe, the
waiter, now invariably kept the same corner table vacant
for them. Sometimes they went on afterwards to see
Dermot McGilray, and once Hilda took Frank to see the
Ashtons. They were charming to him, and it was the

gayest and happiest time she had ever spent with them. Frank talked delightfully, and she sat quietly beside him, proudly possessive. As she put on her outdoor things in Mrs. Ashton's bedroom, Hilda said to her friend: 'Isn't he wonderful! So different from everybody else. He says he has never met anybody like me before, either. Oh! Mrs. Ashton, I'm so happy. We're going to be married as soon as the war is finished.'

Mrs Ashton smiled. 'We like Captain Burton very much, Hilda dear, and there's no question about his feelings for you. As a matter of fact, I knew what had happened from Dermot. You don't think that perhaps you would be a little young as a wife for him?'

'Of course not!' said Hilda, instantly up in arms at the implied criticism. 'Why, you've always said yourself that a man isn't worth knowing till he's at least thirty. And you know I don't like young men; Frank makes them look like suet puddings.'

'You have got it badly, Hilda! It doesn't matter, of course; nothing matters so long as you are both happy. What does your Aunt Helen think about you and Captain Burton?'

'She doesn't know about our friendship yet. I'm not going to tell her until Frank is at the Front. She'll only give me good advice and say I'm not old enough to know my own mind.'

'Yes, I can hear her doing it. But you ought to tell her, all the same.'

'Well, I shan't,' said Hilda firmly, 'though I expect she'll find out. She always does. She and Uncle Phillip used to know Frank.'

'Oh well, I should simply hate to advise you, and it wouldn't be of the slightest use. Whoever yet advised a girl in love! Good luck, my dear, anyway. Your Frank is delightful company, however he may turn out as a

husband. And you've oceans of time. Gracious, it seems no more than yesterday since the only thing in the world you wanted was that schoolgirl hat in John Barkers. And now it's a husband! What funny creatures we are!'

The dreaded evening came at last when Hilda, hurrying to meet Frank as usual, perceived from his expression that he had been drafted, and that any day now he would be cruelly taken from her. She had been so gloriously happy that, as the magical hours had followed one another, she had almost come to believe that the war, for the special benefit of herself and Captain Burton, would somehow obligingly end before his battalion was needed in France; and she had hoped and prayed for this miracle despite Frank's sober insistence that the war would continue far longer than most civilians appeared to think. As they walked along, he broke the news that he had only a few days left, and that, having got special leave, two of those precious days must be spent with his mother and sister, who lived in Gloucestershire. His mother, he explained, was too frail to come to London to see him off, and his sister could not leave her. But there would still be all Sunday, he told Hilda fondly, in which from lunch-time onwards they could be together. Hilda, thoroughly wretched, conceded him to his family, and spent two blank evenings alone in her bed-sitting-room, too restless for any society but her own. For weeks, ever since she had first met Frank, she had lived on the mountain-tops, leaving her room each morning in a fervour of anticipation for the evening ahead with him, and coming back to it only to dream of him until another day began. She would have liked to ask him there for an evening, to demonstrate what marvels she could accomplish, on a single gas ring, in the way of an exquisite and unusual meal; but the Hammersmith Road did not emulate the free and easy manners of Chelsea, and she dared not risk

her landlady's disapproval by such unconventional
behaviour. She tried now to forget the time in reading, but everything seemed meaningless. She gave up
the attempt and just sat thinking about Frank, and
gazing at his photograph on the mantelpiece. He had had
it taken specially for her and his mother — just in case,
he had said ominously. In return, Hilda also had been
photographed, with her hair down, her shoulders romantically swathed in cloudy white chiffon (belonging to the
photographer), and her hands appealingly clasped across
her bosom. Mrs. Ashton, when shown this remarkable
presentment, said that it reminded her of the young
woman in the *Rock of Ages* painting and was not in the
least like Hilda herself. Frank, however, pronounced it
to be almost as wonderful as the original, and said that
he would always carry it with him in the trenches as a
talisman against the Boche. Dear, brave Frank, Hilda
mused lovingly. She took his photograph down, and
held it before her. The peaked hat concealed the splendid forehead, but what a sensitive face it was, with its
stern, deeply-set eyes and astonishingly gentle mouth.
How silly of Mrs. Ashton and Dermot to hint that she was
too young for him! Why, she actually felt years and years
older than he was, and longed to care for him as he longed
to care for her. Her thoughts drifted deliciously to the
time when the war was over, and she was his wife. Unlike
Aunt Helen and Mrs. Ashton, neither of whom ever
seemed to have wanted a family, Hilda decided that she
would have children, a boy first, and then a girl. And she
and Frank would live in a house, not a flat; a solid little
house like the one Walter Grainger occupied, or the
charming houses in Castelnau. And of course they would
have lots and lots of interesting friends, for Frank seemed
to know so many people, in spite of his alleged solitariness.
Hilda's imagination, whenever the issue affected herself,

worked at lightning speed, and already she had furnished the whole house from attic to kitchen. She thought they might even take a small country cottage as well, for summer week-ends. London was still incomparable to her, but the country was in her blood, and in summer there were times when she even remembered the flat, featureless fields about Moss Ferry with nostalgia; at such times she would coax her Aunt Mildred to take day-trips with her in search of wider and greener landscapes than London could provide.

She fell to wondering about Frank's family, and what they would think of her when she eventually became one of them. His father, who had been a country clergyman, was dead. Besides his mother and sister, there was also an elder brother, William, married and living in Yorkshire, for whom Frank seemed to have no fraternal affection whatever. All his family, he told her bitterly, had been sacrificed in order that William might go to Oxford. A marvellous career had been expected for him, but in spite of his parents' hopes, William, now a middle-aged man, was still only a master in a grammar school. Frank, who implied that *he* was the son who should have been given William's glorious opportunities, had left school at sixteen and been placed, against his will, in a local bank. Hilda's eyes had pricked with tears as he recounted the five dreary years he had spent in the bank, hating every second of them. Finally, unable to endure his misery any longer, he had shocked his family by throwing up his post, and, with a few pounds which he had contrived to save, had come to seek a more fruitful life in Fleet Street. He said he had had a great struggle to get on his feet, but that he had enjoyed even the bad times as intensely as he had hated his years in the bank. Frank talked about Fleet Street with so much affection that it took on for Hilda the status of an all-

powerful Being; and when he laughingly said that for all self-respecting journalists there was only one God — Fleet Street — it did not sound to her in the least blasphemous. Eventually he had attained his ambition, and worked for a great newspaper, of which achievement he was justly proud. He referred again, contemptuously, to his brother, and said that if only the degree which William had taken could have been his, it would now be worth several hundred a year to him. Hilda, sad that he should have been so cheated, gazed at him tenderly, and hated the obstructive William with all her heart.

Fathoms deep in love, now that Frank's departure for the Front was so near, Hilda prayed with all the old fervour of her Methodist upbringing that he would come safely through every peril. She repented of her past thoughtless and self-centred existence, and humbly entreated her Maker to visit her with every species of affliction, provided this would make things all right for Captain Burton. Partially consoled by the reflection that she had now done all in her power, she next gave earnest thought to the question of buying a small gift for him to take into battle. She ached to buy him something expensive, and she stared longingly at the handsome, gold cigarette-cases which Messrs Aspreys displayed so temptingly, the largest of which might, just conceivably, she thought, be good enough for him. It was, of course, for the present, only a dream, but she resolved that he should have one as her wedding gift. In such a cause, to deny herself all but the barest necessities, while he was away fighting for her, would be no hardship at all. But what could she buy him now? A book. Nobody could go wrong in giving a book. She pondered over their many talks, and searched her memory for particular books which he had mentioned; but there were so many of them, so diverse in content, that she was at a loss. Poetry, surely, would be the safest,

something that he could turn to for comfort when he was
worn out with fighting. He had talked of Kipling,
Browning, Milton and A. E. Housman, among others.
The choice was so baffling that she was on the point of
telephoning to Dermot McGilray for advice when she
suddenly remembered an old, delightful game they had
played one evening, turning on the question of which
books they would choose to take with them to the tradi-
tional desert island. Hilda had voted for Swinburne,
The Pickwick Papers and Mrs. Beeton's Cookery Book,
while Frank had selected the Bible, *Paradise Lost* and
Boswell's *Life of Johnson*. He had advised her to lose no
time in reading the latter, to which, he assured her, she
would return, as she grew in wisdom, with ever-increasing
pleasure. Of course she would read it. Uncle Phillip had
it, in three large volumes, at the flat, and she would ask
him to lend it to her. But Frank couldn't take three big
volumes to France, so she decided to buy him *Paradise
Lost*, and to write in it very simply: 'To Frank, with love
from Hilda,' so that whenever he opened it he would think
of her.

And now it was Sunday, cold and wet, but Hilda,
engrossed all morning in the important business of making
herself look as attractive as she possibly could, scarcely
noticed the dismal weather. Frank was to call for her at
twelve-thirty, and by eleven-thirty she was dressed even
to her hat and gloves, and feverishly awaiting him. She
stood at the window, her heart jumping every time a
taxi came into view, though she knew that it couldn't
possibly be him. Twelve-thirty came, but still the taxis
passed, and Hilda began to imagine all manner of terrible
things, for he had never kept her waiting before. When
ten minutes had dragged by she was in despair, certain
that he had met with a mortal accident on his way, in
which case her own life too would be over. She crossed

to the mantelpiece and stood before his photograph. She would stand there, looking at him, until one o'clock, and if he had not come by then she would know the worst. At ten minutes to one she heard his knock, and then her landlady going to the door.

'Miss Winstanley,' she called up.

'Yes, Mrs. Roberts, what is it?' Hilda inquired casually, though she was literally trembling with relief.

'Your gentleman to see you, Miss.'

'Thank you very much. Will you tell Captain Burton that I won't keep him long.'

'Very good, Miss.'

Leaving her door wide open so that Frank could hear her movements, Hilda opened and shut several drawers, walked about unnecessarily, took a final, appraising look into the mirror, and then, with *Paradise Lost* tucked into her muff, slowly descended into the little hall.

Frank, presenting her with an immense bunch of golden chrysanthemums, apologized humbly for his lateness. It was due, he explained, to his search for flowers that were worthy of her; and he had, too, run across an old friend who had insisted that they should drink to the eternal damnation of the Boche. Suddenly aware of Hilda's radiant face, he said he was the luckiest man in the British Army to be spending his last care-free hours with such a girl. He was all gaiety and excitement, not at all like a man on the eve of battle, though his battalion was actually, he told her, leaving for France the following night. When they were settled in the taxi, Hilda shyly produced *Paradise Lost*, which seemed to startle him a little. He examined it appreciatively, remarked that he had never before seen such a handsome edition, and admonished her for her extravagance in buying it. 'I'm not worth it,' he protested. 'Oh yes you are,' said Hilda positively. 'I should like to give you something much

more wonderful than a book. And I will, too, as soon as I can afford it.'

Frank kissed her. 'If I come back, and our agreement still holds, you can give me Paradise Regained,' he said smiling. 'I shall never deserve it, but I promise to do my best. I've got something for you, too. Just a little present for a good girl. I bought it in Gloucester, and I hope you'll like it.'

With eager fingers, Hilda opened the dainty box he held out, and stared down rapturously at a tiny, gold wristlet watch on a black moiré band. Like a child unexpectedly given something hopelessly desired, she was unable, for a few minutes, to express her joy. Her thoughts flew back to Moss Ferry, and the bitter disappointment she had once suffered there because of her longing for a solid gold watch. Speech returned to her, and she thanked him profoundly. 'Oh Frank, it's beautiful! How could you have guessed that I wanted one so much? Put it on for me, please.'

He set it by his own wristlet watch, and then clasped it on for her, kissing her wrist as he did so.

'So glad you like it. I noticed that you didn't wear a watch, and took a chance. It will come in useful when you want to get rid of me. And now, where shall we go for lunch? The old place, or would you like a change?'

'The old place, please,' said Hilda quickly. Until she had met Frank she could never have sufficient change and excitement, but it was different now. And they had dined so often, and been so happy, at the little restaurant in Soho that their own special corner table had acquired quite a personal quality; and Guiseppe, the waiter, fostered this delightful illusion by managing to convey to them that they were the only two people in the place he really cared to wait upon. He hurried forward, assuring them that all should be perfect, for he had been expecting

them. The world outside was cold and wet and foggy, but, in this lovely oasis of warmth and soft light, time stood still for Hilda, while Frank was more interesting and charming than she had yet known him. Long after everyone else had lunched and gone, they still sat there. Guiseppe discreetly turned off the lights, save at their table, which he cleared of all but its vase of flowers, ash tray and small hand-bell. Then, courteously indicating that none would disturb them unless they so wished, he too disappeared. The restaurant, dim and ghostly beyond the circle in which they sat, looked like a specimen room in an immense furniture store. Outside, the wicked fog grew thicker and blacker, and the rain drizzled down with steady monotony. Hilda, listening wide-eyed to Frank's entertaining talk, every now and then peered through the window at the outer gloom for the sheer pleasure of turning back to the radiance within. And how comfortable it was, she reflected, just to listen and be her natural self, instead of having to try and look clever as was expected of her by Dermot and his Café Royal friends. She learnt more about London that Sunday than in the whole of the past four years. Frank, quoting from De Quincey, called it 'The Nation of London', and was a mine of fascinating information about such differing characters as Doctor Johnson and Lord Northcliffe, Samuel Pepys and George Augustus Sala, the great Walter dynasty of *The Times* (for which he professed a reverence amounting almost to idolatry), and Gilbert and Cecil Chesterton. To Hilda, it was 'all a wonder and a wild desire', and she sat enthralled, marvelling that she, an ignorant girl of eighteen, should have attracted to herself such a dazzling being as Captain Frank Burton. Young men indeed! What could they give her in comparison? The thought of the morrow, chilling as the fog, kept creeping into her consciousness, but she resolutely pushed it away, back beyond the circle of light.

Glancing proudly at her watch, she exclaimed at the time. It was nearly five o'clock, and they had been there since half-past one! Frank asked if she would like to go out for tea, coming back again in the evening, but she was too contented to move, and suggested that they should have it where they were. 'It will make history in Soho, and I even doubt whether it can be done, but here goes,' he said, bravely ringing the bell. It was answered by Madame herself, all benevolent smiles at this obviously lunatic pair. Tea? But of course they could have tea, she said calmly, and within a few minutes she produced an enormous and coarse white teapot, equally coarse cups and saucers, and a plate of cream crackers. She apologized profusely for the humble ware, unfit to place before such appreciated patrons, but it was all she could manage at the moment. When they came again, she promised them, everything should be of the most delicate.

'There you are,' said Frank, with mock solemnity, 'we *have* made history. This place has never sold a cup of tea in all its days until this minute.'

'And I hope it never will again,' said Hilda fervently, having taken her first sip.

'Except to you and me,' he teased her. 'If reporting was my job I could make quite a news story out of it. Profound shock for proprietress of old-fashioned Soho restaurant! That sort of thing. Never believe one-half of what you read in the papers, Hilda, and you'll grow up to be a wise and happy woman, and live to a ripe old age.'

As the evening slipped unnoticed away, Hilda and Frank, shamelessly breaking their agreement, challenged the future which lay beyond the war, by daring to plot for it. They would become formally engaged as soon as he was out of the army; and married shortly afterwards. There was no sense, he said, in a long engagement. Hilda

promptly concurred with this exquisitely simple plan for the realization of all her dreams. Frank warned her that he would not be a rich husband, but that there would be sufficient if it was really a fact that two could live as cheaply as one. Hilda, who had never given a thought to his monetary affairs, assured him confidently, on evidence known to none but herself, that she possessed uncanny skill in making one sovereign do the work of two, and was altogether a most excellent manager. He was sure of it, said Frank warmly. There was nothing a girl of her intelligence might not accomplish if she gave her mind to it. He was enchanting her with a description of the ancient glories of Carcassonne, where he planned to take her on part of their honeymoon, when they realized that once again the other diners had vanished. Guiseppe, tired but outwardly patient, was hovering near, and Madame, carefully not looking at them, was moving about in the background.

Frank gave a deep sigh and released her hand. 'We must go, Hilda, before they inquire what we would like for breakfast. Anyway, I must get back to barracks. I've several things to do, and a few letters to write.'

He took her home, and in the taxi said such lovely things to her that he alarmed him by a fit of weeping. They said their secret goodbye, for he told her that when he left for the Front next evening there would probably be several other people to see him off, mostly Fleet Street friends. Seeing the state she was in now, he suggested that perhaps she ought not to come to the station, as it would be terrible for him to leave her looking so forlorn; but Hilda was horrified at this proposal, and promised that she would behave with heroic fortitude.

She was on the station the following night a half-hour before the troop train left, and was madly jealous when she saw so many of Frank's friends surrounding him on the plat-

form. Their eyes sought one another continually, but she had no chance to speak to him alone. The train moved, and Hilda, forcing her way to the carriage window, was just in time to reach for his hand and to hear him say: 'I'll write as soon as we are there, darling girl. Pray for me.'

The train gathered speed, and Hilda stood very still, watching it disappear into the night. Four years had passed since, a raw country girl of fourteen, she had come to London full of bright hopes for a further and more satisfying education than Moss Ferry could give her. And only now, as she strained her ears to catch the last faint rumble of the train that was taking her future husband to France, had that education begun.